BETTER DEAD?

The Menace ducked from cover and fired a single shot.

The bullet caught Zhadanov in the shoulder, the Tommy gun sprang from fat hands and the Russian Mobster tumbled back and disappeared between bed and armoire. The gun bounced across the unmade bed and fell to floor with a clatter and suddenly the entire Vegas mansion was smothered in unnatural silence.

The Menace glanced back and saw Olga peeking around the doorframe, long blond hair spilling down one bare shoulder. In his head he heard a sonorous voice repeat a warning for the hundredth time: "Never trust a red, Patrick."

But the voice in his head was wrong. Olga Cherblonya had been vitally important in finishing off Zhadanov. In this one case, Russian interests had aligned with those of America. And what was possible now was possible again in the future.

Zhadanov stirred. The Menace heard a grunt and the soft rustling of silk.

"On your feet, Zhadanov!" the Menace snapped as he crept over to the bed. "I count to five and I don't see both hands, I'm blowing the floor out from under you."

The RED MENACE
#1 RED AND BURIED

JAMES MULLANEY

The RED MENACE series
#1 Red and Buried
#2 Drowning in Red Ink

Editor & Designer
Rich Harvey

Cover Artist
Mark Maddox
maddoxplanet.com

Copyright © 2021 James Mullaney. All Rights Reserved.

"THE RED MENACE" TM & © James Mullaney. All Rights Reserved. Produced by arrangement with the author.

Bold Venture Press edition October 2021

PUBLISHER'S NOTE:
No part of this publication may be reproduced, stored in or introduced into a retrieval system, or transmitted, in any form, or by any means (electronic, mechanical, photocopying, recording, or otherwise), without the prior express written consent of the publisher and the copyright holder.

This is a work of fiction. Names, characters, places, and incidents either are the products of the authors' imaginations or are used fictitiously, and any resemblance to actual persons, living or dead, business establishments, events or locales, is entirely coincidental.

For Ma

Foreword

I'VE known Jim Mullaney for centuries now, and over the many years I've shamelessly gotten shamefully rich off his work on books in my *Destroyer* series. And now he's bailing out and going off to write his own books. So what am I going to do?

Arrrrgh ... Well, if he's going to do it anyway — (and he is 'cause he's a heartless thankless mug) — I'm glad he picked the Red Menace to start with because this first episode, *Red and Buried*, is funny, exciting and stylish ... all the things Mullaney's work generally is, and this book should go a long way to helping him build up the kind of far-and-wide audience someone with his talent deserves. Plus, this story of Podge Becket, his partner, Dr. Thaddeus Wainwright and an enemy from their past, demented Russian Colonel Ivan Strankov who would destroy all life on earth, is as whip-cracking exciting as it gets.

Good luck, pardner.

Warren Murphy,
Two-time Edgar Award winner

RED AND BURIED

Prologue

October 1958

COLONEL Ivan Strankov peered suspiciously at the contents of the sealed glass container and frowned.

There were plants in the tank. Or, rather, there appeared to be the dead remnants of what had once been plants. The stems of the dead husks were curled and oozing white pus, the leaves were shriveled and brown.

The adjacent tank on the laboratory table seemed placed there purely for contrast. This second tank was crammed with plants in flourishing bloom; dark and healthy green. Both containers were labeled with Cyrillic letters and carefully numbered with some sort of diabolically convoluted code that even Colonel Strankov, with his cunning mind and top Soviet security clearance, could not crack.

"What is all this?" Strankov demanded.

Dr. Oleg Plassko was fussing around a table in the center of the room and had barely taken notice of Strankov's presence.

"An experiment, comrade colonel," Plassko said, a hint of distracted frustration in his voice. "A failure for now, I am afraid. But we persevere. We persevere."

Plassko was an odd figure. Thick glasses like the bottoms of Coca-Cola bottles were jammed far back on an upturned, pig-like nose, comically enlarging his already huge, unblinking green eyes and giving the scientist the appearance of a perpetually startled owl. He was barely north of five feet tall but his arms were long and his feet large, as if some malevolent god had pushed down and compressed his torso. Although only fifty-two, Plassko was nearly bald, and the wild fringe of remaining yellow hair brushed the collar of his white coat as he hustled around the lab.

Strankov gave a low growl and returned to his observations.

The colonel did not want to be there, but only those who knew him very well would have detected his annoyance. A grunt, a scowl, a growl. Small tics, barely noticeable. Strankov was used to hiding his displeasure. In the Soviet Union, one did not rise as quickly as had he, and at such a young age, by advertising one's thoughts and emotions. It was not for nothing that Ivan Strankov was a decorated Soviet Army colonel at the age of twenty-six, as well as the youngest recipient of the Order of Lenin and the powerful director of the secret espionage agency known as Motherland.

Where Colonel Ivan Strankov walked, KGB officers fell silent in fear.

There were more glass tanks piled in the corner of the room. These looked as if they had been hastily cleaned and discarded. Strankov wondered if they had contained more plants. He supposed he should read more of what Plassko was up to down here in the Motherland offices at Lubyanka Square. One member of the Politburo was briefly interested in the odd little man's work a few years back and even though that party official had since died Oleg Plassko still had no difficulty finding funding. The unwieldy beast of government could not be stopped once set in motion.

Unlike Plassko, Strankov considered himself a man of action. He had not much interest in beakers and test tubes and glass tanks filled with rotting, pus-filled plants.

"Very good, very good," Plassko muttered. An irritating habit; the scientist often repeated his own words.

There were three other scientists in the room. They had helped Plassko clear off a black-topped central table. Everything in the room had been shoved to one side. Plassko took out several jars of dark material from a refrigerator in the corner of the room and set them to one side. He clapped his hands and looked around, biting his lower lip in concentration. "I believe that we are ready. Yes, we are ready, comrade colonel."

Wordlessly, Strankov marched to the door. He waved one gloved hand into the hallway and a moment later a half-dozen men were hustling into the room.

The first four young soldiers were carting a large wooden box like a funeral bier. The box was six feet long but narrow, and fit easily through the lab's double doors.

"Very good, very good. Over here," Plassko said, gesturing toward the table.

"Mind the gas line. Right there, son, by your foot. Fine, fine. Good. Excellent."

With great reverence the large crate was set on the table in the middle of the room. At a nod from Strankov, the two soldiers who had trailed the others into the room hustled forward and, using crowbars, pried off the lid. The clean silver nails shrieked in pain and once the lid was clear it was leaned against a wall. The soldiers returned and made quick work of the wooden sides. When the box was stripped away, the young soldiers backed away from the object that had been contained within.

The corpse was lighter than the box in which it had been transported.

The body had been preserved for over thirty years. The eyes were closed in permanent slumber. The thick mustache seemed thin close up and was painted black, as was the hair that rimmed the bald pate. A goatee clung to the chin, which was pressed against the starched white collar and necktie.

"Comrade Vladimir Ilich," Plassko wheezed reverently.

If it were a church, the men around the room would have blessed themselves.

Lenin's mouth was stitched tight, as if to stifle more bloody commands which in life had flowed so freely from between the lips of one of history's great monsters.

Strankov's spine was nearly always at a perfect rigid right angle from the floor. The colonel spent his life at attention. Even as he bent to look at the desiccated corpse, the creases in his Red Army uniform remained perfectly rigid lines.

"What is wrong with his skin?" Strankov asked.

Lenin's pale skin was like wax that had dried in the desert sun. It seemed to pucker in places, pulling up from the bone. The dry flesh all around cheeks and broad forehead was crisscrossed with a fine lattice of cracks. Some of those cracks, especially over cheekbones and at the bridge of the nose, had widened into fissures.

"Our great friend and comrade has been dead for thirty-four years, Comrade Strankov," Plassko replied, hustling over to grab one of the glass jars from the counter. "That would take a toll on even the best of us. Even Comrade Vladimir Ilich."

Plassko unscrewed the lid on the jar. If he noticed the stench that immediately flooded the lab, the scientist did not react to it. Three of the soldiers who had been so fascinated by the body of the original Soviet leader retreated to a safe distance.

"Worse than women," Strankov grunted at the trio. "Get out, ladies." The three shamed men did as they were commanded, leaving the other three young soldiers in the room as they shut the double doors behind them.

The other scientists knew what was coming and had braced themselves for the odor, yet one had to excuse himself, then the others until only Strankov, Plassko, and the trio of stronger-stomached soldiers remained.

Plassko remained oblivious to the odor. He stuck his hand in the jar and brought out a mittful of foul-smelling brown paste which he smeared on Lenin's bald head.

"Fool," Strankov hissed. "You should have tested it first on a leg or arm. This is not only your life you…are…dealing…"

But even as he spoke, his words slowed to a shocked whisper before finally dying in his throat.

As Strankov watched in awed silence, Lenin seemed to come back to life.

The gaps in the skin on the Soviet leader's scalp slowly sealed back into smooth flesh. The brown goo gleamed as it was absorbed before completely vanishing. The raised areas in the skin became flat once more and the single patch of forehead on which Plassko had smeared the strange substance quickly took on the healthy pink tone of living flesh. One of the three young soldiers gasped.

"Remarkable, is it not?" Plassko said. He tipped his head, clearly pleased with the result. "I discovered this on an expedition to Peru. Jungle natives use it to preserve their elders. I saw bodies hundreds of years old that looked freshly dead. Amazing." He dabbed some of the brown gunk to Lenin's cheek and the dead flesh soaked it up greedily, turning pink beneath the scientist's smearing fingers. "Of course, the decadent American cosmetics companies would give their eye teeth for its secret if they saw it in use, but that is not how it works, you see. Does nothing to living tissue. Only restores necrotic flesh. Mortuaries. The dead. Only use for this."

He had finished touching up most of Lenin's face. The scalp beneath the hair would be trickier as would be the wrinkled neck. As for the rest of the treatment, they would have to strip the body, careful not to damage it in the process. But for the moment, the face of the late Soviet dictator was the evil mask he had worn in life.

The three remaining soldiers had crept forward in wonder, peering over Colonel Strankov's shoulders. Plassko smiled at his handiwork and sighed contentedly. He glanced at his Russian Army audience. To Strankov he said, "Go on. Feel."

Strankov was irritated that the scientist had read his expression so easily, especially in front of three subordinates. Still, curiosity got the better of him and he reached out and touched the tips of his fingers to Lenin's brow. He was surprised that the skin was cold. It looked so lifelike, yet there was not the warmth or softness of living tissue. The dead skin was hard to the touch. When he removed his hand, there were not the usual white imprints left from retreating fingers.

For a moment, the icy façade of the feared Colonel Ivan Strankov fell once more and he allowed a look of surprise to cross his face. "It feels like plastic."

"Yes, yes. True, true," Plassko said. "It does not revive the flesh, lamentably. It merely restores the *appearance* of living flesh. What a world this would be if we could actually return Comrade Vladimir Ilich to the living, eh?"

It was meant as a rhetorical question, so all were startled when a voice behind Strankov replied, "Well, I imagine he'd pick up right where he left off. You know, murder, savagery, filling the Kremlin swimming pool with blood and entrails. The usual commie summer vacation highlight reel."

The words were spoken in English. An American accent. And the voice. Strankov knew that voice. Unbridled rage instantly stampeded across his face as the colonel wheeled around.

A close-up flash of red; blinding. Strankov should have anticipated it. But here in Moscow, in a basement laboratory in one of the Soviet Union's most guarded buildings, the false illusion of safety had made him reckless.

The soldiers around him were startled as well, stepping back from the figure in red. One grabbed for his sidearm and another followed suit. Strankov opened his mouth to shout to the men waiting just outside the door in the corridor.

"*Gua—*"

The mass of shapeless red took the form of a man in a cloak, and from the rustling fabric shot a single hand, fingers extended. The sharp blow struck Strankov hard below the Adam's apple and the colonel fell back gasping against the table, grasping at his throat. His heel snagged the table's fat base and he tumbled hard on his backside to the concrete floor. On the table, the corpse of Lenin shuddered.

Strankov grabbed for his sidearm. At least he thought he did. He was certain his arm had moved — with all his will he had commanded his right hand to grab his gun — yet, like the phantom pain felt by an amputee, the movement was illusory. The gun remained buttoned tight in its holster and both of his hands remained locked around his own throat.

And he knew in that moment that there was a light scratch somewhere on his neck where the figure across the room had brushed a single finger of one red gauntlet.

It was a paralytic. Mild. Strankov had been dosed with it on two past occasions and both times he had shaken off the effects in about two hours. However, those other two times he had been abroad, once in New York and the other in London. Neither time had Strankov mentioned the paralyzing agent in his reports. What good would it do other than to damage Strankov's reputation in the eyes of his superiors? But here was his domain, which he was supposed to keep secure at all times. Here there were witnesses. Here in Moscow Strankov knew he would not be able to use clever spin and blatant omissions to weasel his way out of terrible repercussions. This would be his doom.

Across the room, the figure in red was now a figure in black. Strankov knew it was only a trick of light. Up close, the cloak and mask were brilliant red, but at a distance of only a few feet the red faded to a deep midnight black. At night, the black material offered perfect concealment and made the man virtually undetectable.

Ultimately the cape and mask were irrelevant. A useful parlor trick to be sure, but the danger was not the cloak he wore but the man himself: The Red Menace.

Strankov knew that his men didn't have a chance. Paralyzed on the floor, the colonel could only watch helplessly as the drama played out before him.

His three men danced around the figure in black.

One soldier aimed a gun. The Red Menace snatched the soldier's wrist and yanked the Russian towards him. The soldier lurched, the gun discharged and the bullet sank into the chest of the second Red Army man.

Screaming in fear at the discharging weapon, Dr. Plassko dived for safety beneath a coat rack next to the remains of Lenin's packing crate.

A split-second after the gun fired, the Red Menace plucked it from the startled soldier's hand and with a smooth, vicious sideways motion brought the gun butt down on the temple of the third soldier. The soldier had not time to remove his own gun from his holster. The blow struck hard and the unconscious man fell nearly in unison with the dying man with the sucking chest wound.

It was over in seconds. The first soldier stood alone in the midst of his fallen comrades, a thunderstruck look on a face that had yet to shed the baby fat of his recent childhood. And then the Red Menace was standing before him.

"Say goodnight, Gracie."

Strankov did not see the blow that sent the final man into oblivion. There was a sudden horrid crack of bone and the soldier was falling.

When the Red Menace swept past the coat rack, from somewhere beneath came a gasp of fear from Dr. Plassko. Hidden hands reached out and Plassko grasped desperately at his own ankles, drawing his cheap shoes deeper beneath the pile of hanging greatcoats.

"What's up, doc?" the Red Menace said, stomping his foot as he passed Plassko.

The coat rack squealed a tiny little squeal of fresh fear.

Shouts from the hallway. A surge of stampeding boots.

The black cape and mask turned red once more, that old trick of distorting light that Strankov knew only too well, and the Red Menace was looming over the Russian colonel. Then he was squatting; then nose to nose with the Russian.

The American wore the same infuriating, idiot smile on his face as always, and Strankov forced all his will into his fingers. If only he could reach his gun he would have blasted the smug smile off the American's face. But though his molars squeaked and beads of sweat broke out across his forehead, his arms remained stuck fast, grasping tightly at his own injured throat.

"I guess you just don't want it bad enough," the Menace said, and the infuriating smile threatened to stretch from ear to ear.

A feral sound rose from Strankov's constricted throat. When he spoke, he could only manage a hoarse whisper. "If you are going to kill me, do it. I do not fear to die."

"Well, Sunshine, ain't that just a stroke of luck on an otherwise gloomy day, because I do not fear to kill you," the Menace said. "Unfortunately, I'll have to take a rain check. This trip's just to let your Politburo puppet masters know that I can reach anyone anywhere, even the director of Motherland. On a personal side note, I'm keeping fingers crossed that I'm ruining your career in the bargain, but you can leave that out of your official report. That's just between us old friends, Strankov."

Pounding at the heavy door. There was a chair propped up against the doorknob. How the American had managed to place it there in silence directly under Strankov's own nose, the colonel had no idea. The shouting on the other side of the door increased. There were many more there than just the three soldiers Strankov had banished from the laboratory. The pounding grew more focused. The walls shook and clouds of dust rose from the rattling frame.

The Red Menace stood. "This has been fun, but I think that's my cue."

"You might escape today, you may ruin me, but it does not matter. You will ultimately fail," Strankov rasped. "You cannot stop march of progress."

"Don't want to. Progress is going along just fine on the fun side of the Iron Curtain. I just want to stop you reds from undermining it." His voice steeled. "You were in Washington again last month, Strankov. I don't want you or any other Motherland goons anywhere near the U.S. again. This is your last warning. It gets bloody after this."

Vicious hammering at the door. The wood frame creaked and the chair legs slowly squeaked across the floor, a quarter inch, then an inch. The door opened a crack and the muffled Russian voices grew loud.

"Comrade colonel!" someone unseen shouted. The chair skipped a few more inches.

The Red Menace winked at Strankov. "See you in the funny papers, comrade cabbagehead." And he was across the room, red costume turning black as he ran.

A small desk was piled high with Plassko's paperwork. The Menace tipped the desk and the mountain of papers cascaded in an avalanche to the floor; documents dumped crazily from fat folders and pencils scattered and rolled in every direction. Beakers from a jostled nearby table wobbled then fell, shattering on the concrete.

A rifle barrel appeared through the crack in the door. It fired blindly, narrowly missing Strankov's head. Pulped wood exploded from the wall an inch away from the Soviet colonel's right ear. "Stop shooting, you fools," the colonel tried to shout, but the paralytic kept his voice a whisper. Another blind shot from a trigger-happy soldier, this one two feet above Strankov's head. Shards of wood fell in the colonel's hair.

The Red Menace swept to the center of the laboratory and lifted the small desk lightly in the air, swinging it high—

Strankov's eyes grew wide. "No," he wheezed.

—and brought the full force of the desk down on top of Nikolai Lenin's rejuvenated face.

The dead dictator's head collapsed with a hollow crunch. A cloud of dust shot out in every direction as if from a stomped-on clod of dry earth. With a bound, the figure in black was up on the lab table, black boots dancing on the bottom of the overturned desk. A hard twist of his heels and the sandwiched head of Lenin made a satisfying crunch.

Across the room, the chair at last wobbled, skidded and fell, sliding across the cement. The door sprang open and two armed soldiers stumbled into the room.

The Red Menace was ready. When the chair fell, his hand was already raised, the fat barrel of an odd-shaped gun pointed across the room. A soft pop and a small object zipped across the room.

The tiny bomb struck the floor before the soldiers and the ensuing explosion launched them back into the hallway like scarecrows. Choking smoke flooded the area around the door and spilled into the hall.

With a nimble leap, the Red Menace was up in the rafters. He swung across the high ceiling from beam to beam and slipped like a wraith through the open transom to the adjoining room just as the entire Red Army piled into the Plassko's lab.

There was much shouting. Men choked on the smoke as they stomped into the room, weapons at the ready. Soldiers rushed to Strankov's side.

"Put a bullet in his brain!" the colonel commanded. The men glanced at one another, unsure why the head of Motherland appeared to be strangling himself. "There!" Strankov growled. He motioned with his eyes to the adjacent laboratory's locked door. A few bullets around the lock and the men kicked the door open and raced into the next room. More gunshots and another broken door into a dusty, seldom-used corridor. Strankov heard their shouts fade and knew that they had gone up the hall, knew that the Red Menace had escaped, knew that his career was at an end.

At the start of the crisis, someone had roused a general from an office upstairs. The old man with the great, bushy mustache swept into the center of the maelstrom.

The general regarded Strankov with contempt as he soaked in the chaos with ancient, watery eyes. Bullet holes in the wall, the lab in shambles, Dr. Plassko being hauled, shaken and pale, from his ignominious hiding place, and the young wunderkind Colonel Ivan Strankov seated on his backside on the floor, refusing to stand for a superior officer. Soldiers pulled Strankov's hands from around the colonel's own throat.

"What is all this, Strankov?" the general demanded. "Get up, man."

"I believe, comrade general, the colonel has been paralyzed," one of the squatting Red Army soldiers offered.

"Ah, yes, yes! I have something for this!" Oleg Plassko announced.

The little scientist flounced to a row of cupboards behind the tank of rotted plants and pulled down a leather valise. He fumbled with the snaps and began pawing through tiny vials, some of which contained leaf samples, others different colored liquids. When he found the vial he was after, he drew some yellow liquid into a syringe and brought the needle to Strankov's forearm. The colonel's racing heart delivered the substance with a single beat and he began to feel a rejuvenating tingle in his fingertips.

And the last words of Colonel Ivan Strankov before he was hauled to his feet, before he was dragged off to a panel of superiors, before the public condemnation that would land him for years in an icy gulag, were a loud proclamation.

"I will kill him!"

1

July 1972

THE cliff was a hundred twenty-eight foot drop to jagged basalt rock and froth-churned ocean. A flock of gulls, mere white specks in the vast blue Caribbean sky, swooped and rose and swooped again on violently erratic pockets of salty air. Sharks had been spotted a mile offshore two days before. A fisherman had caught one in his net and nearly capsized his small boat before he could cut it loose. Jeb Wilson hoped that when they threw him off the cliff, the powerful Atlantic wind that kept the gulls aloft would be strong enough to fling him back against the rocks. He wanted to be dead before he hit the water. Jeb couldn't bear the thought of being a living feast for hungry sharks.

"Do you pray to God, gringo? Because now would be a good time to ask for wings," said the Cuban captain with the thin mustache and the aviator sunglasses. In Spanish, Captain Esteban Suarez repeated his joke to the men who held Jeb's arms, and the soldiers dutifully laughed.

"You're making a mistake," Wilson said. His face was bruised and swollen. It was difficult to form words with his split and bleeding lips. "I'm not who you think I am. I'm just a naval salvage hobbiest. I'm Canadian. From Winnipeg. I've only been to the States two times in my whole life."

"So you have said many times," Captain Suarez said.

"Me?" The Cuban shrugged. "I do not care one way or the other. I just like to throw people off of cliffs." He smiled, and the large silver filling in his front tooth glinted in the sunlight. "And it seems you have forgotten your confession already. What a shame. Betrayal of one's country should matter more to men like us, eh?"

"Betrayal?" Wilson said. "I don't know what …"

Memories swirled through his addled brain like the leaves of wind-whipped palms in the little grove where Suarez had stopped his jeep.

It was difficult to remember what he'd said during the hours of torture. There was the basement cell with the moldy walls and the rusty bars. One chair, crude leather straps for wrists and ankles. And Captain Suarez. The silver tooth glinting in the harsh hundred watt bulb that hung down from the middle of the ceiling. The electric shocks, the broken fingers and toes, the torn-out fingernails.

And a perfect white carnation.

Carnation?

And then Wilson remembered. It was only yesterday. Or was it a week ago? Jeb Wilson's memory could not seem to sort time properly any longer. But he remembered the carnation and the impeccably tailored blue suit. He remembered the starched white shirt, open at the collar, and the sunburned face above it. And he remembered the voice of Nigel Sinclair, a friend from the old days.

"I can't tell you what it is, Jeb," Sinclair said. "I only know that they almost shot us down when my pilot accidentally strayed near the area. Bananas. That's what I'm here for in my dotage, can you believe it? Retired from a life in the service, survive all manner of beastly…well, *you* know, Jeb…and I nearly get shot down over bananas."

They were in a little hidden café in downtown Havana. Although it was quiet down the side alley with its cobbled road lined with Spanish colonial buildings, Jeb could still glimpse the main drag where vintage 1950s Chryslers, Plymouths and Buicks prowled along as if the entire decade of the 1960s had been nothing more than a dream. A sleek powder blue Studebaker that looked as if it had just rolled off the assembly line roared by, flashing past a bright yellow taxi.

Sinclair took a pull on his rum and fanned his sweating face with a tattered menu.

"Lucky to be alive, that's it. Only due to the fact that my pilot was quicker on the radio than those MiGs were with their rockets. Ghastly creatures, these Cubans. But what am I supposed to do? I won't stare at the walls and wait for death or Her Majesty's next government check, whichever comes first. I won't do it, Jeb. Even if I have to accept the indignity of becoming a fruit peddler in my old age. Men like us do not take retirement well. Well, of course, I don't have to tell *you* that."

Jeb was only fifty-one yet he was self-aware enough that he did not take Sinclair's observation as an insult. Jeb Wilson knew he looked old. He was reminded of that fact every time he looked in a mirror.

It was not so long ago that he had been in solid shape. One had to be when the stakes were so high. But after his field days ended, muscle had slowly turned to fat until Jeb scarcely recognized the wreck he had become. His arms were weak, his stomach flabby and he had recently noticed that his double chin was spawning a third. Not that Jeb was obese. He got a little winded climbing stairs, yes, but he could still see the tips of his shoes, which was more than a lot of his contemporaries could boast. He had simply grown old before his time and once the deterioration had started it became difficult to stop until all vestiges of youth were gone and he now no longer cared.

"What do you want me to do with this, Nigel?" Jeb asked, shaking his head wearily. He had ordered a beer but had not touched it. He tapped his finger on the table next to the glass and watched the foam bounce up and roll away from the center.

"Your backyard, not mine, Jeb," Sinclair said. "You can do nothing, if that's what you choose. But so you know, I already communicated all this to our man at the embassy. Insufferable little prig. Can't stand Eton boys. He got the word back to sit tight. London's burying it. Not worth investigating the ravings of a long-retired cold warrior like me. How many similar reports do they get every week from old soldiers all over the world? I'm sure they think I've gone potty from the heat or the boredom."

"I don't know, Nigel." Jeb sighed and ran his fingers through his thinning hair. They came back dappled with sweat and he wiped his hand on his knee. "There's no record of any base out there. What exactly do you think the reds are protecting?"

"Can't say for sure, but there is definitely something there. The jungle is thick. Perfect for concealment. But I know there was at least one large building. I saw it from the side. Wouldn't have seen it if we were directly above. Camouflage netting obscured it. Your spy planes would miss it, no doubt about that. After the MiGs broke off and we were allowed to turn back for Havana, I spotted Russian troops through a break in the trees. Aiming at us, the bastards. They quit as we turned and I lost them in the jungle. They couldn't have mobilized that fast, they must have already been out there patrolling. Something is going on out there, Jeb. I'm not so decrepit that I've lost all my instincts for the game, no matter what Box 850 thinks. I thought America should know, and now it does through you and I am washing my hands of this whole messy business and going back to my blasted bananas."

Sinclair polished off his rum, stood, fussed a moment at his white carnation, and offered his hand. Unlike Jeb's sweating palms, Nigel Sinclair's hand was dry and cool.

"Good luck, old sport. Be safe."

Sinclair left the café and headed down the alley. A moment later he had blended with foot traffic and disappeared around the corner.

Jeb sat alone at the table for another ten minutes before he finally got up and left.

For the next two hours he walked Havana's streets as he tried to figure out what to do with Sinclair's information.

Jeb was still an agent of the United States government, and was sworn to do all in his power to preserve the nation he loved. Although, granted, his was not exactly the most glamorous agency. No one wrote sexy spy novels about MIC, one of the worst kept secrets and most underfunded agencies in the spy game. Mention MIC at a D.C. cocktail party and the response was either jeers or surprise that the agency still existed.

MIC stood for Manpower and Intelligence Coordination. The agency had been set up in early 1950 in response to the first successful Russian nuclear test, First Lightning, in August of 1949. MIC was to be a cop directing traffic, facilitating the smooth flow of information as well as coordinating cooperation when necessary between the various domestic and international American espionage and police agencies. CIA, FBI, Army Intelligence and a dozen other agencies would supply the raw data and the boots on the ground and it was MIC's job to sift through that data. It worked well for the first decade or so. But over the tumultuous previous decade came a bureaucratic shift. America's other intelligence agencies seemed slowly to come to the conclusion that the greatest threat came not from America's enemies but from bean counters, budget cutters and rival agencies. Invisible walls were constructed around the bureaus which MIC theoretically supervised; their staffs became misers hoarding gold.

Nothing ever went away in government, and even as its own budget was slashed and its agents were sent out to pasture, MIC limped on into the 1970s. There were not many MIC operatives left in the field these days and most, like Jeb Wilson, were holdovers from the old days.

Jeb came to Cuba through Canada for several weeks every few months, ostensibly as the owner of a small salvage business. He had made an arrangement with the Cuban government that allowed him to not only cover the costs of his various expeditions, but to turn a slight profit. In exchange, Jeb turned over a few salvaged baubles to the Cubans and greased the palms of a few Cuban officials. In the past six months his Cuban crew had found a pair of two hundred year old wrecks off the coast of the island nation while Jeb supervised the action from a safe distance. Mostly from his favorite hotel bar. Technically he was in Cuba on assignment, but he hardly ever heard from headquarters these days. His MIC job was to keep his eyes and ears open and report back to Washington anything that might pose a threat to the nation.

It was a cozy arrangement, and most days Jeb forgot that he was technically a spy. Now Nigel Sinclair had dumped this thing in his lap and just like that he was out of the salvage business and back in the game.

Jeb's wandering was not as aimless as it seemed. He eventually found himself near a dead end street a half-mile from Havana Harbor. The very top of the lighthouse at Morro Castle peeked over the rooftops. Five old houses, their exteriors all well maintained, sat practically out on the street, two on either side, one facing out from the dead end.

Since his meeting with Sinclair, Jeb had made certain he wasn't being followed. Once he had caught the eye of a curious constable, but Jeb had bought some fish at an open air market and a doll from a sidewalk vendor and the officer had lost interest. When the cop wandered off, Jeb gave the fish to a beggar and the doll to a child. He checked for tails again before turning up the dead end.

The house at the end of the street, like the rest, had no front yard to speak of. Just some tropical greenery, a few colorful flowers and a low wrought iron fence. Jeb puffed as he climbed the three red-painted steps and knocked on the dark green door.

The man who answered was the same age as Jeb but in far better shape. Still, his hair was prematurely white, a stark contrast to his dark skin.

When he saw who was on his doorstep, the man did not smile or speak. He looked up and down his street and, seeing no one, grabbed Jeb's arm and dragged him inside, quickly shutting the door behind his guest.

The foyer was hot. The home was clean but the white paint was peeling. Jeb heard a radio playing Spanish music deep in the house.

"What are you doing here?" the Cuban demanded, his flawless English clipped.

"I need your help, Juan Carlos. Nothing big, I hope."

"Do you have any idea—" Juan Carlos stopped, gathering his thoughts. "I have not seen any of you people in ten years. Ten years. Now you come knocking on my door? No. You have to leave here. Now." He pushed Jeb towards the door.

"You owe me, Juan Carlos. You owe MIC."

"Do not say that name here," Juan Carlos snapped.

Jeb took a deep breath. "Okay, you owe the Red Menace. You do remember him, right?"

It was playing dirty pool, Jeb knew, but it had the desired effect. Juan Carlos's eyes grew wide. "Is he here?"

"Not yet. We have to do some reconnaissance first."

The deception made Jeb feel dirty. Poor Juan Carlos had been out of the loop since Batista's fall. He could not know that the Red Menace hadn't been seen since 1960. Twelve long years. Yet not so long that the name did not inspire fierce loyalty from those who had known him. Within the hour, Jeb was stowed away in the trunk of an old 1950 Chevy Bel Air that belonged to Juan Carlos Pena's elderly uncle.

Jeb could hardly breathe as he bounced around his small prison. When the car finally stopped and Juan Carlos lifted the trunk, Jeb gulped at the humid jungle air.

The car was hidden deep off the side of an abandoned footpath. Juan Carlos held a machete in one hand and he hauled Jeb out of the trunk with the other. Jeb's shirt was sopped with sweat and he felt a chill where the fabric was pasted to his lower back.

Juan Carlos closed the trunk with a careful click, held one finger to his lips and immediately began hacking his way through the overgrowth.

Jeb was grateful for the full moon or he would not have been able to see a thing. Moonlight glinted off the machete as Juan Carlos brought the sharp blade down on vine and frond. Very nearby, the soft footfalls of some unseen jungle animal stopped dead and then raced off through the thick brush.

Juan Carlos Pena's reputation as an anti-Castro jungle guide had not tarnished with age. The old animal paths were still there and, despite the deep shadows cast by the jungle canopy, the Cuban's feet instinctively located them. The two men followed the trails past waterfalls and up hills. Juan Carlos used the machete sparingly for fear the sound would draw attention. After two hours of trekking through the tropical forest, Jeb began to wonder if there was anyone out here whose attention they could attract.

"There's nothing here," Jeb said.

The machete flashed. For an instant Jeb thought that Juan Carlos had betrayed him. He expected to feel the blade strike the side of his head. Instead, a damp hand clamped firmly over his mouth and Jaun Carlos dragged Jeb into some underbrush. He stuffed the machete near their feet and swept the rotting jungle floor over the metal.

Moments later, a foot patrol tromped past.

There were ten of them. Mostly Cubans, with a pair of Russians mixed in. One Russian was older, the other very young. A Soviet advisor and his aide.

The group failed to spot Jeb and his guide. Once they were gone, Juan Carlos grabbed up his machete and the two men hustled after the group.

There were paths made by men now, and so the going became considerably easier. However, a clear path meant much human activity and Jeb knew that it would not be very long before another patrol swept through the area. But what exactly were they guarding?

Jeb and Juan Carlos lagged behind the patrol until the footsteps faded in the distance. Jeb had been puffing as if in the early stages of heart failure for the entire trip up from the hidden Chevy, but with the appearance of the patrol his old instincts had kicked in. His heart quickened, his breathing came under control. Even his own footfalls sounded quieter to his ears as they made their way up the perilous mountain path.

The first scent of salt air was tickling his nostrils and Jeb knew they must have rounded out to somewhere near the ocean when they finally found the spot about which Nigel Sinclair had spoken.

There were some lights on high poles, but black tarpaulins were spread out above them so that the light cast down was hidden from above. Camouflage netting was everywhere. Crude thatch made of palm leaves and light branches covered buildings and were strategically scattered over camo nets. And crawling like uniformed ants throughout the complex were dozens of Russian and Cuban soldiers.

With a nod and a dark expression, Juan Carlos melted back into the shadows. His guide had gotten Jeb to his destination and would go no further. The Cuban would hide here and await the American MIC agent's return. *If* he returned.

Jeb spent the next hour reconnoitering the complex as best he could. He was limited by geography and age, and guessed he'd only gotten a sixth of the periphery mapped out. He had brought a camera with a good telephoto lens and spent much of his time snapping picture after picture. A major road to the south led down a mountain near the sea, but a cliff face on one side and jungle on the other obscured it from aircraft.

Around a central courtyard were barracks and a tin hanger, a few small buildings for medics and officers and something that looked like a bunker. This was the center of the hornet's nest. Men came out of buildings, saluted superiors, and ducked inside other buildings. Foot patrols returned while others marched off into the jungle. Beyond this section of the base, Jeb could see more lights and more activity. There was something else going on in the jungle, but to get there he would have to cross too close to the central hub and there was no way he could do so without being spotted.

It would be dawn soon. Jeb was about to start picking his careful way back to Juan Carlos's hiding place when he spotted two figures exiting one of the smaller buildings. Jeb had seen a man in a white coat enter the structure earlier and had guessed that it housed medical facilities. He directed his lens at the two men.

When he peered through the camera and got a clear, close-up image of the men, Jeb felt his heart clench.

A ghost. Impossible. Not here. It could not be. Jeb blinked, hoping that his eyes were playing tricks. When the image did not change, Jeb allowed a tiny slip of air to pass between his lips.

"Holy smoke," he hissed.

That he had first thought he was seeing a specter was understandable. Colonel Ivan Strankov appeared cadaverous. The Russian could not weigh much more than a hundred pounds. When he spoke, he bared his teeth like a snarling dog. Even his skin looked the wrong color. Jeb wanted to blame it on the weird base lighting, but the skin tone of the fat, pale little man with the thick glasses, bald head and yellow fringe of hair to whom Strankov spoke appeared normal in the light.

Jeb took two dozen pictures of Strankov. Strankov standing in front of the medical buildings, Strankov motioning toward the distant jungle and the unseen section of the hidden base, Strankov walking slowly but steadily, as if a breeze might blow him down, inside the low concrete bunker. The door shut behind the Russian colonel.

Jeb was still trying to wrap his brain around the enormity of this discovery as he made his way back through the jungle to Juan Carlos. The first gray streaks of dawn were lightening the sky when his guide appeared from the thicket. The two men made their way back down the hill, avoiding three foot patrols on their way to the hidden Bel Air.

Jeb did not even notice the bumpy ride back to Havana. In the dark, fiercely humid trunk he thought only of Strankov.

The Russian was dead, or as good as. According to smuggled reports out of Moscow, it had taken the Soviets nearly a year to find a look-alike to generously, if involuntarily, donate his head to replace the flattened mess the Red Menace had made of Lenin's. The Russkies surely would have used that of Ivan Strankov himself if the bone structure hadn't been so wrong. The last Jeb heard, Strankov was locked away in a gulag for life. Yet here was the leader of Motherland, fourteen years after his disgrace and imprisonment, back in uniform and on the wrong side of the Atlantic.

MIC in Washington would need to know.

The sun was hot by the time they reached the capital. Juan Carlos popped the trunk behind an auto body shop, warning Jeb as he climbed back behind the wheel of his uncle's car, "Never contact me again."

Jeb wasn't even listening. As the Bel Air roared off down the road, Jeb hustled in the opposite direction.

In a tiny cottage near the shore he found a friend from the old days. The old man promised to smuggle the undeveloped film to the U.S. Naval base at Guantanamo Bay.

The next two days were sheer agony as Jeb could only sit in his hotel room and wait for a reply. It came after midnight on the third day, delivered by a kid of about twelve whom Jeb had never seen before.

"Interesting pictures of old friend, but vacation photos lack detail. Next time, highlight background landscape."

Jeb shook his head, shocked. "The bastards can't be serious."

MIC had recognized Strankov, but they wanted pictures of the one area of the Russian base Jeb had been unable to reach.

For a few minutes he considered ignoring the order. At his age and in his shape it was suicide to traipse back up through the jungle and straight into the lion's den. Not to mention the fact that he was lucky the Cubans hadn't picked up on his absence the first time around. Castro's thugs had a habit of unlocking hotel doors when one least expected it, even those of supposed Canadian citizens who had bribed all the right people.

Jeb burned the note in an ashtray as he weighed his options. In the end, loyalty to country got the best of him.

The next morning he took a bus out to his salvage operation, which was stationed in a bay a few miles down the shore from the jungle base. His crew had just returned from a fruitless week at sea and he spent the afternoon commiserating with them, heading back for the bus stop as the sun was setting. But when the rattling old bus arrived, Jeb was not standing around with the locals. He had slipped back in the jungle and had begun the arduous, miles-long journey back to the Russian base.

He knew where it was now and so did not need Juan Carlos to guide him. In three hours he was back in the same spot where he'd snapped the photos of Ivan Strankov.

Strankov was not in the main compound this time. Jeb crouched in the forest and puzzled over how he could reach the far side of the base without detection.

It did not take long for him to find the blind spot in their security.

A fresh Russian-led Cuban patrol departed every ten minutes, just as the first patrol in the hour-long cycle was returning. Jeb hoped that gap of ten minute intervals between patrols would be enough for him to sneak through to the other side of the base.

He waited for his chance and when a new patrol had departed and a returning patrol had disappeared inside the main barracks, Jeb slipped from his hiding spot and ran headlong across the main road and through the courtyard.

It was bright beneath the waning Caribbean moon. Nearly everyone was asleep and all the windows in the buildings were dark. Only a handful of the exterior lights remained on, all shrouded from above so as to be invisible to reconnaissance flights. The low light cast the compound in spectral shadows.

As he ran, Jeb imagined Strankov sleeping somewhere in one of the little tin buildings, probably the one with the chugging air conditioning unit. Briefly he wished he had told Juan Carlos the truth, wished that the Red Menace hadn't disappeared over a decade ago. Jeb would have welcomed the return of his mysterious cloaked friend this night. But Jeb Wilson was alone, huffing through the humid Cuban night.

Jungle closed in once more on the far side of the main compound, and Jeb raced into it, grateful for the slap and scratch of branches against his sweating face.

The forest followed an arc around the concrete bunker Jeb had spotted the first time around. Beyond that, on the ocean side, was the closed-off section of the base.

Jeb had crept only a few yards when the alarm sounded.

Shocked, Jeb stopped dead, as if stillness might stop the awful, piercing noise.

The entire base seemed to rouse from slumber, a furious giant suddenly aware of the flea on its back. The staccato shriek blared from loudspeakers on buildings and poles.

Ahn-ahn! Ahn-ahn!

The noise screamed over and over in Jeb's ears, piercing his skull and numbing his brain. It was all he could do to arrest the instinct to flee, to race straight back in the direction from which he'd come. But the compound was alive now. Floodlights flashed on all around, slicing into darkness. Conscripted men in hastily donned uniforms were swarming from every building; officers sprinted amongst them shouting orders and questions in Spanish and Russian.

A running foot patrol suddenly appeared out of nowhere and Jeb fell instinctively to his belly as boots stomped past mere feet from his hiding spot.

A few shouted words were just barely discernable from out the frenzy.

"Loose."

"How?"

"A vent."

Jeb understood Spanish and only a little Russian, but he knew enough to realize that the chaos had nothing to do with him. He stayed put as the drama played out.

Strankov appeared, looking like a corpse that had been roused from its crypt. He waved furious arms and a soldier ran off. A moment later the klaxon stopped blaring. The fat little man with the bald head and fringe of yellow hair waddled desperately out of the bunker. He was dressed and wore a white lab coat, as if he had been working at this late hour. He joined a conference between Colonel Strankov and some Cuban officers.

Strankov's raised voice cut through the renewed silence, and although Jeb could hear the Russian's angry drone he could not catch the words.

Soon people were fleeing back into buildings. Strankov and the little scientist remained outside for several long minutes until a growing whine rose from the southwest jungle. The first aircraft appeared from Havana and Strankov strode into the bunker, forcefully gesturing the chastened little fat man to get in ahead of him.

Jeb saw from the silhouettes against the moon and stars that the two planes were Russian Tupolev Tu-4s. Once they were above the base there came a sudden loud hiss and a moment later Jeb felt his skin grow damp from something more than sweat.

The planes had been adapted as some kind of crop dusters. They methodically circled the area, releasing clouds of vapor from wing-mounted nozzles.

"Great. Poison," Jeb muttered. But the smell that came to his nostrils was not harsh. In fact, the scent reminded him vaguely of...chocolate?

Just what the hell were the Russians up to here?

And suddenly — just like that — Jeb did not care.

This was it. Jeb Wilson had officially had enough. Twenty-seven years in the spy game and he was finished. If MIC wanted to investigate this further, that was fine with him. MIC, CIA, whoever. He didn't care. He was out of it. Fifty-two years old was too old for the game. A real retirement. Maybe make a real go of his phony salvage business cover. Maybe collect seashells in Florida and sell them to tourists. Something else. *Anything* else. Far away from this godforsaken sweaty island jungle.

The Tupolevs were circling in the distance for another run. The main square in front of the buildings was empty. Jeb broke cover and ran for all he was worth back across the road. He thought he heard a voice shout behind him but he did not stop to see.

Back into the jungle and down the hill. Foot patrols pounded the overgrowth, radios squawking. At one point the planes roared above, heading back to Havana.

Still, Jeb ran. In the sultry predawn he avoided Cuban street patrols. From alleys to backyards to courtyards, all the way back to his hotel. The wee hours skeleton staff was easily avoided and Jeb made it up the stairs and back to his room without being seen.

He turned the key in the lock, grabbed the knob, heaved a sigh of relief...

...and tripped and fell flat on his face on the threadbare carpet when the door was wrenched open from the inside.

Jeb rolled onto his back and found himself staring at the unblinking black eyes of six Russian Kalashnikov rifles.

"There was a time when the Americans would send more than an out of shape relic to spy on me."

The accent was Russian, the voice was one Jeb had heard only on surveillance tapes, and then more than a decade ago. He had heard the same voice at the jungle compound that night.

Colonel Ivan Strankov was sitting on the edge of Jeb's bed, legs crossed crisply and a cigarette smoldering between long fingers. A Cuban captain wearing a broad grin and sporting a silver filling in his front tooth stood at his side.

Jeb knew that Strankov couldn't be more than forty. Yet up close the Russian looked eighty. His face was drawn, his skin leathery. And the pigmentation was off — horribly so — like the ugly mess a child achieves from mixing all the watercolors together.

"I'm not—" Jeb began.

"No," Strankov snapped. "I have limited time and patience." To the Cuban captain he said, "Take him, Suarez, and break him."

Jeb was dragged from his hotel room and dumped in the back of a truck. In twenty minutes he was strapped to a chair in a basement room in the capitol building while the Cuban, Suarez, gleefully beat, burned and bled him.

For hours he kept his cover. "I'm a naval salvage hobbiest. Check with your own government. Minister Perez, Foreign Relations Minister. State Committee President Yedra, National Bank of Cuba. Canadian. I'm Canadian. From Winnipeg."

How many times he told the story he did not know.

"Ontario?" Suarez said at one point late at night.

"What?"

"You just said you were from Winnipeg, Ontario."

"Yes….no. Winnipeg, Manitoba."

The first crack in the dam. It was not long after that he broke; shattered completely. Much sooner than his younger self would have thought. He told them everything. His two trips to the secret base, Juan Carlos, the pictures back to MIC. When the soldiers dumped Juan Carlos Pena's mutilated body at his feet, Jeb scarcely noticed.

He was a mass of bruises when Strankov pulled him back by the hair and blew a puff of cigarette smoke in his face. The Russian was so discolored he was nearly purple. In a moment of lucidity that shocked him from his delirium, Jeb knew that he was not the only one in that cell who was near death.

"You think you know something? What is happening here?" Strankov shook his head and smiled a mouthful of long, yellow teeth, like the teeth of a very old wolf. "Pitiful."

And then he was gone. Out of the cell — a gaunt shadow of his former self, but spine still rigid — without a backwards glance at his prisoner.

Jeb remembered the hot sunlight and a courtyard. Voices in Spanish, a language he knew as well as English, yet for some reason his brain could not process the words any longer. Hands grabbed him, lifting, dumping him in the back of a jeep. A drive that could have been minutes or hours. Hard kicks to the belly and he was rolled out of the jeep, dropping like a fat sack onto the ground. The ocean air tousled his hair, the salt mist stung the fresh wounds on his pale skin.

A fresh, horrid pain in his chest. He saw a short knife blade and a close hand carving something into his flesh.

Captain Esteban Suarez was standing before him once more, slipping a knife back into a sheath on his hip. The unforgiving Cuban sun beat harshly on Jeb's pale skin, the endless ocean stretching out to the far horizon, gulls swooping, and a lethal hundred and twenty-eight foot drop to violently churning sea.

"You know, Mr. Manitoba or Mr. Ontario, whichever senor prefers—" Suarez flashed his silver filling. "—for the right amount of money, I could be persuaded to let you go. You say you know the President of the National Bank?"

"What?" Jeb said, hope flickering in his heart. "Yes. Yes, I know him."

"Oh." Suarez snapped his fingers. "But we are not allowed to take the bribes. I'm so sorry, this had slipped my mind." The flash of silver and Captain Suarez lunged forward, shoving both hands hard in the center of Jeb's chest.

Solid ground became empty air. Jeb fell.

Gravity drew him straight down into the sloping rock face. He struck, bounced, struck the side of the cliff once more and was a limp bag of broken bones by the time he slammed the basalt rocks that lined the bay.

Suarez was back in his jeep and driving away from the seashore as Jeb Wilson's lifeless corpse slipped slowly from the moss-and-blood slick rocks and vanished beneath the churning water. And for just a moment the white caps were stained red.

2

"That's not true, Brad, my family did not in fact lose *a* fortune in steel, my family lost *two* fortunes in steel. Believe me, when my grandfather lost a fortune it stayed lost. The only one worse than granddad was my father. A real financial Houdini, dad was. Give him a dollar and he could turn it to pennies like that."

Patrick Becket snapped his fingers and flashed a winning smile of perfect white teeth. The small crowd gathered around him chuckled approvingly.

The louvered vents and high ceiling fans churned the chilly recirculated air in the big Hawaiian hotel ballroom. The men in their tuxedos took no note of the air conditioning, but the silent women in their sleeveless gowns shivered at the cold.

"No, I wish it was a joke." Becket gestured to his tux. "What I wouldn't have given to have had this for my prom. Instead I looked like I'd mugged Arlo Guthrie. My mom said it'd be fine, but you know the night's a bust when your date gets a poison ivy rash from her corsage. In the meantime dear ol' dad's on the back phone screaming at his broker about the million he's just lost on magic beans futures."

More polite, insincere laughter from the half-dozen hangers-on.

A soft voice at his shoulder. "Excuse me, Mr. Becket?"

Patrick Becket turned to find Milo O'Hara standing anxiously at the edge of the crowd. Becket's personal accountant was wearing a pinched expression and an off-the-rack business suit. O'Hara did not meet the eyes of the tuxedoed bluebloods, not that the crowd could be bothered to waste so much as a glance on him.

"Oh. Milo," Becket said. He checked his watch. "Is it that time already? I'm sorry, but will you ladies and gentlemen please excuse me? Tennis tomorrow, Brad?"

The men said their goodbyes and peeled away one by one, their shivering feminine ornaments clinging more tightly to their sleeves than cufflinks.

On his way to the door, Becket apologized to several men who tried to engage him in conversation, throwing up his hands in surrender and nodding to Milo in a helpless manner that wordlessly expressed, "Sorry, not my idea, I'd love to stay and chat, but I'm a hostage here."

In the lobby, with the big ballroom doors closed tightly on the dreary gathering at his back, Becket's fingers immediately tore at his bowtie. "Thank God," he announced, heaving a sigh of relief. "Another minute and I'd've drowned myself in the punch bowl. Whatever I gave you for a raise this year, Milo, double it."

Becket strode across the gleaming lobby of the Paradise of the Pacific Hotel, past wealthy guests with expensive baggage, drunks returning with cheap local escorts, wait staff and bellmen. A placard on an easel angled to face the main doors read "Welcome To Guests of Becket International, Inc." The logo of a dark blue B bracketed by light red I's was like a family crest pasted large in the center of the billboard.

When the company was about to go public, Milo O'Hara and others had suggested the logo be abandoned in favor of Patrick Becket's own face. Becket was ruggedly handsome in an old Hollywood way, with a lantern jaw, sandy hair and intelligent, mischievous eyes. Becket had steadfastly refused. Patrick Becket was the name of his company but not the face. For most of the time he remained as aloof as his position as head of IBM's major competitor in the computer business allowed. Even this, the annual week-long meetings held for major shareholders was torture for Patrick Becket, which was why he had arranged in advance for rescue by Milo.

A doorman in a red uniform with gold piping opened both the door and his hand as Becket passed, earning ten dollars for his trouble.

The Honolulu night was warm but dry. It felt good to breathe natural air again.

"Thank God it's over." He dug at his collar, unbuttoning his top button.

"There's some paperwork we need to go over, Mr. Becket," Milo said. He hustled to keep up with his employer, who was striding past manicured shrubs in terra cotta pots. Becket made a beeline for the side parking lot.

"Tomorrow, Milo. You know how many phony smiles I've had to force this week? It feels like my jaw's been wired shut."

The parking attendant wasn't on duty. As they walked past the dark booth, a little window sign announced the hotel employee left at nine.

"It's on your way home, sir," Milo insisted. "Mr. Haverford's plane leaves at noon tomorrow, and we could have those contracts we discussed out of the way tonight and run them past legal first thing in the morning before he leaves. Five minutes at the office, Mr. Becket, and I promise I'll—" The accountant gasped and stopped dead.

The parking lot had seemed deserted. Mostly rental cars of guests and a few employees whose exceptional work in various departments had earned them a bump up from the regular employee lot to one of the six coveted temporary spots nearer the hotel. It was from the shadows next to a boxy Rambler that the three men emerged.

The hippie fad had spread its pollution to Hawaii's tropical paradise. The three punks wore torn bellbottom jeans and sandals. Two sported tight tie-dyed T-shirts while the third wore a hideous blouse that looked like a polyester flower shop. None of the buttons were buttoned, and his loose shirt tails flapped in the ocean breeze.

The one with the flower shirt was small, and he slapped a tire iron menacingly in his open palm. The pair in tie-dye did not need weapons to intimidate, they merely needed to loom above the rest of the mortal world like overly-muscled sequoias.

Milo raised his hands and took a step back. He glanced at his boss, but to his shock he found Patrick Becket appeared entirely unruffled.

It was his sheltered life. Had to be. Despite what he always said about his ancestors' inability to maintain their fortunes, Patrick Becket had never wanted for anything in his life. He had lived always in a pampered bubble. For Milo O'Hara's employer, muggers and murderers existed only in the abstract. Becket might be aware of the existence of bad men who would club you over the head for your watch and wallet, but only as newspaper filler or the stuff of movie melodramas. If anything the CEO of Becket International, Incorporated seemed amused to encounter three muggers in the dead of night in a lonely parking lot with no sign of rescue in sight.

"Put your hands up, Mr. Becket," Milo suggested in a whisper.

Becket held up a staying finger, as if interrupted at the office water cooler. "Hold that thought, Milo."

And when Patrick Becket addressed the trio of toughs, it took all of Milo O'Hara's willpower not to release the contents of his bladder down his Woolworth's slacks.

"Well, aren't you the prettiest little things," Becket said to the two bruisers. Both men had long, tangled hair that hung in greasy strands over their broad shoulders. "Are the boys out here treating you right? You know, you mainland gals have to watch out. There are bad men on the islands. Fly out on daddy's credit card did we?"

One of the hulking goons growled and took a step forward, but their little leader held a small hand against his rippling chest and the big man stopped.

"No," the little punk sneered, "but as a matter of fact we'll be takin' yours, mister. Along with whatever else is in your wallet." He snorted, but only one of two goons joined in with a hearty guffaw. The other was as silent as stone.

The spokesman for the group was a native Hawaiian, with a broad nose and dark skin. He handed his tire iron to the nearer goon who was glowering at Becket and flicked out a switchblade, metal glinting in the parking lot lights.

"That's fine," Milo told the mugger. "My friend and I don't want any trouble. I am unarmed. I am reaching for my wallet now." The accountant was snaking a shaking hand to his inside jacket pocket when the unthinkable happened. His boss apparently chose that moment — the worst possible moment — to go completely and utterly insane.

"I've got a better idea, Tiny. Why don't you do yourself a favor and take your scary, clicky little knife thing there along with Thing One and Thing Two, and get the hell out of here while all your kneecaps are still intact? I'll give you—" He checked his gold Rolex. "—five seconds." Patrick Becket's voice was perfectly level, as if he were addressing a toddler who could not grasp the concept of coloring between the lines.

Milo O'Hara's wallet was out and held high in his shaking hand. The leather was slick with palm sweat. "Mr. Becket, *please*," he begged.

But it was too late. Patrick Becket was a dead man. Milo could see it in the murderous eyes of the little man in the ugly shirt.

The little punk was used to taking everything he wanted from the rich tourists who visited his island. His police record stretched back ten years to his first juvenile offense, and he had beaten and robbed dozens of vacationers not just on Hawaii, but on Maui and Kauai. He had not yet murdered a man, but there was a first time for everything.

"You got a big mouth, mister," Tiny said, licking his lips as the gears in his brain turned and his eyes telegraphed his lethal decision. "You shoulda kept that big mouth of yours shut." The knife was already level to the ground, Becket's belly lined up and wide open for an attack. With a triumphant whoop, the little mugger lunged, plunging the blade deep in the soft guts and pulsing organs of this big-mouthed tourist.

At least that's what he thought happened. He was sure the knife would find an easy target. But as he darted forward for his certain first kill, something strange happened. Two very strong hands snapped out and latched tightly onto his forearm.

Suddenly Tiny's victim wasn't where he had been. The tourist had skipped to one side and grabbed the would-be killer's arms. And then he was yanking, hard.

The mugger's forward momentum launched him past Patrick Becket and straight through the driver's side window of a parked car. Glass shattered, decorating the parking lot with tiny shards that glistened in the mercury vapor light, and the punk spilled hard into the front seat, face and hands torn and bloody, legs kicking futilely at the night air.

Milo O'Hara stood in stunned disbelief, wallet still held above his head. The accountant was not the only one amazed. As their boss kicked air and moaned, the two monsters stood in slack-jawed shock. Their hesitation lasted just an instant too long.

Becket sent the heel of his dress shoe hard into the right knee of the nearest behemoth. There was a horrid crack, like thick ice settling heavily on a winter pond, and the man went down, his leg bent at an unnatural angle. Three rabbit punches in rapid succession brought a furious spurt of bright red blood from the man's nose.

"Aaaaargh!" the final beast cried, and charged.

The goon swung the tire iron in his huge hand. Becket ducked easily below the weapon and, coming up fast, stabbed the leading edge of his hand, knuckles bent like a spear, against the man's throat. The tire iron clanged to the ground and the mugger grabbed instinctively at his own neck. Becket quickly snatched two handfuls of long hair and jerked down. The head dropped sharply and met Becket's knee with a vicious crunch. The final mugger was unconscious before he hit the pavement.

It was over in less than ten seconds.

Milo O'Hara was still offering his wallet up, but there were no longer any takers. He gulped at air for a moment, remembered eventually that breathing was necessary to survival, pulled in a deep lungful of air, and on the exhale managed to hiss, "My God" before again forgetting temporarily how to breathe. "My God. I mean— My God."

"Yes, mine too. Put that away, will you, Milo. You look like a tourist."

Milo's hands were still raised. Becket guided the hand still holding his wallet high above his head back inside Milo's jacket.

The man with the broken kneecap groaned and Milo jumped.

"My God, Mr. Becket. The police. We should…I'll call the police."

Becket did not object, but for the briefest instant Milo thought he saw a frown brush his employer's brow, as if the attention of the Honolulu police was the last thing on Earth he wanted to deal with. Milo trotted away but did not get far before he heard howls of pain and renewed groans from behind. When he turned he found that the short mugger had been dragged out of the car and was sitting on his backside on the asphalt.

The chief mugger was bleeding profusely from a head wound. The dark river of blood looked like motor oil in the weak parking lot light. He was cradling his right hand as if it was broken, although Milo could not see how it could have been damaged in the fight. The second conscious man was holding his hand up under his armpit as well and gritting his teeth against fresh pain. The third man groaned as he regained consciousness and drew his hand instinctively toward his chest.

Patrick Becket was in the process of tossing away the tire iron that had somehow found its way into his hand, and he beckoned Milo to return.

"Forget the cops, Milo. The boys are swearing off mugging. Go on now and scoot, you little rapscallions. Join a youth choir or something. Off you go."

The muggers hauled themselves to wobbly feet. The monster with the broken kneecap leaned heavily on their ringleader's shoulder. The three men were escapees from a horror movie graveyard as they shuffled away, trails of dribbling blood staining the pavement. They disappeared through the beachside palms.

Becket was marching confidently over to his car, a green Mustang parked near the line of light poles that bisected the parking lot.

"Find out who owns that car and buy them a new one," Becket said, an added little spring in his step as he hopped behind the wheel. He stabbed his thumb back at the Rambler. In addition to the shattered window, the old car's door was buckled in, and there was blood and glass all over the front seat.

As his employer revved the Mustang's engine, Milo suddenly felt very tired, the inevitable crash after a rush of adrenaline and fear. "It's an old car, Mr. Becket. Just a hotel employee. A couple of bucks for the window and a little detailing should suffice."

"A new one," Becket insisted. "Whatever they want, let 'em have it." He considered for a brief instant. "Just, Milo? Make sure it's something in red."

With a grin at some private joke poor Milo could not hope to understand, Patrick Becket threw the car in gear. Milo O'Hara was left alone to cough in a cloud of acrid rubber smoke as the Mustang tore out of the lonely hotel parking lot.

3

His hand was an arrow directed with crossbow precision at a single spot. He watched in slow motion as it shot forward and struck the Adam's apple.

The attacker outweighed him by a good sixty pounds, but that didn't matter. It never had in the old days. The blow stopped the big man in mid-charge. The hulking mugger's eyes shot open wide and he grabbed his throat...but suddenly the giant hands were small and the fingers long and thin and the man was no longer the hippie mugger from the Paradise of the Pacific Hotel parking lot. The hair was now short, the features sharp and rat-like. He was shorter too, and wore a uniform. Russian Army.

Strankov.

The Soviet colonel was sitting on the floor in a Russian basement lab, paralyzed hands clutched comically at his own throat and Becket's own hands were no longer bare.

The red gauntlets had a life of their own. They grabbed Strankov by the uniform jacket and shook violently, as if trying to awaken the Russian colonel from slumber.

Strankov's eyes glared hatred. Still, Becket held tight and shook until Strankov screamed and vanished in an oozing red puddle on the concrete floor.

The shock jolted Becket and his eyes sprang open.

The weird dreaming images of the mugger and the Russian colonel scampered back to the recesses of Becket's subconscious mind, replaced by gently rolling Pacific waves pressed between a cloudless blue sky and a hot strip of perfect white sand.

Funny that he'd dream about Strankov. He hadn't given the Russian colonel much thought for over a decade. The attempted mugging in the parking lot the previous night had apparently shaken loose some very old memories. Old and best forgotten.

Becket wore a pair of green swimming trunks that matched the green cushions of the wooden chaise lounge on which he lazily sprawled.

There were a few white scars here and there on tan skin, evidence of very old wounds, but he considered most minor scrapes. The only visible sign of a major injury was the white patch on the left side of his chest. It started like a starburst that trailed around and petered off on the side. But the wound was ancient; long ago healed.

A silent phone sat on a glass table, plugged into a line that ran back to the house. The great, high rear wall of Patrick Becket's Hawaiian estate loomed behind a row of gently swaying palms. A beach umbrella shielded him from the worst of the Pacific sun and a cooler of bottled spring water on ice was at his side.

Another long, insufferable day in paradise.

His right shoulder ached. He rubbed at it gingerly and tried rotating the arm but the pain persisted. There were days when it was much worse, and after the unexpected workout last night he was happy he didn't have to call his doctor this morning.

"Ain't life grand?" he sighed to the ocean.

With his thumb, Becket popped the cap off a mineral water bottle. He was taking a lazy swig when he noticed a lone man walking up the otherwise empty beach.

The stranger was no beachcomber. He stood out like a sore thumb in his two piece suit and sport shirt. He carried a briefcase in one hand and mopped his desperately sweating brow with the damp handkerchief which he held tightly in the other. Black dress shoes struggled in soft sand as he crossed over to where Becket lay.

"Mr. Becket?" the young man asked.

"This is a private beach," Becket said, hiking his dark sunglasses up to his forehead. "*My* private beach. Since I'm the only one lying out on the beach that I own, and since you know my name, you already know I'm me. If you know something, son, make it a statement, not a question. It's irritating the other way." Becket dropped the glasses back over eyes that were now closed.

"Ah, yes," the man said. He was in his late twenties and seemed put off that a man of only forty-two would call him 'son.' "Good morning. It's nice to meet you, Mr. Becket. My name is Kirk. Simon Kirk. I'm the director of MIC."

"Kirk? You Harmon Kirk's kid?"

"One of them," the young man said.

"How is old Harmon?"

"On a new assignment, actually. Unrelated to MIC."

"Harmon finally busted out of the loony bin, huh? Good for him."

"Yes." Kirk sat without an offer from Becket in one of a pair of Adirondack chairs which were arranged under the umbrella. "Actually," he said, popping the hasps on his briefcase, "my father is the one who suggested I get in touch with you."

"Have you seen this *All in the Family* show?" Becket asked. He lifted his glasses once more, but he did not look at Kirk, who seemed baffled by the non sequitur. A white wisp of cloud stretched thin across the otherwise flawless blue sky, and as he spoke Becket watched it slowly disintegrate. "God, that Meathead son-in-law is unbearable. Here's this fat mooch living under his father-in-law's roof, and all he does is scream at the guy. Every night he starts another screaming match. The father-in-law — Archie — is supposed to be the villain of the thing. But all I do is watch wondering why he puts up with this halfwit commie know-it-all. The fat slob eats all Archie's food and lives rent free while Archie works at a miserable job every day to support his family, and he has to come home to that ungrateful jackass who isn't even a blood relative, and he puts up with it and *he's* the bad guy? That fat turd would have a bruise on his rear end the shape of my boot and be out my front door in two pinko seconds."

"Mr. Becket, I'm not sure what—"

"My friends call me Podge."

"Podge."

Podge tipped his head, considering. "You can call me Mr. Becket.

What it has to do with you, young Master Kirk, is that I have the greatest electronic and human security in the world on this estate, yet you just waltzed up to me on my private beach which means my people let you in here. No one phoned ahead, which tells me you told them not to, probably with threats of IRS audits or some other abuse of government power. Which tells me that you're a fan of theatricality, which would make sense for someone who would seek me out after all this time. You're reaching in that briefcase because you have something in there that you think I'm going to find absolutely fascinating. And what I'm telling you is that *All in the Family* is on tonight and even though I hate it I never miss an episode, so you're going to have to take whatever offer you were planning to make and stick it back in that briefcase and hightail it back out the way you came. Make sure you let the electronic gate hit you in the keister on the way out."

"Jeb Wilson is dead," Kirk announced. "He was murdered last week."

Podge slowly peeled off his glasses. Kirk's youthful face seemed suddenly to be that of a much older man.

"One of our boats found him floating out at sea. They thought at first he was a refugee who drowned while trying to flee Cuba."

"Cuba? What the hell was Wilson doing there? He was old enough to have a stateside desk job by now."

"There aren't enough MIC stateside jobs to go around any longer," Kirk explained. "We don't have the budget we had back when you worked for the agency."

"*With*, son," Podge corrected angrily. He glanced around but the beach was empty and there was not a single sail out on the waves. Still, he lowered his voice. "I don't know what your father told you my relationship with the agency was, but I never worked for, I only ever worked with."

"He did make that clear," Kirk said. "I apologize. Be that as it may, the current MIC is a shell of the agency you knew. Every couple of months we hear threats from Congress and rumblings out of the White House that we're being closed down. Our current budget is a fraction of what it was in the Fifties. We've tightened our belts to the point where we can barely breathe. Wilson wasn't necessarily too old, but I admit he was in lousy shape to be a field agent. Still, I had no choice but to keep him active. I have to use the tools that are available to me, even if they're inadequate to the task."

Podge bristled at Kirk's use of the word "inadequate" to describe Jeb Wilson, and opened his mouth to speak. The MIC director quickly raised a staying hand.

"I know he was your friend, and I don't mean to insult his memory," Kirk interjected before Podge could say a single pointless word in defense of Wilson. "He was a good soldier who died because of my orders. I simply needed someone better than him, someone more up to the task. Not that he completely failed in his final mission, he absolutely did not." The director of MIC reached into his briefcase and brought out a handful of photographs which he handed to Podge.

They were aerial photos, taken from a high-altitude reconnaissance plane.

"This is an area of jungle north of Havana," Kirk explained. "Our spy planes were rerouted there last Thursday as a result of Wilson's initial report."

Podge saw only jungle. If Kirk hadn't mentioned Cuba there would be no way of telling by the geography exactly where the tropical forest was. There were a few white circles drawn here and there on the photos around areas that might have been hints of structures peeking from the overgrowth, but without magnification Podge couldn't be sure. At a glance, the pictures were unspectacular and he said so to Kirk.

"Agreed," Kirk said. "However, this is the same area of jungle one day after." He passed over another set of photographs.

Podge saw a burned-out area, like desert. It appeared as if there had been a fire that had laid waste several acres. By the shape of the charred area, the blaze looked deliberate. No natural fire burned like that. It was a nearly perfect circle carved in jungle.

In these photos there was no thick overgrowth to obscure the manmade structures. There were tin huts and cinderblock buildings dotting the entire landscape. Podge could see the frozen black shapes of tiny men dragging branches up onto the roofs of buildings.

"Well, I assume you know whatever did this was an accident," Podge said.

Despite himself, he found the photos intriguing and the interest was clear on his tan face. The expression was not lost on Kirk, yet so engrossed was Podge in the pictures he did not look up to see the small smile that flashed across Kirk's face.

"They went to a lot of trouble to keep that base hidden," Podge said, more to himself than to Kirk. "No way they'd open it up to the world like this on purpose, especially if they knew Wilson had reported it. They tortured him, didn't they."

It was a statement of fact, not a question. Any vestige of a smile vanished from Kirk's face. He nodded sharply and turned his face to the vast Pacific Ocean. "We even know who did it. One of Castro's monsters, a captain named Suarez. He carves an S on all his victims. We found one on Wilson's chest." Kirk sighed. "It's an ugly world out there, Mr. Becket. Much worse than it was when you helped us out all those years ago."

Podge ignored him. He was back to studying the photos. "Napalm."

Kirk tore his gaze from the waves. "Our experts say no. It's not really burned, although you can't see that on those smaller images. The area appears to have simply withered overnight. Complete deforestation, but not by fire. Look at the last pictures in the cycle. Those were taken just after dawn. It appears as if they've adapted some Russian refueling planes as some kind of crop dusters. See the clouds spreading from the wings? They're dumping something that is arresting the spread of whatever killed the rest of the foliage. I don't know what it is, but they are definitely not stopping napalm with crop dusters. It's unlikely as well that it's radiological or chemical."

Podge tapped the photos together on his bare belly and handed them back to Kirk.

"I don't know what this has to do with me. I liked Jeb fine, but I hadn't seen him in over ten years. And he never knew who I really was. If you thought his murder was going to drag me into something foolish, you're wrong. You've wasted your time, son."

Kirk reached back into his briefcase one last time and produced his trump card. He handed another photo to Podge. Unlike the rest, it was not an image taken from a spy plane. The grainy photo had been snapped from the ground. It was a picture of a man.

Colonel Ivan Strankov was a ghost who had somehow escaped Podge's dream. He was much older and so emaciated that it seemed impossible he could still be drawing breath, yet here he was, alive and back in uniform.

"One of Jeb Wilson's final acts on this Earth was to get that to us," Kirk said. He laid out many more photos of Strankov. Appearing in several was a little fat man who tickled some memory at the back of Podge's brain, but he could not process the information now. His eyes were locked on Colonel Ivan Strankov.

"Your last encounter with Colonel Strankov kept him away from the U.S. for fourteen years," Kirk said. "At least nine of those were spent in a gulag. How he managed to worm his way out of that and regain his old rank, we have no idea."

"Strankov was always a survivor."

"We do know that his old Motherland agency has been mostly folded into the KGB. He's no longer its director. Mr. Becket, you know better than I do the danger Strankov represented back in the old days. I'm hoping—" He paused for a deep breath, and on the exhale blurted, "I'm hoping that a final visit from the Red Menace will end Strankov and whatever he's got going in Cuba once and for all."

Podge stifled a laugh. "You realize this is 1972, right, kid? Only stick-up men wear masks these days."

"Okay, maybe you can do it without the mask."

Podge was no longer looking at Kirk, nor at the ocean or sky. He stared blankly at the empty air. "And then it's only pantyhose pulled over their heads," he muttered. "What kind of sissy-Mary bank robber wears a pantyhose mask? I stopped a gang in '58 that was using stolen Army tanks to rob banks around military bases. Now *those* guys had panache. Put these modern pantyhose bandits in a cell with those guys and see how fast the girlie-assed Nancies end up drowned in the cell toilet."

Kirk could sense that Podge was weakening and moved in for the kill.

"You just need to find out why Strankov is there, Mr. Becket, and what is going on at that base. Also what caused the damage to the jungle, and if it's all something that the U.S. needs to worry about. MIC agents are no good for this job, not after Jeb. The Cubans and Russians will make my people as soon as they land in Havana. But in addition to your computer company, you *do* own the largest private security company in the world. That's the ticket. I know Castro has tried to hire your people at your satellite office in Brazil before. It's the perfect cover."

"Except I don't work for commie rat bastards, and they all know it," Podge said, shaking his head. "What, you want me to call Castro and tell him I suddenly want a job I've refused for five years? Even that khaki sack of crap will figure out it's a setup."

Kirk grinned. "You won't be working for him right away. We also know you've had queries from dictators all over the world. Take a random job from, say, Africa. The rest will get the word that you've altered your business practices and contact you. Castro is sure to be one of the first in line. He thinks all Americans are money hungry, so he'll just assume your capitalist nature got the best of you. You'll be *invited* to Cuba. And while you're setting up a new system for Castro, the Red Menace can take out Strankov."

Podge could not believe that he was even considering Kirk's insane scheme. It was ludicrous. The kid was right; it was a far uglier world than it had been in the Red Menace's day, and Podge had gotten out well before civilization had begun its rapid descent into madness. Plus he was twelve years older now, no longer a kid in his twenties but an older and hopefully wiser man who understood there were limitations — not just physical in nature — on what any one man could do.

Still, there were the three muggers in the hotel parking lot last night. Podge had handled those punks like the old days. Even so, good sense won out.

"I'm sorry, Kirk, but I can't. It'd be like digging up Max Baer and shoving him in the ring with Mohammed Ali. I don't have the edge anymore."

"What if I told you I can give it back to you?" Kirk said. He did not wait for a reply. The young man reached into his briefcase one last time and pulled out a bulky black walkie-talkie, into which he said only three words: "Send him out."

A few moments later, a man appeared from out a set of rear gates in the high wall at the back of the estate.

He wore black slacks and a white shirt, untucked. His steely gray hair was parted with engineering precision. He looked to be in his sixties, but was thin, tan and appeared to be in excellent shape. He carried a black doctor's bag in his hand and it swung smoothly, as if it were a permanently attached appendage. When he reached the two men sitting under the umbrella, he peeled off his sunglasses wordlessly and dropped them to the glass tabletop. His thin lips were drawn into a disapproving frown.

In contrast to the new arrival's frown, Simon Kirk's grin threatened to spill off both sides of his face. "You know Dr. Wainwright, of course," he said to Podge.

Podge's face was unreadable as he stared up at the older man. "There's some things in life you never forget, kid," he said after an interminable pause during which Kirk's smile slowly melted in the heat. "Your first car, your first crush, and the first guy who ever killed you."

4

September 1956

THE explosion launched a brilliant orange fireball into the Las Vegas night sky and rattled windows in casinos on the Arrowhead Highway two miles away. The blast took off the roof of the guard building, launching bodies onto the driveway and lawn and firing knife-blade fragments of glass and Spanish tile through the air.

The quartet of Mafia guards charging from the main building caught the worst of the blast. Slivers of tile ripped through soft flesh. Guns flew from dead hands and the bodies skidded to a bloody stop on the sprawling front lawn.

The Red Menace slipped from the safety of the pool house, hopped the small wall next to the driveway and darted up the drive.

Zhadanov must have been alerted to the assault. Not only were the grounds crawling with armed Russians, but all the estate lights had been turned on. The black cloak and mask worked best in shadow, and the Menace was clearly visible as he ran.

He heard the zing of a bullet as it whizzed by his head, heard the soft thwack as it struck the grass. From the angle of that one shot, the Red Menace knew instinctively where the sniper would be and he found the man crouching behind a fat chimney on the uppermost roof, rifle with silencer peeking out around the brick.

The Menace darted left, feigned right but jumped even further left, narrowly avoiding the second bullet which zipped past in the precise spot his head would have been. The sniper wouldn't fall for that move again.

As he ran, the Menace slipped his gun from his belt holster. The Russians had tried many times to copy the unique barrel-in-barrel design, but had failed repeatedly.

With a gloved thumb, the Menace flipped the dial above the butt a single notch, aimed up at the roof and squeezed off a single shot.

The gun popped and the gas-propelled miniature grenade soared up past the floodlights to the roof. The ensuing explosion pulverized brick and ripped a Cadillac-size chunk off the third floor roof. The gunman fell amid the raining remnants of the chimney, flopping in a lifeless heap on the patio. The hail of heavy debris scattered lawn chairs and tables and shattered the French doors.

The Red Menace ran past the body, boots crunching glass underfoot, and ducked through the shattered doors.

A hail of bullets heralded his arrival inside and he barely missed getting cut to ribbons, diving for protection behind a gaudy silver sofa and scampering on hands and knees to the safety of the marble wet bar.

Bullets chewed the sofa behind him, sending bits of nylon and stuffing dancing in crazed puffs of fluff throughout the living room.

He found two people already hiding behind the bar.

Jeb Wilson was hunched with his back against the small fridge, automatic in hand.

Beside the MIC agent crouched Olga Cherblonya.

The beautiful Motherland agent pressed her hands to her ears to muffle the sounds of gunshots, but seemed otherwise unfazed by the chaos around her.

"Fashionably late," Jeb said. "We had to start the party without you."

"I missed my streetcar," the Menace said with a grin. "You okay, Wilson?"

"Still in one piece," Jeb replied. He pulled a deep breath into his barrel chest and jumped out from cover. Bracing his gun on the bar he squeezed out three shots in rapid succession, then dropped down to safety once more.

From the shouts across the room it was clear he'd hit one of the gunmen.

The words were in Russian and Jeb growled in disgust as he slapped in a new clip. "Russian mafia. Now I've seen it all."

Thanks to the Red Menace, MIC had learned of Zhadanov, the high level Russian agent planted in Las Vegas. He was supposed to infiltrate the Mob and await further orders, which would be issued once the great Soviet takeover of the U.S. came. But Jimmy "the Weasel" Zito from Portland, nee Anatoly Zhadanov from Minsk, had gone rogue. The brutal Russian had murdered his way up the chain of command to become one of the greatest Mob kingpins in the western United States. In his lust for power, Zhadanov had started a bloody Mafia war that had spread to several major American cities. It had gotten so bad that the Russians had decided to pull his plug and had sent Olga Cherblonya to stop him. For now the Russian beauty was an arms-length ally.

"Zhadanov is upstairs," Olga said, in a smoky voice and exotic accent that had been a mesmerizing siren song to many a foreign agent. She sat on her right hip, long legs tucked up beneath her backside. She had kicked off her high heels and was now barefoot, and her sequined silver gown sparkled in the bright light cast by gaudy chandeliers. "Main stairway is through those doors."

"Piece of cake, darlin'," the Red Menace said with a wink. His gun was in his gauntlet once more and he repositioned the tiny dial with a practiced flick of his thumb. With a soft pop of compressed gas propellant, a fat pellet launched across the room and struck with a loud plop the wall above the archway that led into the foyer. The tacky wallpaper instantly erupted in flames. The combustible liquid landed on the silk curtains framing the door and splashed down on the two remaining thugs. Fire immediately burst out on curtains, clothing and hair. The men screamed and dropped their guns, attempting to slap out the flames.

Jeb popped up from behind the bar and sent both men to eternity with two quick, clean shots to the forehead.

Jeb, Olga and the Red Menace ran across the living room. Jeb was first through the burning archway. He took it at a leap, landing on his shoulder and rolling to safety behind a carved granite statue of Dionysus, the Greek god of fertility.

When he glanced around the statue, something blocked his view.

"God, I hate these commie perverts," Jeb muttered, and with a single

.45 slug made Dionysus a whole lot less fertile. "Clear!" he shouted.

The Red Menace came next through the wall of fire, shielding Olga Cherblonya with his cape.

Another of Zhadanov's henchmen suddenly appeared at the top of the stairs, a machine gun clutched tightly in pudgy hands. The man screamed Russian expletives as he let loose a volley of gunfire that ripped furiously at marble balusters and railing. The Red Menace and Jeb fired simultaneously. Their choreographed fusillade caught the big gunman in the chest. The gun dropped and so did the gunman, end-over-end down the staircase. He landed in a heap at the Menace's and Olga's feet.

"Strong start, but lousy on the dismount," the Menace said.

The trio took the stairs two at a time.

They met no further resistance on the staircase. The long upstairs hallway was empty as well, save for ugly pornographic tapestries and pedestals on which priceless Ming Dynasty vases doubled as ashtrays.

"If I was a tacky turncoat Russkie, where would I hide?" the Red Menace asked.

Olga glanced up and down the hallway and bit her lip. "We try here?" she suggested tentatively, pointing left with a delicate finger.

The Red Menace nodded. "Take the other end," he told Jeb.

The MIC agent raced off right while Red and Olga took the left.

There were many doorways to check, and the guest bedrooms, closets and bathrooms all turned up empty. One room held a king's ransom in coins, jewels and bundled piles of cash.

"Now there's something you don't see on the collectivist farm," the Red Menace whispered. He closed the door silently and they continued down the hall.

"Zhadanov was loyal communist until your decadence transformed him," Olga insisted. "It is capitalist system to blame for what he has become."

"Whatever floats your Battleship Potemkin, Comrade Knockers."

They had reached the last door. The Menace held a gloved finger to his lips and motioned for Olga to stand back against the wall. Once she was safely out of harm's way, he stepped in front of the door, gave a vicious kick with his heel, and dove out of the way of the sudden explosive hail of bullets that launched from within the room.

The barrage chewed apart a garish tapestry on which an embroidered Zhadanov frolicked unclothed amongst a bevy of B-girl wood nymphs.

In the hall, Olga winced as the gunfire continued and the Red Menace shielded her with his body. "Hey, if he hadn't done it, I was ready to," the Menace said to her, nodding to the tattered remnants of the tapestry.

"Is not time for the joking," Olga snapped, fingers plugging her ears. The gunfire from the bedroom was petering out.

"Is time for you to stay put," the Red Menace suggested firmly.

The gunfire had stopped and the Red Menace heard the distinctive click of a magazine snapping in place as the gunman reloaded. The Menace took advantage of the brief pause, diving into the room and sliding on his belly behind a paisley fainting couch.

Zhadanov was standing by the bed wearing a purple silk robe open over a pair of striped silk pajama bottoms. The Russian's hairy belly hung over the waistband, his fat fingers were covered in rings that looked like diamond-encrusted ashtrays, and his jet black and usually perfectly Brylcreemed pompadour was a wild mess.

"I ain't comin' quietly!" the Russian screamed in the flawless American Mobster accent he had learned from imported Edward G. Robinson movies at Moscow University spy school.

Zhadanov trailed the Red Menace with a hail of bullets that tore wallpaper to shreds, ripped pictures from the wall, blasted tonics and powders on the bureau, and shattered the huge, gilded wall mirror that stretched from bureau to closet.

The Menace ducked from cover and fired a single shot.

The bullet caught Zhadanov in the shoulder, the Tommy gun sprang from fat hands and the Russian Mobster tumbled back and disappeared between bed and armoire. The gun bounced across the unmade bed and fell to floor with a clatter and suddenly the entire Vegas mansion was smothered in unnatural silence.

The Menace glanced back and saw Olga peeking around the doorframe, long blond hair spilling down one bare shoulder. In his head he heard a sonorous voice repeat a warning for the hundredth time: "Never trust a red, Patrick."

But the voice in his head was wrong. Olga Cherblonya had been vitally important in finishing off Zhadanov. In this one case, Russian interests had aligned with those of America. And what was possible now was possible again in the future.

Zhadanov stirred. The Menace heard a grunt and the soft rustling of silk.

"On your feet, Zhadanov!" the Menace snapped as he crept over to the bed. "I count to five and I don't see both hands, I'm blowing the floor out from under you."

On the bedside table was a small picture of a woman who could only be Anatoly Zhadanov's mother. The woman was the spitting image of the Russian spy but for the Babushka and darker facial hair. Mama Zhadanov's face had more Russian moles than the British Secret Service.

The frame was solid silver and highly polished, and had the Red Menace not glanced at the picture he would not have seen the reflection of Olga Cherblonya, a snub-nosed .38 in one delicate hand, creeping in behind him.

The Menace dropped and spun. Too late.

Olga's first shot only grazed his chest. He had twisted sideways so the bullet that was meant for his heart only tore away a chunk of meat beneath his shirt and scraped a painful path along his side, exiting the back of his cape.

But something was wrong. A flesh wound should not have caused such excruciating pain in his chest. His heart. The bullet must have struck between beats. It felt like it would burst out of his chest. The gun dropped from his hand and he fell flat on his back to the carpet, gasping for breath, clutching one hand at his chest.

Olga advanced, a wicked grin of triumph on a face once beautiful, now the victorious visage of a some hell-sent demon. From the corner of his eye the Menace saw Zhadanov pulling himself up on the other side of the bed, a pistol in hand, palm pressed to his bleeding shoulder.

"You let the mook shoot me," he groused to Olga.

"Drop ridiculous accent," she commanded. "You need this cover no longer. We have succeeded in mission. You leave this hateful land tonight and return with me to Russia in triumph as hero of the people." Olga cast a murderous shadow of the Menace's prone body. The smile was gone as she raised her revolver and took careful aim at his forehead. "Goodbye,

Red Menace."

Point blank range. No way he would escape this time. When the gunshot came it was a hollow clap in the Menace's ears. He was dead.

So why could he still see Olga?

She loomed above him for an eternal moment before the .38 flipped over in her hand. It hung from the tip of her index finger for an instant, and in the next instant she was spitting a spray of crimson and the gun was dropping to the floor.

And a voice was calling loudly to him, but this time it was not in his head.

"I told you never to trust a red, Patrick."

Olga's lifeless body collapsed to the floor to reveal a tall, gray-haired man standing in the doorway. Dr. Thaddeus Wainwright's thin lips were drawn into a characteristic disapproving frown.

Zhadanov took a shot at Wainwright from across the room, but the doctor did not even seem to notice. He merely leveled his automatic and squeezed off a single shot without a sideways glance, as if tossing a piece of trash into a corner wastebasket. The bullet slapped Zhadanov in the forehead and this time when the Russian Mobster collapsed behind the bed he did not get back up.

Wainwright hustled to the Menace's side. "I warned you not to trust the girl," he scolded, tearing open the younger man's shirt. His black bag was suddenly at his side, and the Menace knew that the doctor must have had it near him in the hall. "Soviets are a cancer, and you don't form an alliance with cancer. You don't bargain with it, you don't reason with it. You kill it."

Practiced fingers found the wound. The fingers were cold. Why were they so cold? And why was Wainwright so far away? It was as if the Menace was looking up at his friend from the bottom of a deep well. The darkness came then, a total blackness like nothing from this Earth and a great sense of falling, falling into nothingness.

Sudden bright light, stabbing his eyes like tiny needles. Wainwright's fist pounding his chest once more, restarting the heart.

In his hazy vision, the Menace saw Jeb Wilson run into the room, saw the MIC agent's face fall when he saw the Red Menace dying on the floor.

"I'll call an ambulance!" Jeb yelled.

"No," Wainwright snapped. "My equipment is in a van downstairs. Help me move him."

Wainwright grabbed the Menace under the arms while Jeb took the legs. The Red Menace must have passed out on the way because the next thing he knew he was in a well-lit van with windows painted black and Dr. Wainwright was above him in rolled-up shirtsleeves. There was no one else present and the Menace's mask had been removed, replaced by a plastic oxygen mask and a horrible odor. Wainwright was giving him more than just oxygen, and Podge knew that he was being treated with one of the doctor's many remarkable discoveries.

"Stinks ... like ... cat ... scat," Podge breathed.

His voice was scarcely a whisper and he did not know if Wainwright heard him.

The doctor continued working with practiced efficiency. He dragged a device over to the gurney on which Podge was lying and hooked something that looked like an enormous suction cup attached to a rubber-coated Slinkie over Podge's chest. When he flipped a switch on the black box to which the cup was attached, the lights inside the van dimmed.

Wainwright grabbed up a syringe, tapped out the air and sank the needle into Podge's arm. The hum that issued from the machine abruptly grew more insistent, what could only be warning lights began to flash upon its surface, and the last thing Podge saw was a shocking look of worry on Wainwright's face and a sheen of glistening sweat on a brow that he had heretofore thought imperturbable.

Then the blackness claimed him and Podge was falling into infinity once more.

5

1972

Podge Becket had no idea if the rutted runway at Entebbe International Airport was the result of wounds suffered in the previous year's insurrection or if the Ugandans were just lousy at mixing blacktop and operating steamrollers. Either way, he gripped the arms of his seat for white-knuckled life as his private Learjet bounced crazily through water-filled potholes until the plane finally came to rest nose-first in Lake Victoria.

Dr. Thaddeus Wainwright remained unruffled throughout the rough landing, and only folded up and set aside his copy of *The Wall Street Journal* when it became impossible to follow the bouncing text.

Wainwright was sitting across from Podge and both men looked out their respective windows at the tiny portion of the African nation that was visible.

"I see we've arrived in hell," Dr. Wainwright announced.

"I bet you a million bucks hell smells better," Podge said.

When the door was opened, the stairs lowered and the first whiff of Ugandan air rushed into the cabin, Podge crinkled his nose and said, "I prefer that in cash."

Once they had deplaned, Podge saw that it only seemed as if they had landed in Lake Victoria. It was actually a massive, water-filled pothole from which the crack Ugandan airport staff was trying to pull his jet with some rope and a donkey.

"And I see I've already spent that million you owe me," Podge said.

Fortunately for Podge and Wainwright, the airport beggars that existed in most of the Third World were not there to annoy them. Unfortunately for the beggars, this was because President Idi Amin had had them all dragged off and shot.

Podge's security people were already on the ground in Uganda for two days and were hard at work in the capital of Kampala. A Ugandan Armed Forces officer of about thirty-five was waiting with a driver on the tarmac next to a gleaming black Rolls Royce.

The officer's uniform was spotless and Podge wondered how long he had to pound it on rocks down at the river to clean off all the blood. That was the question he wanted to ask. Instead he forced a smile and offered his hand.

"Hello, to the famous Mr. Patrick Becket," the officer said. "I am Robert Mpala and I am honored to make your acquaintance. Please, get in."

The air conditioned interior of the Rolls Royce was a welcome relief from the heat and stink of the airport and Podge wished he could spend his entire trip in Uganda hiding out in the back of the car. The Rolls sped along a highway that had been built by the British to last for decades only to be chewed up in days by tank treads after the Brits abandoned the country the previous decade.

"Would you gentlemen care for a drink? We have fine spirits as well as American Coca-Cola. Nothing but the best for guests of our Glorious President Amin."

Wainwright snorted.

"Is something wrong…it is Dr. Wainwright, correct?"

"No, nothing. I just thought of a joke Patrick told me on the plane about this dim fellow who used glowing adjectives to describe the most horrible things. He saw a superlative car accident, a brilliant mugging, and a magnificent dead dog in the road. Of course, it has nothing to do with anything *you* said. Carry on about your glorious president whatever-he-is. I'm going to take a nap before I think of any more jokes."

Wainwright settled back in the seat, closed his eyes and pretended to fall instantly asleep. Feigning sleep so as not to be annoyed was one of the doctor's old habits. Another was sticking Podge with uncomfortable moments like this one.

Mpala stared daggers at Podge from across the rear seat of the Rolls.

More than a decade ago, when Podge was in his twenties and traveling the world with Wainwright, he would have attempted to fill these Wainwright-engineered awkward silences — of which there were many — with nervous conversation. But Podge was now older, wiser and much, much richer.

"I might as well take a nap, too," Podge said. "Wake me when we reach Kampala, Jeeves. And try not to gnaw on my foot while I'm asleep."

Podge felt as if he had scarcely closed his eyes when he felt a hand gently nudging him awake. Mpala was gone. A new, friendlier face was smiling through the open door.

Wainwright was already out of the car, black bag in hand, and was standing next to their fresh guide.

"Hello, I am Captain Edmund Nwatoo," said the Ugandan, in a flawless British accent. "I will be your guide while you are visiting the Command Post."

"What happened to the other guy?" Podge asked sleepily as he stepped out onto the gravel driveway.

"Oh. I think he was not feeling well."

"Probably someone he ate," Wainwright suggested.

Unlike Mpala, his replacement did not seem insulted at the suggestion. "Tish-tosh," said Nwatoo, waving a hand in the warm air. "Rumors and propaganda meant to discredit our great leader. Now, I believe you are here to supervise your people, so let us get cracking." He ushered them down the drive toward the main gates. "If there is anything you desire while here, Mr. Becket, I shall do my level best to deliver."

"Don't believe him," Wainwright warned. "I already asked him to deliver up some democracy. He said Amin is still working on it. Funny, he's been working on it for over a year now and hasn't found it yet. Probably can't see it behind that stack of bones."

"Piffle and rot," Nwatoo said, his smile unshakeable. "The West is filled with liars who come up with propaganda and fools who believe the lies. Present company excepted, of course. Would you care to freshen up, or begin work straight away?"

Podge opted for work, and so Nwatoo brought them to the main entrance.

"Here are the new cameras. They are quite lovely," the Ugandan said.

A team of Podge's security staff from his South African offices had descended on the former Government House, now the Command Post of Idi Amin, earlier that week. The men wore white overalls with the legend "Becket Security" on the backs. Thick wires ran next to trenches dug through manicured grounds, across driveways and to the fence that encircled the entire compound. Under the watchful eye of Ugandan soldiers, Podge's men were installing the latest in camera technology on the heavy fence posts.

The cameras were bulky silver boxes that delivered grainy black-and-white images to TV screens in guard booths. Each guard booth covered a stretch of fence and the guards inside had a limited view of only one small part of a grid. However, a room in the main building was under construction and would be the central hub to which all the camera images would be channeled.

"You need to reinforce the guard booths," Becket said, "and set some men back farther from the gate. One truck stashed with explosives takes out everybody you've got stationed out here now. Circles within circles, that's how you've got to play it."

"Your people have already suggested we build secondary guard quarters and reinforce all the existing guard houses at each entrance," Nwatoo happily replied.

Podge nodded and headed out through the gates. Nwatoo waved a hand above his head and a contingent of a dozen Army Forces soldiers followed Podge, Wainwright and their Ugandan guide outside the Command Post.

Nwatoo seemed pleased when Podge personally walked the perimeter of the presidential palace and questioned his workers to make sure that there were no blind spots between cameras through which enemies might slip.

"I didn't know we'd be hiking halfway to Tripoli," Wainwright groused.

"You could have stayed at the car," Podge said.

"Those soldiers were looking at me like lunch."

"Lies," Nwatoo, volunteered cheerily, tagging along behind the two men, the dozen soldiers trailing along in his wake.

"I suppose I shouldn't complain," Podge said. "At least you're talking now. You've barely said two words since you finished torturing me back home."

Since their meeting with Director Kirk on the Hawaiian beach, Wainwright had spent days as a racehorse trainer putting Podge through his paces.

For six days before they even left the Islands, Podge was forced to climb ropes, ladders, drainpipes, trees, and whatever else vertical Wainwright could find. The pain in Podge's shoulder quickly became unbearable and, tongue clucking unhappily, the doctor had pawed through his ever-present black bag and delivered an injection that had blessedly banished the throbbing ache.

Podge was forced to run over rooftops on his estate, jumping from building to building. Wainwright spent one afternoon on the beach shooting at Podge, but after it was over he assured the younger man that it wasn't a training exercise. "I have to have some fun for myself, Patrick," insisted Thaddeus Wainwright.

Throughout it all, Wainwright timed everything on a stopwatch, shook his head unhappily, and made little pencil ticks in a notebook.

There were multiple daily injections and blood tests. Wainwright issued the shots with great trepidation. "I've still only gotten the formula to work perfectly on me," he had said four days earlier in the unused maid's quarters off Podge's kitchen. The servants either stayed in another building or lived off the estate, so Wainwright had taken over the rooms, turning them into his personal suite as well as an infirmary.

"It works well enough on me," Podge replied as he pressed some gauze to the needle mark and folded his fist back to his shoulder.

"Not perfected, Patrick," Wainwright insisted. "There's still something about my body chemistry that is unique and I'm no closer to finding out what it is than I was a decade ago. I can push you to the limit, but I can't get you beyond it."

It was with reluctance that he finally concluded Podge was physically fit enough for one last mission. However, he insisted on accompanying his patient to Uganda. "Someone needs to patch you up if you get your damned fool skull caved in."

Now it was a week later, Podge Becket and Dr. Wainwright were touring the perimeter of Uganda's presidential palace, and Wainwright finally brought up something that had been irritating him since they were reunited on the beach a week ago.

"You told Harmon's son that I killed you," Wainwright announced suddenly.

Podge was conferring with his African office director from South Africa who was overseeing the Ugandan Becket Security job.

"What?" Podge asked. He dismissed his South African employee, who returned to duty supervising workmen who were electrifying the palace fence.

"I didn't kill you in Las Vegas," Wainwright said. "I saved you. It's irritating when you say things like that. I am a doctor, after all. I have a reputation to think of."

"You're kidding," Podge said.

"I restarted your heart. You were clinically dead, you know. And that had nothing to do with me or my equipment. In point of fact, some of those devices — devices I invented, mind you — have been adapted for use in hospitals around the world. I take my profession very seriously, Patrick."

"Tell you what. Next time I die, assuming you bring me back, I'll be more grateful. How's that?"

"Next time I might be less inclined to bring you back," Wainwright said.

They had completed the circuit and were back at the main gates. Podge led their party back inside the Command Post. Nwatoo was still dogging their steps and had listened to their conversation with fascination.

"You are a medical doctor?" the Ugandan captain asked. "Where did you go to school, if I may ask?"

"Harvard."

"Ah, it is such a small world," Nwatoo said, beaming. "Our Glorious

Leader's personal physician who is my most excellent friend went to Harvard Medical School. Perhaps you know him. Dr. William Gudmunga?"

"No, thank God," Wainwright said.

"Are you certain? You and he appear about the same age."

"Very unlikely," Wainwright droned.

"May I ask what year were you at Harvard?"

"The first one."

A cloud of confusion brushed Nwatoo's brow. "Sir?"

"Ixnay on the honestynay," Podge suggested.

"Fine," Wainwright said with growing impatience. "The second one. Who cares? Why are you still here, you annoying little man? Go away."

Podge nodded. "Yes, that's much better."

Nwatoo decided that the two Americans were eccentrics. He and everyone in the Command Post certainly had experience dealing with unconventional behavior. And Patrick Becket seemed to know his business, and that was all that mattered to Uganda's Glorious Leader. Nwatoo kept a smile plastered to his face and continued the tour.

Podge gave advice to the Ugandans on equipment, training, and the proper positioning of soldiers all around the grounds and buildings. The main observation room inside was a beehive of activity. Crates bearing the Becket Security logo were stacked up in the hall, and technicians and electricians hustled to install dozens of TV monitors.

The end of the tour brought them to a large state dining room. Running up the center of the room was a gleaming ebony table lined with fifty exquisite antique French chairs. At the far end sat the Glorious Leader himself, resplendent in a bright green uniform with gold piping, giant epaulettes spilling from each shoulder and enough medals and ribbons on his chest to decorate the Rockefeller Center Christmas tree.

"Haloo, my friends," Idi Amin cried enthusiastically as Nwatoo ushered Podge and Wainwright up to where Uganda's president sat. "Welcome, Mr. Patrick Becket! I did not think I would ever have the pleasure. I have tried to engage your people for over a year now, but they have always had prior commitments. I was starting to think I was not important enough for you." The president laughed heartily. "And now, to have you here in person, I am honored. Come, sit, join me for lunch."

There were steaming silver chafing dishes arranged on the table before Amin. Standing at the ready were waiters in impeccable uniforms with napkins draped over their forearms and a sommelier holding a bottle of 1818 Chateau Lafite Rothschild.

Podge shook Amin's offered hand and was pleased with himself for heroically resisting the urge to stick a fork in the dictator's head. Wainwright lifted the lid on the largest chafing dish and suspiciously queried, "What kind of meat is this?"

Amin beamed. "Acholi. Very good. Very young. Like veal."

Nwatoo shifted his eyes. Suddenly the ceiling mural was the most interesting work of art he had ever encountered.

Podge's eyes were flat. "The Acholi are an ethnic group here, aren't they?"

"Bah, pigs," the Glorious Leader said, spitting on the floor. A waiter instantly sprang forward to mop up the glob of saliva. "As people, they are less than pigs. But as a main course, they are superb. I have a French chef who makes the most delightful sauce from their squeezed eyes. Make you strong, see what your enemies see." Amin bounced a thundering fat fast off his own barrel chest and laughed heartily.

Podge and Wainwright begged off lunch.

They refused quarters at the Command Post, opting to take their chances at a hotel in the city. Their bags had been sent ahead and were waiting in Podge's rooms.

The suite had once been the epitome of British elegance, but was now a shabby shadow of its former self. There was grime ground into the carpet, the windows were opaque with filth and the sheets look like they hadn't been changed since the British buggered off in 1962.

"Tell me why I'm not back on my plane, assuming the airport donkey didn't drop dead of a heart attack, and flying the hell out of this fat ghoul's cannibal smorgasbord?" Podge demanded.

"Because you signed on for this," Wainwright said, calmly taking a seat in an overstuffed chair. He reached into his suit jacket pocket. "Harmon's son is smart, like his father. He's right that this job will attract others. It will only be a matter of time before Castro sends for you. In the meantime, you put up with it."

Podge felt like smashing something. In a fit of anger, he grabbed up a lamp from an end table but before he could break it he noticed the cloud of dust shaken loose from the shade, the broken bulb and the startled rat that ran along the baseboard and vanished behind a shabby sofa. The moment of fury passed and Podge's shoulders relaxed.

"Ah, who'd even notice?" he said, replacing the lamp to the table.

"I must say, I'm glad to see you haven't become a complete cynic," Wainwright said. He lit a cigarette from a silver case and tossed the smoldering match to the scarred coffee table. "There's only room for one on the team, and the position is taken."

Podge flopped on the sofa. He heard the rat and some friends scratching around inside the wall. "Why are you back with MIC anyway, doc? I thought you were dedicating your life to studying medicinal plants on Ceylon or something."

"The beauty of my particular life, Patrick," Wainwright said, blowing twin clouds of smoke from his nostrils, "is that I have more of it to dedicate than anyone else on Earth." Although he looked to be a very fit sixty-year old, the sadness in Thaddeus Wainwright's tone suggested a much, much older man. "Besides, someone's got to keep you from killing yourself. I knew when Harmon's boy sent his people to collect me that all he'd have to do is ask and you'd be back running around in that cape like some middle-aged maniac, especially when they told me about Wilson. And those MIC dolts haven't got anyone who'd give you a fighting chance to get through this alive."

"I have more than just a fighting chance."

"A chance," Wainwright insisted. "And barely that. But not without me. Alone, you wind up like Jeb Wilson in under a week. With me, you buy a few more days, which will hopefully take you beyond the end of the mission because, Patrick, the safe money says more than ten days and you're a corpse."

"Have you considered the possibility that I've gotten smarter with age?"

"I'm the only person who gets smarter with age," Wainwright insisted. "The rest of you are all idiots. Why else would you say yes to

Harmon's boy?"

Podge intertwined his fingers on his belly and closed his eyes. "In my defense, Thaddeus, I've been very bored lately. Wake me if there's a revolution."

Wainwright let a slender cloud of smoke slip from between his pursed lips.

"Did I say ten days?" he muttered. "Make it three. On the outside."

6

THEY spent five days in Uganda.

Fortunately, Idi Amin left for Russia after the first day. The Ugandan president had an important Moscow meeting with high ranking Politburo members. He hoped to secure more funding for his nation lest insufficient Soviet sponsorship result in Uganda becoming something worse than a brutal, backwards, nightmarish hellhole.

Podge's people were wrapping up their work on the afternoon of the fifth day when Podge received word that a special envoy had landed at the airport and was on the way to Kampala by helicopter. The person they were to wait for at the Command Post was a representative of Presidente Fidel Castro of Cuba.

"This had better work," Podge said as they waited near Amin's helipad. "I already need to shower for a month to get the stink of one dictator out of my hair."

Captain Edmund Nwatoo was hustling around the perimeter of the landing area giving orders to soldiers and glancing up at the African sky.

"Just stay sharp," Wainwright warned. "These Cuban devils killed Wilson and won't hesitate to kill you. You're good, Patrick, but you are no longer a kid."

Podge had been feeling butterflies in his belly, and the sudden paternal concern of the usually taciturn Dr. Wainwright did nothing to dispel them.

"It was easier when it was just the Russians," Podge said.

Wainwright was watching the sky. The faint sound of rotor blades rose up over Kampala and quickly grew louder. "It was never just the Russians, Patrick. America has always had more enemies than just the Soviets, and she seems to have more inside her borders these days than outside. Don't trust anyone except me and you might live through this. Here he comes."

The Russian-made helicopter swept in from the southwest, flying low over surrounding buildings. It buzzed over windblown trees and settled like a giant nesting metallic bird to the helipad. Nwatoo ran to open the door.

The Cuban who stepped out could have convinced Adam Smith to burn his manuscript of *The Wealth of Nations* and stock up on copies of *The Communist Manifesto*.

Podge had never thought a communist uniform could be sexy, but the woman who ignored Nwatoo's outstretched hand and scanned the grounds for Patrick Becket's face could have made radical redistribution of wealth her talent in the Miss World competition. The judges would have eagerly surrendered their bank accounts to Third World peasants even as they tripped over one another to award her the crown. That she would accept the crown there was no doubt. Even among a world of equals there had to be some whose power, wealth or beauty made them more equal than others. The proles would not complain if the crown, sash and scepter of the new communist world order were on the brow, shoulder and in the delicate hand of the Cuban major who had just seen Podge and Wainwright and was even now walking across the lawn toward them.

Wainwright darted a concerned eye at Podge. "For the love of God, Patrick, close your mouth," he hissed.

Podge hadn't realized his jaw had dropped. "I expected some dumpy revolutionary with cigar ash in his beard. Holy cow, doc."

"I've been married twelve times. My last 'holy cow' was eight wives ago," Wainwright said, voice low. "And recall your last one was Olga Cherblonya, and that misbegotten infatuation required four weeks in the hospital and six months recuperation."

The woman stopped before them and offered a no-nonsense hand. "Hello," said the beautiful Cuban soldier. "I am Major Ameriga Isabella Blanco."

She smelled of soap, not perfume, but the lack of flowery fragrance was somehow sexier. Her skin was naturally soft and not coarse as a revolutionary's should be. Her womanly curves threatened to pop the buttons of her khaki blouse.

"Viva la rack," said Podge, shaking her hand.

Major Blanco's hand tensed and she frowned, simultaneously confused and suspicious. "Excuse me?"

"I believe— Dear God." Wainwright took them both by the wrists and pulled their hands apart. "I believe the major is here to talk business, Patrick. You!" he called to Nwatoo. "The irritating fellow with the idiot's grin. Find us someplace where we can talk. Preferably somewhere you are not barbecuing Watusis for brunch."

Nwatoo offered an obsequious half-bow and hurried up to the building. Major Blanco strode after the Ugandan. Podge offered Wainwright a broad wink and fell in directly behind the Cuban soldier.

Wainwright clasped his hands behind his back and, a fresh hint of worry brushing his brow, trudged up in the wake of the others.

AN AGREEMENT was reached in less than ten minutes.

MIC director Kirk's plan had worked perfectly. Fidel Castro had heard that Podge's security agency had relaxed its rule on the nations with which it would do business and the Cuban dictator wished for an estimate for services as quickly as possible.

Podge informed Major Blanco that he and Dr. Wainwright — Podge's most trusted employee advisor and personal physician — would personally fly to Cuba immediately to meet with Becket Security's honored new client.

Their bags were packed for them by hotel staff and forwarded to the airport, and they all flew to Entebbe International Airport on Major Blanco's helicopter.

At the airport, they found Podge's personal jet safely out of the pothole into which it had tipped on landing earlier that week. Unfortunately, they faced a fresh setback.

"Where the devil are the tires?" Wainwright demanded.

The Learjet jet sat on its belly on several huge slabs of cement. Spindly naked metallic legs stuck out from beneath with no wheels in sight. Their luggage was dumped in a heap on the rutted tarmac next to the crippled plane.

"Ah, now this *is* awkward," Nwatoo said, his cheery smile plastered flat on his dark face. "The Glorious Leader needed them for his aircraft, you see. He only borrowed them. He will return them when he returns from Moscow."

"You may fly with me," Major Blanco offered, seemingly unhappy to have to make the offer. Her Russian transport was refueled and awaiting takeoff.

"Are we sure swimming for Havana isn't an option?" Wainwright droned.

Podge signaled for his people to load their bags onto the Cuban-bound plane and instructed his flight crew, which had been staying in Kampala and was unaware the plane had been dismantled, to arrange for new wheels and to get out of Uganda as soon as possible. "Forget about us, we'll make our own arrangements. Take everybody from Becket Securities home," he insisted to his pilot. "Call me as soon as everybody's out." There was a worried undertone in his voice that only Wainwright noticed. "I'll leave the number where I can be reached in Cuba with the office in Honolulu."

Captain Edmund Nwatoo waited beside the open door of the Cuban plane.

"Goodbye, my dear new friends," the Ugandan said, in a deeply sad tone.

Podge shook the young man's hand, thanked him for all his help, and entered the plane behind Major Blanco.

"You seem like a pleasant enough imbecile," Wainwright said to Nwatoo. "Pleasant, weak, intelligent...they all get you dead in places like this. Escape this godforsaken country before you're diced up in Monday's stew."

"Alas, this is my home, so I stay," Nwatoo said. "But so long, my rude, racist, imperialist friend. I fervently hope that your plane does not crash in the middle of the ocean or that some other horrible, painful evil does not befall you."

And for the first time in their brief acquaintanceship, the smile that passed between the two men was sincere.

On the plane, the door shut tight behind him and the aircraft already taxiing down the runway, Wainwright quickly took his seat next to Podge. He set his black bag between his shoes.

The amenities on Major Blanco's plane were a far cry from those on Podge's private jet. The seats were cold steel, the fuselage was a thin sheet of perspiring metal, and the bathroom was a rusty bucket. Major Blanco gave a little superior smirk at the two men as she strapped herself in. Clearly she expected the American capitalists to complain about having to give up the creature comforts of the Learjet.

The engine whined to a crescendo and the plane bounced off the runway and screamed into the hot African sky.

"Not as bad as I thought," Podge said to Wainwright.

"You mean that the wings didn't fall off and the whole mess explode on the runway?" the doctor asked. "Yes, a real testament to the skills of our communist rivals. Say whatever else you want about their barbarian system, they defied conventional wisdom and actually managed to get a pig to fly. Bravissimo, Comrade Marx."

"Don't mind him," Podge said, smiling to Major Blanco.

"I do not," Major Ameriga Blanco sniffed in reply. "I expect nothing from American reactionaries and am therefore never disappointed." She stuck out her superior chin at Wainwright. Wainwright offered a placid smile and both middle fingers.

"Speaking of America," Podge said, interrupting before the pantomime war resulted in someone getting tossed out of the plane at 20,000 feet, "you've got an unusual first name for a Cuban major."

"My great-great-grandmother was Italian, descended from Vespuci," Ameriga explained. "She married a Cuban diplomat in Rome and returned with him to Havana during the last century. My family is proud of the name and has passed it on to each generation. Until me, the name had been a gift to the men of my family only, but the son that my father had hoped for never arrived."

"Are you sure Castro didn't have him dragged out of the womb and shot?" Wainwright asked.

Podge shot him a hard look. "Knock it off, doc," he said.

"Killjoy." Wainwright folded his arms across his chest and studied the bathroom bucket and Podge turned his attention back to Ameriga.

"Your family must be very proud of you."

"Pride is a meaningless concept when applied to the individual," she said. "I am proud of Cuba, her people and her great communist mission. I know that you, Mr. Patrick Becket, do not share my ideals. You are going to Cuba purely for capitalist gain. I am here to escort you to Havana and to be your liaison with state security while you are in the country. I do not need to engage in small talk with a person who is the antithesis of everything that my nation and I believe in, nor need I endure the insults of his lackey."

They were at cruising altitude. Ameriga unbuckled her seatbelt and marched wordlessly up to the cockpit.

Podge raised an eyebrow and shot a silencing glare at Wainwright, but the doctor was casting a curious eye around the cavernous interior of the plane for this lackey of which Ameriga spoke. Finding no one, he turned his attention back to Podge.

"Communist *and* crazy. She's lucky she's got looks," Wainwright said.

"You could try to be nicer," Podge said. "By the sounds of it we're going to be stuck with her as our shadow while we're Cuba. And I saw her eyes. This is a smart one, doc. It's not going to make my job any easier." He tapped an anxious hand on his thigh.

Wainwright noted the nervous gesture but did not call attention to it. The doctor understood better than anyone the pressure the younger man was feeling right now, and attempted to offer him a distraction from what was to come.

"By the way, what was that back at the airport?" Wainwright asked, voice low. "Worrying about getting all your people out of the country. I am assuming that you left some kind of present for the Glorious Leader."

"Let's just hope they don't dissect all the new equipment they just paid a bundle for before we're done in Cuba, or we might be taking a short walk in front of a firing squad." With his toe, Podge dragged the bathroom bucket across the floor and pushed it in front of Wainwright. "Now why don't you stop pestering me and try reading something on the john? We've got a long flight ahead of us and I didn't buy this first class seat to listen to your jibber-jabber the whole way."

7

THE communists and their fellow travelers boasted that the Republic of Cuba was heaven on Earth. From the air, one almost believed the lie was true.

The Caribbean sun bleached white long strands of perfect beaches, the sea was vast and blue and the jungle was lush and green. Even Havana appeared beautiful from above; a jumble of quaint buildings, some of vaguely European style, some very old contemporaries of architecture found in Madrid and Barcelona.

Podge didn't expect the landscape to be awash in blood. In a place like Cuba, the little deaths of little people took place a few murders at a time, the remains invisible to the naked eye flying far above the beautiful landscape. The bodies were buried, the land absorbed the blood and the sea washed the stains away.

But despite the lie of its natural beauty, the island was a prison for its people with the invisible bars of the cage formed from the bones of their countrymen. This was the domain of Fidel Castro, this was the evil system that had murdered Jeb Wilson.

Ameriga had spent much of the flight in the cockpit. Once the plane began its descent she had reluctantly rejoined Podge and Wainwright in the back.

The airport in Havana was in better shape than the one they had departed in Uganda and they came to a smooth stop near the terminal.

The air inside the main building was thick and became even stickier when they exited through the main doors. It felt to Podge like he'd walked face-first into a hot, sopping wet blanket.

A vintage Packard painted drab green was waiting for them out front, a Cuban army private standing at attention beside it. "I will drive," Ameriga said, demanding the keys. "See to it that their luggage is brought to the Revolucion Grande."

Ameriga drove through the heart of Havana, a city which had seemingly been bypassed by the previous decade. Podge took note of the large tailfins on the old cars. At one point they passed an old man whipping an ox from the seat of a wooden cart.

"It feels like 1956 all over again," Wainwright commented.

Podge knew what his old friend meant. 1956 had not been the best year for the Red Menace. Podge brushed his hand against his side, feeling the roughness of the ancient wound beneath his thin cotton dress shirt.

Signs painted directly on walls as well as billboards and flags bore the stern image of Fidel Castro and the phrase *Socialismo o Muerte!*

The oppression of *socialismo* meant that every Cuban had been touched by government-sponsored *muerte* in one way or another over the past thirteen years.

The Packard left the dense human activity of downtown Havana and headed into the hilly suburbs. The entire island nation seemed caught between the stalled prosperity of the past and the drab gray of the long totalitarian twilight. Old homes were falling into disrepair yet their owners did their best to keep them patched together.

Then suddenly the neighborhoods became more prosperous and the military presence became more pronounced and Podge knew that they had passed into the realm of the ruling elite. There were checkpoints on every corner, and soldiers with German shepherds patrolled lawns and streets. In the most prosperous enclave, Ameriga turned up the longest driveway to the highest wall, and when the soldiers rolled back the massive gate the Packard was waved onto the grounds of Fidel Castro's estate.

The sympathetic foreign press accepted the claim that the man called el Jefe lived a modest lifestyle. The man himself, Fidel Castro Ruz, stood on the east portico of his modest twenty-seven room home, flanked by a pair of Cuban Army soldiers. The dictator bounced from one boot to another like an anxious child awaiting the arrival of Santa Claus. When the Packard drove around the circular drive and stopped before him,

Castro broke away from the soldiers and hustled up to the car.

"Hola, amig—Hijo de puta!" He kicked a wandering peacock out of the way. "Amigos, welcome!" he cried with great enthusiasm as he yanked open the rear door.

Up close, Fidel Castro looked like a pile of month-old dirty laundry and smelled like an outhouse. His beard resembled a tumbleweed from the back lot of an old MGM Western. His arms flailed wildly and he used his lit cigar to punctuate the air. He took no notice of Major Ameriga Isabella Blanca, who had rapidly circled the car and now stood at attention at the front bumper.

"Patrick Becket himself has come to Cuba," Castro said, pumping Podge's hand as he climbed out of the Packard's back seat. "Honored I am that you have taken the time to personally see to my humble request. You are Dr. Wainwright, correct?"

"A pleasure, sir," Wainwright said, his gritted teeth squeaking enamel as he shook the dictator's hand. The instant Castro's back was turned, the doctor rubbed his palm vigorously against his trouser leg.

"You will do me the honor of—" Castro took one step that ended in a horrific squawk and a flurry of loose feathers. This time the unfortunate peacock ran off flapping colored wings. "Take that bird away and have it shot!" Castro screamed in Spanish.

The pair of soldiers hustled out of the shade of the portico and ran across the lawn and into the underbrush after the desperately fleeing bird.

"Please, come!" Castro enthused, with a grand wave of his arm that sent cigar ash scattering to dust on the driveway. "You must be starving after your long journey. We will discuss the many ideas I have to enhance my security over lunch."

His grand march through the mansion's side door was punctuated by the sound of gunfire erupting somewhere in the bushes accompanied by a fatal avian shriek.

Podge shrugged. "Still beats Amin's idea of lunch," he said off Wainwright's disgusted scowl. "You joining us for eats, Goldilocks?" he called to Ameriga.

"I will be here when you return," she replied. She slipped on a pair of sunglasses and said not another word.

"Suit yourself. One less Chatty Kathy fighting over the drumsticks."

After Podge and Wainwright disappeared inside the mansion, Major Blanco stood at silent attention near the Packard, her eyes unreadable behind her dark glasses.

NEITHER peacock nor person, Podge was pleased to discover, was on the menu. Even Thaddeus Wainwright seemed to enjoy, albeit reluctantly, the satisfying lunch of rice, beans, pork and fruit. After they had eaten, their small group began the tour of the grounds of Castro's estate. Podge took special note of the locations of permanent sentries, filing the information away in the back of his mind.

The Cuban leader had heard of the impressive services provided by Becket's company to leaders around the world, services which until very recently had not been available to the enemies of the United States.

"Although I am not an enemy of your country," Castro insisted, bouncing across the grounds. Podge, Wainwright, Ameriga and a trio of soldiers hustled to keep up. "The American government might call me an enemy, but I am not. I am for the people. All people, everywhere, including the American proletariat. I am a common man myself. Is it true you did security for Buckingham Palace? What is the queen like?"

"Have your physicians ever suggested that you cut down on sugar?" Wainwright asked. "Apropos of nothing, of course."

"No," Castro said, shaking his head. "A moat," he announced brightly. "I would like a moat. Can you build me a moat?"

"That's really not the sort of thing we do, Mr. President," Podge said. "We do offer some advice, suggestions to our clients on how to enhance security. But primarily we're more of an electronics firm. High-tech gadgetry, that sort of thing."

"Si, si," Castro said. "Like James Bond. Run by the computers."

"Some, yes, depending on the service, " Podge replied. "But mostly not."

"But you, Senor Becket, are involved in the computers, it is my understanding."

"The computer business pay the bills," Podge said. "Security is just something I do on the side. More an avocation than a vocation."

"Ah, but you are too modest. Becket Security is the greatest personal security firm in the world. Laser beams! Can we put them on the roof? Like the *Star Trek*?"

"I'm sorry, but that technology doesn't exist," Podge said.

Castro was a picture of sad disappointment behind his scraggly beard.

"Nixon has laser beams," Castro pouted. "Che told me."

"We can give you something called motion detectors," Podge offered. "A beam of light is sent to a detecting device, and if the beam is broken — say by a person walking through the beam — the connection is broken and an alarm is sounded."

The bright smile returned. "It is like a laser beam, this motion detector?"

"It's a beam of directed light," Podge said. "It's really not—"

"I'll take ten. No, twenty." Castro clapped his hands delightedly. "Major," he barked at Ameriga, "Make a note that I will be purchasing twenty of the most advanced motion laser beam detectors from Becket Securities, Incorporated."

Ameriga was carrying a notebook at the ready, and she quickly jotted down a few scratches with a stubby pencil.

Major Blanco was now the height of military professionalism, her earlier hostility towards Podge and Wainwright gone, at least for the duration of the tour. El Jefe was clearly delighted with his visitors, and overt rudeness to Castro's guests right now could result in prison or worse. Still, Podge's occasional smiles and friendly nods in her direction were met not with return smiles but with a face devoid of all emotion.

Ameriga's raven's mane hair was pulled back and she wore a drab olive green army cap. Her pursed lips were dark even without lipstick.

"She's something, isn't she?" Podge whispered to Wainwright as they walked.

"Yes, if by something you mean insufferable," Wainwright replied. "She reminds me of wives two through five and number eight. *Especially* number eight. Besides, remember, Patrick, your last female communist friend." He nodded to Podge's left side and his ancient, hidden scar. "Don't trade a Russian disaster for a Cuban one."

Ahead, Castro's ears perked up. He seemed crestfallen. "Russians? You have not done work for Brezhnev?"

"No," Podge promised. " Moscow hasn't called me yet."

This seemed to please Castro no end, and he remained an ebullient mass-murderer for the rest of their tour. There were some slight disappointments along the way. The fact that Podge could not deliver killer robots with machine gun arms was deeply upsetting. Also that there would be no bird-mounted flying cameras, boomerang land minds and vaporizing ray guns. But despite the small frustrations, in the end Fidel was happy with Podge's initial list of hardware suggestions.

"There is the matter of my consultation fee," Podge said.

"Whatever it is, I will pay," Castro assured him.

When he found out the amount, the dictator's face paled slightly behind his beard.

"Quality costs, Mr. President," Podge said.

"Of course," Castro replied. He sent for a finance deputy who promised el Jefe that the Cuban treasury would deposit the full amount in Podge's Zurich bank.

They parted in Castro's driveway with Podge asking for building blueprints and detailed sketches of the grounds. "All the better to deliver you the excellent service that dignitaries around the world have received from Becket Securities," Podge said.

Castro charged Ameriga with seeing to it that Podge received all he required before racing off late to a meeting with his Council of Ministers.

"If you gentlemen would please wait here while I arrange for the blueprints to be sent to your hotel," Ameriga said. She did not wait for a reply before abandoning them in the hot sun beside the Packard while she ducked inside the mansion.

The lonely pair of peacock executioners kept a wary eye on the two Americans.

"You aren't actually going to do any work for this maniac," Wainwright said, keeping his voice low enough that the soldiers could not hear.

"We'll do what we have to do to get the job done," Podge said.

"Building a sociopath murderer an impenetrable fortress is probably your least good idea in a week of very bad ideas," Wainwright said.

"You think so?" Podge said. He was eyeing the sun, which had begun to dip low in the sky. "Wait'll tonight. I only wish I could have just asked him what was going on up in those hills. It'd sure make this trip a lot easier."

"He's crazy but he's not that crazy, Patrick. Whatever secrets they're hiding you'll have to uncover on your own."

They waited a few minutes longer for Major Ameriga Blanco to reappear from the side door of the mansion. "The arrangements are made," she announced when she finally stepped back out into the hot sunlight.

She shooed the two men into the Packard for the return trip to the city.

A sweating government functionary in a white suit in desperate need of dry cleaning was waiting on the sidewalk in front of the Revolucion Grande Hotel. The man handed Major Blanco an armload of documents and a single scrap of notebook paper before hustling off to his waiting taxi.

She dumped the documents into Wainwright's arms, despite the doctor's protests that he did not want to get involved and, after scanning the single small sheet of paper, handed it over to Podge. "Your plane has left Uganda," she informed him.

Podge scanned the note. The Learjet had flown out two hours after they had departed and was in Johannesburg. His entire security team was back in South Africa.

Podge crumpled the note and stuck it in his pocket, careful to mask his relief. "Say, why don't you and I leave all this fun and excitement in Dr. Wainwright's capable hands and sneak out for a drink? My capitalist treat."

"Not very bloody likely," Wainwright said.

"You were just paid half a million dollars to do this work," Ameriga agreed.

"Yes, but I'm a delegator, you see, I'm not really a hands-on kind of tits. Did I say tits? I meant boss."

He smiled. She scowled.

"How 'bout meeting me halfway?" he suggested, offering a lopsided half-smile.

She hissed a stream of angry Spanish — the only word of which Podge could make out was "puerco" — and, turning on the heel of her boot, marched back to the Packard.

"She's deeply, madly in love with me," Podge informed Wainwright.

Wainwright shifted his armload of government documents. "You're an oaf, but congratulations at least on getting rid of her. You're right, she's intelligent. That's dangerous. Not having Cuban state security breathing down the back of your neck should make tonight at least a tiny little bit easier." He headed for front doors of the hotel.

With a discreet glance, Podge took silent note of the half-dozen men who were at that very moment watching him from strategic positions up and down the street. They were in cars, on sidewalks, and sitting at a café across the street.

"Yeah, doc. Should be a piece of cake."

8

Their luggage had been searched.

The practice was common in totalitarian regimes, and the only difference from country to country was whether or not the host nation wanted its guests to know about the invasion of privacy. In this case, the Cuban government did not want Podge aware it had riffled through his shaving kit and underwear. Everything had been neatly removed from their bags and great care had been taken to replace each item in the precise same spot. But even professional snoops weren't perfect.

A twisted collar here, a misaligned pant crease there. To the trained eye, even one a decade out of practice, it was not difficult to see if one's bags had been tampered with.

Podge was not worried that the official government snoops in Uganda or Cuba would find his greatest hidden prize. No enemy ever had.

The special false bottom in his suitcase was undetectable, and if by some bit of freak luck it was ever discovered it would simply look as if the lining of the bag were coming loose. Only careful manipulation of a hidden lock opened a secret compartment.

If an enemy ever tried to open the false bottom, a canister of colorless, odorless gas would release and render unconscious any nearby living creature. The range would vary depending on the location, but in the case of the Revolucion Grande Hotel, Podge estimated that at least three floors would succumb to the gas.

Podge successfully avoided rendering the seventh, eighth and ninth floors of the Grande unconscious and slipped from the secret compartment a bundle of carefully folded red cloth. He gave the fabric a vigorous shake and it spread out wide across the bed of his hotel suite without so much as a single visible wrinkle.

"You know, I never really realized how silly this thing looked," he called out to the living room as he reached back inside the suitcase. He placed the matching mask next to the cape. "Oh, geez," he muttered.

Both mask and cape were bright red, almost glowing. He stepped back several feet and watched the luminescence fade and the red change over to midnight black.

"And it would have made a hell of a lot more sense just to make it black all the time." He stepped forward and the cloth turned red once more, back again and the cloth once more faded to black. "What were we thinking?"

"Not we," Wainwright replied. "*You.* I made the mistake of telling you about the strange properties of those berries I found in the Philippines, but you're the one who insisted I use the dye on the cape. I, if you don't recall, argued vigorously against it."

Podge changed into a pair of black slacks and matching shirt. He was glad Wainwright was in the other room as he dragged the cape around his shoulders. He checked his reflection in the big mirror above the bureau.

"Holy cats," he muttered.

Podge had never been embarrassed to don the cape back in the old days. He was much younger then, as had been the world. A creeping cynicism had bled into every corner of society since the 1950s and the innocence of those long-ago years had been replaced, bit-by-incremental-bit, with a world that Podge no longer recognized. So sinister were the subtle forces of change that even Podge, aware that they were taking place, did not realize how deeply they had taken root in his own attitudes. It was as if someone had crept into his house and replaced everything he owned with exact replicas. It might look like his home, but there was an indefinable, otherworldly strangeness to it.

Never in the past thirteen years had he felt more starkly the utterly changed world around him than he did in that moment, standing in his old cape before the mirror in his Havana hotel room and feeling the complete fool.

Better to do it fast and get it over with.

Podge went to work on his other suitcases. Other hiding spots yielded a dozen mismatched pieces of black metal. Some bits were hidden in plain site as parts of handles, hinges and protective metal corners. With expert hands, Podge assembled the parts into his familiar gun. He loaded in the more exotic weaponry, finishing up by slapping in a clip of conventional bullets.

He had tested the weapon regularly in Hawaii over the past decade, the only aspect of his previous life he had allowed into his current one.

He slipped the gun in his holster. Spare clips and assorted weapons he stashed away within the folds of his cape. The last was the mask and gauntlets which he held in one hand as he walked out into the suite's living room.

Wainwright had spread the Cuban documents, including blueprints to Castro's house, out on the coffee table and was writing hastily in a yellow notebook. As was always the case, the doctor's pen never seemed able to keep up with his brain. His hand was scribbling seemingly with an independent will as he looked up at Podge.

On an armchair next to Wainwright was a small silver box adorned with the Becket Security logo. The machine was about the size of a two-slice toaster and emitted a gentle hum. The Cubans who searched their luggage hadn't known what it was, and so had no way of knowing that the machine, when switched on, would effectively render neutral any listening devices that were hidden around the suite.

Podge was relieved when Wainwright didn't make some smart-alecky remark about the cape. Although the hint of worry on the older man's usually bland face did nothing to help relieve the squishy feeling in the pit of Podge's stomach.

"How many did you see outside?" Wainwright asked.

"Lots. I guess the front door is out of the question."

Well, let's just hope they leave me alone. I have enough with all your homework to worry about without a bunch of pineapple herders poking their noses in on me."

"The lackeys will stay put unless they're told not to. The ones I saw are staked out for the night. We might be Castro's new best friends, but they're still gonna keep tabs on Americans. The only one we really have to worry about is Major Blanco. Hopefully she's gone for the night." Podge turned to go.

"Get me samples of the dead plants," Wainwright instructed. His pen continued to fill lines of the yellow legal pad even as he spoke. "Also, I'll need some leaves from the living plants around the perimeter. With luck, I can find out from them whatever it is they sprayed to contain that infernal defoliant they released up there."

"You gonna wish me luck?" Podge asked anxiously.

"I am, and I do," Wainwright said. His hand was still writing and he turned his attention to it, as if checking it to make certain it hadn't made any errors while he was not watching. "Do me the great favor of not getting yourself killed tonight, Patrick. There are very few people in this world who are worth a spit. I'd hate to be left alone to deal with the morons and lunatics who constitute the rest of the human race."

Podge watched the top of his old friend's gray head as he hunched over his work.

With a tight nod, Podge tugged on his black gauntlets. There was only one thing left.

Podge lifted his mask and pulled it down snug around his ears.

It was the first time he'd donned the mask in thirteen years. He thought it would feel strange and so was surprised at how normal it felt. Like pulling on a favorite childhood shirt that he should have outgrown decades ago but which somehow still fit absolutely perfectly. It covered tightly both hair and face down to his nose.

Without another word, the Red Menace turned and slipped into the dark spare bedroom. Wainwright heard the door to the balcony open and the brief sound of honking horns and the hum of evening traffic before the door clicked shut again.

"God help us," the doctor said to the empty room.

With a worried exhale, Thaddeus Wainwright threw down the pen and fished in his pocket for his silver cigarette case.

9

THE Cuban night was hot. The kind of oppressive tropical heat that felt like a damp blanket was smothering the entire city.

As usual the communists had gone to great lengths to stamp out all vestiges of joy, but the Cuban people had clearly not read the memo. After a decade of Castro's oppression, Havana was still a vibrant city of lights and music. The street traffic was thinner than was common for a major Western city, but automobiles still rumbled by in a steady stream. As the Red Menace jumped from balcony to balcony on his way to the fire escape, he noted a great deal of foot traffic on the sidewalks far below.

His feet found the fire escape, landing softly on the old rusted metal.

He wasn't worried that Major Blanco's agents would see him. The cape would conceal him from a distance. He climbed swiftly to the roof, a shadow among shadows.

Across the gravel roof, past air vents and a skylight. A cable ran from the roof of the Revolucion Grande Hotel to the Hotel de la Revolucion. The Red Menace tested the strength of the cable with one hand. Finding it secure, he tugged a wire from his right gauntlet, tossed it over the cable and slid on the makeshift zip-line from one hotel roof to the next.

The black cape billowed dramatically behind him, catching the updraft between the two buildings. He landed as silent as a cat.

The roof door was unlocked. The stairwell was dank and poorly lit. He crept down five floors rapidly, pausing only when the first floor door banged open.

He heard sounds of revelry from the first floor ballroom. The event was some sort of big state occasion, for in the brief moment the door was open he saw several Cuban military uniforms passing along the carpeted hallway.

Two young lovers were making out in a corner alcove on the first floor landing. He was a major with a wedding ring, she a lithe young thing without one.

They didn't stay long. The two stumbled upstairs in a clumsy embrace, never noticing the masked figure who crouched in the corner of the second floor landing.

Their footsteps clicked to the third floor where another door opened and quickly closed. The stairwell was silent once more. The Red Menace moved on.

The basement was unlit. He used a small flashlight to find his way through a labyrinth of moisture-soaked walls.

It was true that owners of buildings around the world, in no matter what country one visited, were concerned with people breaking in, not out. The old iron door was sealed, but the lock and handle were on the inside. The Red Menace found a crowbar on a tool bench and popped the door with a minimum of both fuss and shattered brick.

Once outside in the alleys of Havana it was an easy matter to find and hotwire an unlocked Cadillac Le Mans. Less easy was the trip through a city thick with army patrols, but by avoiding the main thoroughfares the Menace reached in an hour the foot of the jungle hills on top of which the secret base was hidden.

He ditched the car and continued on foot.

MIC Director Kirk's spy plane surveillance photos gave him a clear idea of the best route to the top, and so it was that three hours after he left Wainwright at the hotel, the Red Menace found himself up the hillside and crouching at the edge of the burned-out patch of jungle.

The Russians had hacked foliage away from the surrounding jungle and dragged it to rooftops as camouflage. Most of the building lights were off, yet the few that remained plus the bright starlight illuminated looming shapes of manmade structures.

An effort was being made to cover the brown patch of ruined jungle with palm fronds and tree branches, but with such a large area to cover the task was ongoing and surely taking longer than the Soviets would have liked. Even this late at night he could hear the sounds of soldiers chopping away at thick growth while a steady stream of men labored to drag brush from a worn forest path on the far side of the clearing.

The noise of distant work obscured the nearer sound of marching feet and the Red Menace sucked in a lungful of air when a group of Cuban soldiers suddenly appeared from the jungle three yards from where he was hiding. For an instant he was afraid the sound of his labored breathing had caught their attention, however they gave not a glance in his direction. Only once they had marched past did he exhale.

His knees ached and he shifted position to keep his legs from going numb.

Every step of the way had taken longer than expected. The climb up the hill had stolen his breath, and he was winded and sweating.

If he was not the man he once was he was grateful that at least his cape and mask had not changed. He made a mental note to thank Wainwright for inventing the special fabric that did not hold in the heat. If he'd been draped in the black blanket he had worn during his first days as the Red Menace back in the Fifties, he would have passed out from heat exhaustion halfway down the hill.

When the patrol was long gone and he was once more alone, the Menace crept forward to the very edge of the clearing and grabbed a handful of dead foliage.

The plants had definitely not been burned. Whatever had killed them had transformed them into soft mush. Even the hard stems were rotted and limp. When he squeezed them in his fist, pulped gunk spilled out of his gauntlet like old, wet spaghetti.

Scattered around the clearing were the remnants of larger trees, their trunks jutting up like the ribs of massive prehistoric creatures. But the leaves were long gone, joined with the mass of rotting compost on the forest floor. The bare trunks had lost nearly all their branches, and those that had not dropped were hanging limp, like arms without the support of bones. The tops of the trees were slowly curling downward and it was clear to the Red Menace that they would soon fall to join the rest of the putrefying jungle waste.

He circled the clearing to the right until he was close enough to reach out and touch the trunk of a fifty foot blue mahoe. The tree's trunk was spongy down to a hard core inches deep, and his retreating glove left an imprint in the surface from which oozed a white liquid. The Menace cleaned his gauntlet on some nearby palm fronds and waited to see if there was a reaction, but the living leaves failed to curl up.

By every best guess — from Wainwright to Director Kirk's expert consultants — the killer agent worked remarkably fast. If transferring some of the liquid from one plant to another did not kill the leaves on contact, the Menace had to assume that the Russian planes had successfully rendered inert whatever had caused the damage.

Two weeks of boots tramping around the clearing had crushed most of the dead vegetation to pulp. The Menace found a few intact stalks and slipped them inside some small plastic vials which he corked and tucked away inside his cape. He also took a few clippings from the undamaged foliage around the dead zone.

No sooner had he collected Wainwright's samples than the ground began to rumble and the drone of truck engines rose from out the night.

A moment later, amber headlights sliced the darkness.

His path had led him close to the ocean side of the base. He was aware from the aerial photographs of the road that ran up along the southern perimeter but was surprised that he had come so close to stumbling out onto it. In the darkness, in a strange environment, it was difficult to get his bearings.

For a moment the Red Menace retreated back into the brush.

The trucks appeared, a caravan of four big Russian Army vehicles. The canvas backs were open at the top and the beds were laden with freshly harvested brush.

The Russians had apparently grown weary of the slow camouflage progress that was proceeding onsite and had enlisted other teams to pitch in the effort. The first two trucks rumbled past. Further along the road they were waved along by Cuban sentries.

The Menace could see the first truck driving deep onto the base, heading in the direction of the distant area that Jeb Wilson had failed to penetrate.

Instinct took hold and the Red Menace was running even before his conscious mind realized it. The second truck was being waved onto the base and the third was rolling past. He only needed to time it just right…

Branches slapped his face and he swatted them angrily back with gloved hands as he raced determinedly forward. The forest ended on a short bluff into which the road had been cut, and when the jungle's muddy edge began to crumble beneath his boots the Red Menace jumped. There was the awful, exhilarating feeling of empty air beneath him for a split-second, and in the next he was crashing into the pile of brush that was packed inside the fourth and final truck.

He had twisted in midair to wrap himself in the cape, hitting with his shoulder, rolling so that the cape unfurled as he sprang free. The sturdy cloth did not tear, but sharp branches jabbed hard through the material. A short knife blade of a rough-hewn branch struck the ancient wound on his left side and he gasped at the pain.

He grabbed at his old scar. His fingers came back slick, and not from sweat.

The wound was not life-threatening. The toughened skin that formed the scar had kept the machete-like branch from piercing deep.

The truck squeaked to a stop on protesting brakes and the Red Menace drew his cape up protectively.

A few bored words exchanged in Spanish. A flashlight beam shined perfunctorily across the rear gate of the truck but not inside the bed. This time the Menace did not need to hold his breath, this time his entire body seemed to instinctively still. He waited.

After only a few seconds the truck was waved forward.

The final truck in the small convoy bounced through potholes and up the road, unknowingly carrying its hidden cargo to the next checkpoint on its way inside the top secret Russian base.

10

COLONEL Petr Bolgevik did not trust Colonel Ivan Strankov. Not in the least, and certainly not as director of the most important strategic Soviet inroad in the Western Hemisphere since the glorious October Revolution and the founding of the Soviet Union.

Not that trust came easily to Petr Bolgevik. As an officer in the KGB, mistrust was Bolgevik's bread and butter. Trust was for the weak, for the foolish, for the West. In training he had been taught to trust only in the great communist mission. As for those charged with seeing that mission realized? They were men and, his instructors had drilled into his brain, all men were fallible and, therefore, untrustworthy. Bolgevik took the lesson to heart. The KGB colonel believed in communism, not men. And the man he believed in least of all these days was Red Army Colonel Ivan Strankov.

Bolgevik was colonel in rank, but not in uniform. He was the head of the plainclothes KGB unit at the Cuban base which Strankov commanded.

Bolgevik was a much younger man than Strankov. He had been alive during the Great Patriotic War, but as a baby, a toddler. The guns had fallen silent on the Eastern Front, the Germans had retreated from outside Moscow and Leningrad, and the Iron Curtain of the Cold War had descended before Petr Bolgevik's first childhood memory.

Technically, Colonels Bolgevik and Strankov were of equal rank but in reality this was nonsense. Bolgevik had compiled a mental list of several reasons Strankov should be considered the subordinate officer, the primary reason being that Bolgevik was KGB. The most powerful men in the Politburo feared the clandestine agency and the harm its agents could do to reputation, let alone life. Add to that the fact that Strankov had spent a decade in a labor camp. This humbling experience should have sent Strankov stumbling for the shadows in fright at the mere sight of Colonel Bolgevik.

As if that weren't enough, Bolgevik had been the first of the two colonels assigned to the Cuban base. He had been stationed in Cuba during the earliest days of planning and had watched the first trees being cut down, the stumps being hauled from the ground and the first trenches being dug. In fact, Bolgevik was in Cuba a full two years before Strankov was even released from the Siberian gulag. The pecking order was firmly established before Strankov arrived. Or at least it should have been. But since his first day Strankov acted as if the base were his private domain.

Finally, as the disgraced head of the failed agency Motherland, an agency that had been largely folded into the KGB after Strankov's removal from power, Strankov should have realized the supremacy of the KGB over all he had once commanded.

Yet in not a single matter did Ivan Strankov demonstrate the least awareness that Bolgevik was his superior. Never did he show Petr Bolgevik the deference that was the KGB colonel's due. That, however, would soon change. If Colonel Bolgevik had played his cards right, this warm Cuban night would be one of the last Strankov spent in Cuba.

Bolgevik had left the apartment of his Cuban mistress after midnight and returned to his quarters on the Russian base. There was a note tacked to his door.

SEE ME IN MY OFFICE AT ONCE. STRANKOV

Bolgevik tore the note down and scowled.

"Your impertinence has doomed you, comrade colonel," he muttered, through tightly clenched teeth.

He considered ignoring the note. He had no idea how long it had been tacked up. Strankov could be long in bed by now.

But the trucks were still driving up the bay road with their loads of camouflage and the chainsaws were still running day and night in the jungle, and with all the activity Bolgevik would have a difficult time getting to sleep.

The KGB colonel crumpled the note, stuck it in his pocket, and struck out across the compound for the entrance to the main bunker.

The sentries stood at attention as he passed between them. Bolgevik skipped lightly down the stairs and ducked down the nearest side corridor. The hallway was chilly, as usual. He rapped his knuckles on the unmarked steel door at the end of the hall and was surprised when the knock was answered.

"Come in, Comrade Bolgevik."

It irritated Colonel Bolgevik that Strankov would know it was him, as if Bolgevik had nothing better to do in the middle of the night than come running like a servant answering his master's call. He was scowling as he pushed open the door.

The room was dark but for a single desk lamp which brightly illuminated a stark white circle on the desk directly below. The shadow of a thin man was barely visible seated behind the desk, beyond the splash of light. Cigarette smoke filled the office and fingers of smoke curled through the light, although Bolgevik could not see evidence of a lit cigarette in the darkness. One lonely butt was stabbed out in the ashtray on the desk.

"Do you treasure loyalty, Comrade Colonel Bolgevik?" the shadow of Ivan Strankov asked. The base director's voice creaked like a rusty hinge.

Bolgevik flashed an oily smile. "I see what this is," he said. "My report has reached the right eyes in Moscow. There is no need to play games, Strankov."

"Game? This is no game. This is life."

An envelope appeared from out the dark, slapping hard on the metal desk and sending twisting streams of cigarette smoke dancing crazily across the splash of light.

Petr Bolgevik's jaw dropped a fraction of an inch when he recognized his own handwriting in the phrases "TOP SECRET," "KGB EYES ONLY" on the envelope. The end had been torn open and a typed sheet of white paper hung from the hole.

"I put that on a plane to Moscow two days ago," Bolgevik sputtered.

"It is a state security matter. What do you think you are playing with here, Strankov?"

"I," said the shadow seated at the desk, "was a fan of loyalty once upon a time. When I was young and stupid like you. Fortunately I still engender loyalty from others even if I myself do not feel it for anything these days."

"You have loyalty, Strankov. You have it for yourself. You have staffed this site with old Motherland cronies and officers so young they fear to question you. You have shut out the KGB in virtually everything you do. You have the Cubans fooled into thinking you have a direct line to Comrade Brezhnev at the Kremlin up here in your mountain bunker. And those experiments you have allowed Dr. Plassko to conduct. I only just found out that you lied in your report to Moscow of the events here last month. You should not even be associating with Plassko, one of your failed cronies from your failed agency. Moscow was right to banish him to the University of Havana. They should have put him in the gulag and left you both there to rot."

Such accusations from a KGB official would be enough to freeze the heart of any sane Russian. And in this case both men knew that these, unlike most KGB accusations, were all true. Bolgevik was furious and breathless by the time he finished, and he puffed his chest out defiantly to await the traitor Strankov's feeble, bleating defense.

At first was a very long moment of silence. Bolgevik briefly wondered if the man behind the desk had dropped dead. It was possible. Strankov was clearly in terrible health. The charges might have been enough to finish him.

All at once, a cleared throat. Not fear. Just a contemplative repositioning of phlegm.

A hand snaked out into the light, fingers grotesquely discolored, and brushed the envelope. "So you say." The hand retreated and there was a rustling in the shadows. "I do not have time for arguments, for second guessing, for secret notes to Moscow questioning my command from some KGB junior officer seeking advancement."

Bolgevik growled and waved a furious hand. "I do not care about advancement, Strankov. I care only for the glorious communist mission. Whatever fleeting sense of accomplishment it has given you to intercept that letter, you have only delayed the inevitable. What is more, by tampering with a top secret KGB communique, you have made matters worse for yourself. Whatever it is you think you are doing here in Cuba, it is over. You are finished, Strankov."

Bolgevik puffed out his chest even further and gave the shadow lurking behind the desk a victorious sneer.

The KGB colonel thought he heard a soft click, magnified by the claustrophobic darkness of the otherwise silent office. He was not sure he heard the sound. And an instant later, when the bullet scrambled his brain, the ability to hear, speak or send letters to Moscow was forever lost to young Colonel Petr Bolgevik.

The silenced bullet slapped young Petr Bolgevik in the forehead, splattering skull and gray matter on wall and door. Bolgevik collapsed as if all the bones in his body had instantly turned to jelly.

Colonel Petr Bolgevik kicked feebly at the floor, as residual impulses fled his body along with the trail of thick black blood that dribbled off into the dark crevices of the small office. Eventually the kicking stopped and the body was still.

The desk light snapped out.

In the darkness behind the desk, a drawer opened and closed. The sudden blaze of a match briefly illuminated a ravaged face. The flame was abruptly extinguished.

In the darkened office, the soft inhale and exhale of a pair of struggling lungs was accompanied by the gently floating orange tip of a lonely cigarette.

11

Private Ernesto Cruz had been stuck on guard duty nearly nonstop for the past three weeks. The longest he had slept in that time was one four hour stretch over a week ago. The rest was stolen catnaps here and there, and the best of those didn't amount to a full hour. At least he was not alone. Everyone was being pushed to his limit since the incident that had destroyed a huge patch of jungle and set off alarm bells throughout the Cuban government. Not that it made Private Cruz feel any better to know everyone else was as exhausted as he. It was taking all his effort just trying to stay awake.

By the time the latest caravan of trucks laden with jungle brush arrived at his checkpoint, Private Cruz was practically seeing double.

It seemed as if the entire Cuban army had been put to work like slave labor in the literal coverup that had followed the accident, with teams of soldiers hacking away at jungle brush for hours on end. As bad as his extended guard duty shifts were, he much preferred it to the tough physical labor most of the men were enduring out in the forest.

The latest truck drivers were blinking away sleep as he waved them onto the base. They were like dead men, none speaking so much as a word as they passed. From this final checkpoint they bumped across the acres of dead forest to the far side of the clearing where teams of sweating Cuban soldiers swarmed the trucks and unloaded the cargo.

"How many is that tonight?" Cruz asked as the latest set of tail lights briefly stained the jungle red. He yawned, a huge gulp of air that exposed his back molars.

"Nineteen," Private Ramondo Ruiz replied. "And do not start yawning again. I am tired enough as it is. You will put me to sleep."

A new truck drove up and Ruiz shined a flashlight beam across it.

"These Russians, they are demanding too much of us," Cruz said. He rapped the side of the truck and the driver put the vehicle in gear and drove off.

"You were not here when this base was constructed," Ruiz replied, he stifled his own yawn with the back of his hand. "Now *that* was two years of hard labor the likes of which you cannot know. The cargo ships smuggling in the supplies every day. Even submarines many times each week. The work was done almost entirely at night at the beginning so that we could not be seen from the American planes. Only when the tunnels were started were we able to work during the day. But then we were forced to work underground, like burrowing rats. This? This is nothing compared to that."

"I would still like to know what happened. Have you heard anything?"

The last truck pulled up to their checkpoint. Private Ruiz shook his head. "From the Russians? Are you joking? We are supposed to be comrades, but I would not trust that Strankov to tell me if my hair was on fire and he had the last bucket of water on Cuba. What was that?"

Cruz was yawning once more. "What?"

"I heard a noise," Ruiz said. Suddenly he was no longer tired. Alert, rifle at the ready and the flashlight tucked up with the gun's butt in the crook of his arm, he nodded for Private Cruz to circle the front of the truck.

Cruz unhitched his rifle from his shoulder and crept around the front bumper as Private Ruiz moved stealthily around the back.

Private Cruz strained his ears but all he could hear was the soft purr of the engine, the chirp of jungle insects and the occasional outburst from distant chainsaws.

Then a footstep. The crack of a branch very close by.

Cruz froze.

He swore he heard someone moving, the rustle of fabric. It sounded very near but though he strained his senses he could see no one in the nearby jungle.

A flash. A brilliant streak of crimson at the corner of his eye. And as quickly as it came, it was gone. The night seemed darker in its wake.

More footfalls, these passing away into the dark, then swallowed by the jungle.

Sudden movement at the rear of the truck. Cruz snapped his rifle up with a start, leveling it at the silhouette.

"Do not shoot!" Private Ruiz snapped. He lowered his own gun and swept his flashlight around the area.

Cruz took in a sip of air and lowered his rifle, slipping his finger from the trigger. He winced at the flashlight beam that raked across his face.

"Did you see anything?" Ruiz asked.

Cruz hesitated. The red splash from the truck's taillights illuminated the road behind the truck and stained the left side of Private Ruiz's face. This must have been the flash of red he had seen. His tired eyes were playing tricks on him.

"No, nothing," Private Cruz said.

Private Ruiz hooked his rifle back over his shoulder. "I could have sworn I heard something," he said, yawning.

"You have been on duty too long," Cruz replied, shouldering his own weapon. He no longer felt like yawning. "You are jumping at shadows."

Cruz rapped his palm on the passenger door and the truck headed up the last leg of the long road and into the patch of deforested jungle.

THE GUARD had nearly spotted him. The road was too narrow, the jungle too close and dense to slip into without being heard. The Red Menace had no choice but to wait until the Cuban private's back was turned and then make a break for it.

As he ran up the road he cursed again the arrogance of his own youth. The cape and mask had been a dramatic combination back then; the legendary Red Menace sweeping up to an enemy from out of nowhere in a blinding flash. But the hubris of youth seemed ridiculously reckless to him now.

The Menace heard the engine rumble behind him and he ducked for cover behind the nearest building, a small latrine used by the Cuban conscripts.

The truck in which he'd stowed away rolled slowly up the road. Before it made it as far as the latrine, the bright yellow lights abruptly veered left and the big truck took the bumpy road through the forest of dead trees and composting foliage.

Alone once more, the Menace broke cover and raced across the compound. With the base lights off he was utterly invisible to distant eyes.

He had studied Jeb Wilson's photos well, memorizing the layout. He hustled alongside the air conditioned quarters where Strankov surely slept at this late hour.

An image of Strankov came to him unbidden. Sitting on the floor in a Moscow basement, hands clutching his own throat.

I don't want you or any other Motherland goons anywhere near the U.S. again. This is your last warning. It gets bloody after this.

He'd given the Russian colonel fair warning. For more than a decade the peace had been kept between them, although he could mostly thank a Soviet gulag for that. But there was not a statute of limitations on such things, not between old enemies. Strankov was back and the bill would come due. But not just yet.

The Red Menace bypassed the colonel's private quarters and slipped over to the low concrete bunker.

There were two soldiers guarding the single door, their eyes trained dead ahead. A single weak incandescent bulb in the alcove outside the door was not long for this world. It buzzed on and off, alternately washing the area in flickering amber, then switching off completely. A swarm of confused insects flapped around the sputtering bulb. Into the dim light of the alcove behind the two soldiers crept the Red Menace.

He hugged the wall. If he could stay just far enough back, could remain just out of view. That he'd nearly been spotted at the checkpoint had rattled him. The infernal cape had to remain outside the field of vision of these two, had to stay black as night.

One of the soldiers suddenly shifted and the Menace's hand snaked instinctively under his cape for his gun.

The soldier repositioned his weight on his right foot, muttered a complaint about the flickering bulb, and continued staring out at the night.

The Menace relaxed his grip on his gun butt.

The door was not locked. He opened it and darted quickly inside, hoping the sound of the bolt clicking did not catch the attention of the guards.

A moment passed and the door did not fly open. He was safe.

A short corridor ended in a long flight of steps. He hustled down to the next level, his boots making not a noise on the concrete stairs. There was another corridor below, this one long. There were closed steel doors all along its length as well as other corridors that snaked off in all directions.

It was much cooler in these secret tunnels below the jungle. The Russians were keeping the air frosty. His shirt was wet with sweat and the sudden cold chilled him. He unstuck the damp cloth from his back as he walked.

Black stenciling adorned many of the doors, text in both Russian and Spanish.

The Red Menace found one marked Dr. O. Plassko. The name rang a bell, although he could not remember where he'd heard it before. He slipped inside the room.

It felt as if he'd stepped into a sauna. The room was every bit as oppressively humid as the jungle he'd just escaped. Even more so after the cool journey he'd just taken through the air conditioned corridor.

Dull purple lights glowed eerily from shelves all around the room. He found a switch next to the door and when he flipped it on, a half-dozen rows of florescent lights buzzed on above his head and flickered on into the far distance. And along with the florescent room lights, a light also snapped on in the Red Menace's brain.

"Oleg Plassko," he muttered, nodding. He remembered now where he'd heard the name before. He had not made the connection with the fat little man who appeared in several of Jeb Wilson's photographs. Plassko was a Motherland scientist; a botanist of no particular distinction. At least that's what his MIC dossier had read back in the late Fifties. Plassko was present during Strankov's last ill-fated meeting with the Red Menace. The Menace had scarcely given Plassko a second thought. Apparently Strankov thought more highly of the botanist than had the analysts at MIC and the Red Menace, at least if this underground facility was any indication.

The large room with the buzzing florescent lights in which the Red Menace stood was a greenhouse. Hundreds of large glass tanks were lined up on simple wooden shelves. At a quick glance, all of the nearest tanks appeared to be filled with plants. On each tank was stuck a single strip of masking tape, and on each strip of tape was scribbled a code of numbers and letters.

The Menace remembered the lab back in Moscow. He'd been preoccupied with Strankov, of course, as well as having to deal with a substantial contingent of Red Army soldiers, but he vaguely recalled several similar plant-filled tanks in the basement room at Motherland headquarters over a decade ago. But that little lab was nothing compared to this major operation deep beneath the Cuban jungle.

"What are you boys up to?" the Red Menace asked quietly.

The center of the room was a laboratory. There were tables with beakers, test tubes and Bunsen burners. There were more tanks on the tables, these ones sealed tightly. Thick gloves were built into one side of each of the glass tanks which allowed an individual on the outside to manipulate items within the tank without fear of contamination.

Lining the bottoms of the sealed tanks were plant samples that appeared to have been taken from the area of dead jungle. Scalpels and tweezers inside the cases had been used to dissect and inspect the rotting plants. There was a spiral bound notebook lying open on the nearest table. The Red Menace glanced through the first few pages but it was written in a crazy Russian scrawl, and although he could speak the language and recognize some written words, the mess in the notebook was indecipherable to him.

Although...

There was one word recurring that he recognized: *smyert*. As he flipped through page after page he saw it dozens of times. It appeared to be the conclusion to what he guessed were many separate experiments. It was the Russian word for death.

The Red Menace did a quick search around the lab tables and found stacks of books and thick, bound files. Plassko's life's work. Two small refrigerators were jammed in between the towering stacks of paperwork, and inside the fridges were dozens of tests tubes, all loaded with a green goo.

He took a test tube out, tipped it and tapped the side. The gunk was thick and rolled like exceptionally slow molasses to the corked end. He replaced the test tube and took one from a rack way back in the fridge, hoping that it wouldn't soon be missed.

He slipped the glass test tube into one of his own small plastic vials, marked it carefully along with the samples he had retrieved from the jungle outside, and secreted the collection of samples beneath his cape. Assuming the Menace managed to get off the base alive, Dr. Wainwright was going to have his hands full.

He had hit the light switch and was opening the door back into the hall when he heard the sound of footsteps echoing up the corridor.

The footfalls were slow, but determined. A sharp, steady click-click that ricocheted off the cement walls and carried away down the long hallway.

The sound launched the Red Menace back in time.

The footsteps of most men were smooth, with the ball of the foot rolling to toes in a flowing motion. This was a distinctive tread: the sharp click first of the heel, followed by the castanet snap of the toe.

Through the crack in the partially opened door, the Red Menace saw striding up the corridor one of the most hated ghosts from his past.

Colonel Ivan Strankov was the very personification of Death himself.

The Russian's face was drawn, his cheeks sunken so deep one could see the outlines of his teeth. In the pictures Jeb Wilson had taken, Strankov appeared unhealthily

thin, but the photos did not do justice to the walking cadaver the Russian had become. There was no meat on long bones. Just paper thin flesh and gristle pulled tight.

And the skin. The color of Strankov's skin was like no human's. It was simultaneously ashen and dark purple, changing tone as it dipped in and out of the cavernous furrows of his leathery face.

Strankov was alone; a solitary corpse to haunt the halls of the secret base.

Yet not quite as alone as the Russian thought.

The Red Menace closed the door as the Russian passed and then quickly slipped out into the corridor behind Strankov.

The hallway lights were dull behind metal cages, the amber splashes up the center of the corridor too frail to illuminate the Red Menace as he skulked along the shadowed concrete walls. Strankov marched along, a specter trailed by a ghost.

The base was far larger than the brains at MIC had guessed. The first hallway led to another which fed a network of corridors. The Red Menace gradually became aware that they were inexorably heading toward the northeast.

Wilson hadn't photographed the northeastern section of the base. Even the aerial photographs taken by America's spy planes had been unable to get a clear shot of that inaccessible area. The northeast section had been spared the ravages of defoliant, and so was still protected by dense jungle.

By the Red Menace's best guess they had traveled half a mile in the direction of the remote corner of the base.

The corridors ended in a few offices and a staircase flanked by two closed steel doors. Strankov started up the long stairs. Halfway up he paused and for an instant and the Menace was afraid the Russian had heard the sound of soft footfalls behind him.

Colonel Strankov stood there for a long moment, just leaning against the wall, a hand pressed to his chest as he breathed. The Menace stood stock-still at the bottom of the stairs.

The Russian looked for an instant as if he might keel over and tumble down the steps. All at once the momentary weakness was banished, the arrogance returned, and Strankov straightened up once more and finished off the flight of stairs, disappearing from sight on the upstairs the landing.

The Red Menace swept rapidly up behind him.

He was back at ground level. A single door was open on the short hallway.

Inside, Strankov stood with his back to the door, his hands clasped behind his back as he stared out a long, narrow window.

The view from this room was of the section of jungle unseen from the air. Here the outside lights remained on. Netting and natural forest camoflage still prevented the world from seeing what the Russians had built in the jungle outside of Havana.

But the Red Menace saw.

Draped in nets, trees and jungle vines was the unmistakable concrete slab of a hardened ICBM missile silo. In the distance he saw another. Strankov and his Soviet masters had smuggled nuclear missiles into Cuba.

"Holy macaroni."

The Menace wasn't aware at first that he had spoken aloud. He realized he'd messed up in that infinitesimally brief moment when the soft whisper escaped his lips and Strankov's shoulders stiffened. As the Russian's unseen hand reached for his belt, the Red Menace was already moving, darting down below the control console in the middle of the room, out of Strankov's line of sight.

And, cursing his own stupid blunder, he waited for his old enemy to pull the alarm that would rouse the entire sleeping base and bring the whole Cuban Army rolling into the bunker like oranges.

WHEN HE heard the English language curse whispered into the air behind him, only years of practiced stoicism prevented Colonel Ivan Strankov from jumping out of his ravaged skin. Instead of panicking, he reached instinctively for his holster.

Strankov wheeled, gun in hand.

He found that he was alone in the darkened room.

Surprise, then a frown crossed his discolored face. He'd heard the voice. Soft, yet clear as day. He considered sounding the alarm. But what if he was wrong? He was so tired these days, and it was so very late at night.

There was a wall-mounted intercom next to the window that overlooked the missile silos. One hand had been snaking for the buzzer, but he drew it back.

Ivan Strankov's index finger gently caressed the trigger of his handgun as he left the window. He crept slowly around the computerized control console, then jumped.

"Do not move!" he snarled.

Strankov was certain he would find someone crouching down on the other side of the console, but there was nothing there but three empty chairs.

Wilson, the dead American agent, had not made it this far. The bunker was guarded at every entrance. The Cubans would insist that it was impossible for base security to be penetrated again. Perhaps he had imagined the voice after all.

Yet for some reason — caution, instinct — the gun stayed in his hand.

Another sound. Fabric rustling.

Someone was moving in the room!

And as a familiar tingle churned the pit of his stomach, Strankov saw out of the corner of his eye a sudden flash of red.

It could not be real. His enemy was long gone, vanished into ancient history. It was a trick of the light, a flash of an old, buried memory.

By the time he realized that the memory was indeed real, it was too late. A wash of crimson rose up suddenly out of the nothingness.

No time to turn, no time to shoot. Too late to react when the sharp blow struck his temple. The room lights blazed brightly for an instant and then all light was extinguished and Colonel Strankov dropped like a soggy turnip to the bunker floor.

THE RED MENACE pressed his fingertips to Strankov's neck. There was a pulse. Weak, but steady. That the pulse was so feeble was unsurprising. Strankov had aged decades in the fourteen years since the Menace had last seen him.

The Red Menace pulled his gauntlet back on and glanced around the room.

It was late. The base was a ghost town. Still, something as important as the missile control room would be checked in on regularly by patroling soldiers.

In a perfect world he would have found some way to get Strankov back to Wainwright. The doctor had a dozen serums in his bag of tricks to loosen the tongues of men. And there was now much to learn from Strankov, not only about whatever it was that had killed the plants outside, but details about this secret Russian missile base.

Casting a wary eye at the missile silos outside the control room window, the Menace lifted Strankov in a fireman's carry and carted the unconscious man out the door and down the stairs. Strankov was as light as a sofa cushion and the Menace carried the slumbering man easily through the hall and to a vacant downstairs room.

It was a supply closet. There was a stack of chairs in one corner. The Menace took one down and lashed Strankov to it with some extension cords.

The Menace slapped the colonel gently a few times on the cheek.

"Wake up, sleepyhead. The shock of your life is staring you in the kisser."

The Russian groaned and the Red Menace took a step back. He kept an ear trained on the closed door and the hallway beyond, ticking off the agonizing seconds as he waited for his old enemy to come around.

12

"You are a very lucky man, Ivan Ivanovich!"

It was his grandfather's voice. He did not know why it was coming to him now. The old man had been dead for twenty years.

Strankov's grandfather often shouted as if he were deaf and unaware of his own raised voice, even though his hearing was perfectly fine. When he had asked as a boy, his grandmother waved a weathered hand and told young Ivan Strankov to ignore him. "He has always had a big mouth, that one, ever since we were first married forty years ago. Do not give it a thought. He is just an odd one, your grandfather."

Yet little Ivan Strankov was a clever boy and he did think about it. He wondered why it was only sometimes that Dedushka Boris talked loudly even though he was not angry, while most of the time he spoke in a normal tone. As he grew and became busier with school, and military service and a life outside his little nuclear family, he wondered about it less until it was just a tiny buzzing question buried deep in the recesses of his busy brain. But the nagging question he'd had about his grandfather since childhood came back in force one fateful afternoon when he was a grown man.

"It is not many young men who meet the great Comrade Stalin!" his grandfather loudly enthused that particular afternoon so many years ago. "A great hero of the Revolution! Did you know that I once met Comrade Vladimir Ilich? Now he was a great man! But not as great as Comrade Stalin, the greatest hero of all!"

The old man's rheumy eyes darted desperately back and forth.

There were other old men sitting at benches in the park, chess boards laid out carefully on makeshift tables. A few ducks waddled forlornly around the worn grass near the little stagnant pond, but as this was communist Russia there were no spare scraps of bread to feed them. Starving humans took precedence over hungry birds.

A few irritated faces glanced up from chessboards at Dedushka Boris Strankov's raised voice.

"Grandmother said you had something to give me," Strankov said. A single disdainful glance at the old chess players and their sagging faces returned to their games. They had learned long ago not to challenge a man in uniform.

"Ah, yes," his grandfather said, his voice abruptly dropping to a normal level as he fished around in the pockets of his tattered greatcoat. When he produced the old World War I medal from a hole in the lining of his pocket, he beamed. "Pinned on my blouse by Vladimir Ilich himself!" the old man shouted. "You, a great hero of the Revolution in your own right, must take it. Here, young Ivan Ivanovich."

Hands coarse from years of hard living and gnarled from arthritis pressed the medal into the young man's hand.

Strankov's hands were soft and pink. In his memory, he saw himself. His skin was perfect, his face unlined. Not the haggard purple flesh of recent years.

Strankov was a young captain in the Red Army and just returned a hero from the Great Patriotic War. Young Captain Strankov had led a battalion into Berlin and had been one of the first on the scene at the official end of the Third Reich.

"I hear from the grandson of Yuri Dzyuvo that you brought Hitler's body back to Moscow!" Grandfather Strankov shouted proudly. The chess players were no longer paying attention. Only a duck looked up and quacked at the noisy old man.

"That is not something Dzyuvo should have discussed, nor should you," Captain Strankov warned.

The old man was like a turtle retreating into the shell of his greatcoat. "Of course," he said, his voice suddenly normal once more. "We are just so proud of you, your grandmother and me." And the voice rose again.

"If only your father were alive to see you now. The great young Captain Strankov, returned from victory over the fascists!"

He yelled it so loudly that the startled duck flew off into the middle of the pond.

His grandfather had always been a big, burly, fearless fellow. However, on that frosty October morning, Ivan Strankov detected something in the old man's voice that he had never noticed before. Apprehension. As if he were afraid of his own grandson.

It was a surprising discovery. Like looking day after day for many years at a familiar landscape painting hanging on the wall, only to suddenly find a group of picnickers sitting in the foreground. Like his grandfather's fear, the picnickers had been there all along, yet had gone unrecognized on a conscious level.

Even as he thanked his grandfather for the medal and was leaving the park, Ivan Strankov was thinking back to all the times his grandfather had raised his voice throughout the years. At the road he glanced back to find the old man in heated conversation with some of the old chess players. Now that Strankov was out of earshot, his grandfather's voice was hushed and did not carry across the pond.

On his ride back to Moscow, young Captain Strankov's analytical mind began to sort through memories of his grandfather.

Strankov's mother had died in childbirth, his drunken father had died of blood loss when he cut off his hand attempting to fix a tractor when Strankov was still an infant. His father's parents were already old when Strankov was born, but had kindly taken in the little orphaned child.

The shouting, Strankov realized, came only when his grandfather was discussing the Party and the leaders of the Soviet Union. He never spoke a disparaging word, only ever shouted the most glowing praises. Why would a man raise his voice only under those circumstances? To prove loyalty to anyone nearby. And who would be so desperate to prove his loyalty to the state to strangers? A man with something to hide.

By the time he had reached his office at GRU headquarters, Strankov had already decided to have his grandparents watched. Three days later he received a report from the agents assigned to keep tabs on his grandfather. The old man had been arrested in a tavern for the crime of treason against the state.

Ivan Strankov met his grandmother at the precinct where his grandfather was being held. The old man was howling somewhere in the depths of the prison as the grief-stricken woman threw herself on the desk of the local constable. Great, fat tears streamed down the deep furrows of her leathery face. When her grandson arrived, she clung to him as a drowning woman would a life preserver.

"Please, what is happening Ivan?" she cried desperately.

Strankov peeled her sausage-like fingers from his bicep. "Let me talk to the men," he said, coldly, efficiently.

She panted and nodded, backing away and wiping her eyes with the sleeve of her cheap cloth coat. Her grandson — her surrogate son — was a very important man. A great soldier in the Patriotic War, already a Red Army captain at the age of twenty-three, and an officer with the GRU, Soviet military intelligence. This she had insisted to the constable in his uniform and the government agents in their plain black suits before her beloved young Ivan Ivanovich had arrived. Now they would see. Now these evil little men would be punished for arresting an innocent old man for the crime of having a foolish tongue loosed by too much vodka.

"Do you have the charges?" Strankov asked the local KGB agents. He was passed a paper which he scanned for less than twenty seconds. "Very well," he said, nodding in satisfaction. "Have him tried quickly. I want this over with fast. The old fool has already embarrassed me enough."

His grandmother's face collapsed. "Ivan, you cannot."

"He has openly criticized the government many times," Strankov told her. "Under questioning, his associates admitted that he has shown open contempt for the Politburo and specifically for comrades Lenin and Stalin going back decades."

Somewhere in a back cell his grandfather had heard Strankov's clipped, emotionless declaration.

"Bastard!" old Boris Strankov's disembodied voice raged. "Ingrate! You did this to me, to your own blood! I feared you as a child! We both did! We saw what you were even then. A cold, vicious, cruel, heartless monster! If he did this to me, to the one who raised him, who tried to love him as a son, he will betray you! All of you! He will betray the state, he will betray Russia! You are fools to not slap this treacherous fiend in shackles right now, this very minute! I curse you, Ivan Strankov! Damn you to hell!"

The old man continued to hurl invective, and at a gesture from Strankov one of the plainclothes men went back to the cells. There was a grunt, then silence.

"Deal with this matter quickly," Strankov said. "I have a train to catch."

His grandmother had been watching the proceedings as a horrified and silent spectator. It was all too much to believe. But when her grandson turned to go, casually abandoning his grandfather to a monstrous fate, the floodgate of tears suddenly burst open and she fell to her knees before him. "Please, Ivan!" she screeched.

His mouth was a pencil-thin line as he hauled the old woman to her feet and dragged her from the constable's small office.

"You knew," he snarled once they were alone outside. "I should have figured it out long ago, the shouted glowing praises followed by the whispers. I had to figure it out, but you *knew*. You are lucky I do not have you shipped off to a gulag with him."

At this his grandmother became inconsolable. She wailed and tore at her coat and when she would not stop crying he simply left her on the steps of the police station and went back inside.

"Also, there is a Corporal Yuri Dzyuvo who lives in the same building as the old man." He refused to call he who had raised him "grandfather." He pointed to the KGB men. "He was under orders not to discuss our time in Germany. Have him arrested for treason as well, and find out how much his family and friends know."

The men in the dark suits nodded and Strankov went back outside. His howling grandmother's face was awash in tears and she attempted to grab his leg as he passed. He skipped around her grasping hands and headed down the road for the train station.

His grandmother died three days later. She was the lucky one. His grandfather survived six years in a Siberian gulag before he succumbed. In his last breath he cursed the young man who had so easily betrayed his own flesh and blood.

Ivan Strankov never knew his grandfather's last words and only learned of the man's death months after the fact. In the intervening years

Strankov had risen steadily up the military hierarchy and by that point had achieved the rank of colonel.

Ivan Strankov's ruthlessness was legendary. It was said that he would murder his own mother for advancement, and those who said it did not know how close to a literal truth the statement was. It was mercilessness which his superiors decided was the most important quality for director of a new agency that was being formed to combat the capitalist threat. At the ripe old age of twenty-nine, Comrade Captain Ivan Strankov became the first director of the agency known as Motherland.

America's President Eisenhower had recently sanctioned the creation of an agency called Manpower and Intelligence Coordination. The agency, known by the shorthand MIC, was to oversee the intelligence apparatus of the entire U.S. government. This meant that MIC would have access to the intelligence of the entire Western world.

MIC was the honey pot of intelligence. To learn her secrets would be to learn every vital secret possessed by the enemies of the USSR. Motherland was created as the Russian counterpart of the Manpower and Intelligence Coordination agency, its purpose to infiltrate and exploit as a Soviet resource the intelligence of MIC.

Early on in the process of forming his fledgling agency, now *Colonel* Strankov had been called before select members of the Politburo and intelligence services. It was evident by their demeanor and questions that the old graybeards were afraid the new cock-of-the-walk would be stepping on their toes.

"Yours is a very broadly defined mission," said the director of the GRU. "Is there an end game, and how will we know if you have achieved it?"

"I will report directly to the general secretary on operational matters," Strankov had replied. "The how, when and where of those operations, comrade, is a state secret."

"What is the budget of this Motherland?" asked the defense minister.

"It will be whatever it needs to be to attain our goal," Strankov said. "The exact amount, I am afraid, comrade field marshal, is a state secret as well."

"You have, as far as we know, limitless resources and direct access to Soviet funds and personnel around the globe," said a first deputy chairman. "That is great power, captain. Who exists in the government to oversee your actions?"

"Checks and balances, is that what you mean, first deputy chairman? I will let that remain an American concern. My concern, as I am sure is true for all of us, is that the glorious Soviet Union be successful against capitalist world hegemony."

It was a skillful performance. Even Strankov was a little concerned that his tacit reference to an affection by the first deputy chairman to the American concept of checks and balances might be a bridge too far. However, after that meeting there were none in the government who dared speak a sour word against Motherland or her director. Ivan Strankov and his secret agency were simply too powerful a force to be questioned.

After establishing Motherland's Moscow headquarters and drafting top agents from all over the Soviet military and intelligence services, Strankov's first espionage task was to ferret out the weakest link in the MIC chain.

In every large government organization there was always someone unhappy with his job, dissatisfied with his superiors, angry at some fleeting administration policy. It could be a secretary, an analyst, a field agent or even someone in a high leadership position. The individual need not have any influence, they need only offer the crack in the metaphorical door through which an enemy might slip in undetected.

The problem with MIC was its infernal director. Harmon Kirk had been chosen personally by President Eisenhower to head the new agency.

Kirk was an old hand in the wartime Office of Strategic Services who had helped establish its civilian successor, the Central Intelligence Agency. Kirk himself was incorruptible, and Strankov knew from the start that he had no hope of turning MIC's director. What he hadn't planned on was Harmon Kirk's unerring ability to enlist nothing but unfaltering American patriots into the ranks of his agency.

Every attempt Strankov made to recruit a double agent was rebuffed, usually resulting in the body of another Motherland agent rotting in some Third World landfill.

In desperation he had even ordered an MIC janitor kidnapped, threatened and eventually tortured, but the man was a retired Marine whose son was saved by Kirk during World War II and he stubbornly refused to break.

Brainwashing MIC agents also failed. The most sophisticated techniques available to Motherland were tried on three agents on three separate occasions and all were sent back to the US as double agents. MIC had uncovered them each time. Harmon Kirk's counterespionage experts used complicated mathematical formulas to determine probabilities that somehow led them unfailingly to each brainwashed subject.

After two years of ceaseless effort it was clear to Strankov that he would not be able to fulfill the primary goal for which Motherland had been established. Still, whenever he was asked, Strankov told his superiors the same thing.

"Everything is going exactly according to plan."

Since only Ivan Strankov knew exactly what the plan was, and since he theoretically had operational authority over every agent — covert or otherwise — in Russia, no one dared press the issue.

Repeated failed attempts at infiltrating MIC forced Strankov to alter the mission of Motherland. If they could not infiltrate, they would exist to counter MIC.

For a little while Strankov enjoyed some successes. MIC agents turned up mysteriously dead here and there around the world, with nothing that could be traced back to Russia. World leaders who were enemies of the USSR who were certain of safety because MIC was overseeing their protection suddenly found their palaces penetrated, their loves ones threatened, their pets and mistresses killed. One nation flipped from West to East simply because a sultan found his prize Pekinese floating in his bedroom fish tank, a wadded up copy of Pravda shoved down his throat.

Little things. Nothing so grand that it risked heating up the simmering Cold War.

Not exactly the stuff for which Motherland had gotten into business, but tangible successes with which, if asked, Colonel Ivan Strankov could satisfy his superiors.

His was not the perfect mission he had envisioned for himself. After all, Ivan Strankov was a genius, a colossus in a world of inferior little men. But it was enough to keep the dullards of the Kremlin at bay.

Until that day in 1955 when the man who would become his great enemy made his first appearance at the periphery of Motherland's operations.

Strankov had dismissed as fantasy the initial reports about the skulking figure in the black cape which could somehow magically change to red.

It was only when Motherland's office in Lebanon was driven through with a bulldozer and its station director hung by his ankles from the walls of the Russian embassy draped in an American flag that Strankov was forced to sit up and take notice.

"He called himself the Red Menace," the station director said after being recalled to Moscow. Motherland did not countenance failure, at least not from its agents in the field. The disgraced man was in chains in a dingy prison cell, the bloody rope marks where the masked man had bound him burned into the flesh of his bare ankles. "He does not work for the American government in Washington. He said he is just a citizen who does not like communists." The man's eyes were dead, his voice flat. There was no sense lying since his fate had already been decided.

"He told you all this, did he?" Strankov demanded.

"Actually, he said he was an 'average Joe who hates commies,'" the station director said. "This was after he drove a bulldozer through my wall and retrieved the three British oil executives we had taken prisoner at your order."

The scheme had been part of an attempt to secure a new Mideast oil pipeline for Russia. It was a large enough debacle that even the Kremlin had taken notice.

There were others after that, growing more numerous as the months and years went on. In Africa, South America. Once in Alaska, in London… that last catastrophe had ended with Strankov personally experiencing the effects of the paralyzing venom that the Red Menace secreted in his gauntlet.

Motherland was not the masked man's only target. Plans of the KGB, East Germany's Stasski and every Iron Curtain country were undone. Double agents in France, Italy, Belgium, all over the Europe and the world were exposed. The Red Menace targeted everyone whom he deemed a threat to the United States.

The activities of the mysterious American vigilante directed the Kremlin's eye squarely on Motherland.

Strankov's agency, like MIC in the U.S., was supposed to be able to sift intelligence data from every Soviet espionage agency and aim Russia's entire spy apparatus like a spear.

Capturing or killing the Red Menace became Motherland's top priority. And for a few years Strankov was able to hang on, to stall for time while hoping that someone down the line got lucky and delivered him the head of the infernal nuisance.

It all came undone that evening in 1958 in Oleg Plassko's laboratory.

The Red Menace had not only stolen in and out of Motherland headquarters, he had paralyzed its director in full view of a dozen troops and a Soviet general. There was no wriggling out of the noose for Ivan Strankov.

After the Red Menace's Moscow visit, the destruction of Lenin's body, and Strankov's public humiliation, an investigation was led into Motherland. It did not take long for his enemies within the Russian security apparatus to smell blood in the water. The first few to come forward were a trickle, followed by a river, followed by a tidal wave that swamped Motherland and washed its incompetent director out into the open. The truth that had been evident all along if any had but sought it out became clear. Ivan Strankov was an utter fraud and failure. Nearly his entire reign as director of Motherland had been devoted to covering up one blunder after another.

Fate's final twist of the knife was to send Strankov to the same forced labor camp to which his grandfather had been banished years before.

Eight years of backbreaking labor. A diet of subsistence gruel. Five broken bones, incompetently set. Three toes lost to frostbite. Strankov did not fear the afterlife of eternal hell of which the religious spoke, for he had already lived it in the Siberia wilds. And then one day… salvation.

Strankov did not know why he was dragged out of his prison cell that morning. He assumed more work hauling lumber or mixing mortar.

Perhaps a beating. Every day was the same in its dreary, nightmarish predictability. But on that day there was no work. Instead, he was put on a truck and then in a train. In two days he was back in Moscow.

He was given a hot meal, cleaned up, and handed his old uniform. The clothes hung on him like fresh blankets flung over an old scarecrow. The former director of Motherland was taken to a large office in the Kremlin and found himself standing before the desk of First Secretary Leonid Brezhnev.

The Soviet leader looked like a melting snowman in an ill-fitting blue suit. His great black eyebrow was a misplaced mustache glued over a set of dull eyes that held not a glimmer of warmth or human intelligence.

"The Soviet Union welcomes back its friend and comrade Colonel Ivan Strankov," First Secretary Brezhnev said, as if Strankov had been on extended vacation in a dacha on the Black Sea these past eight years. "See to General Valtroikin for your new assignment. Good day, Comrade Colonel Strankov."

A bewildered Strankov quickly learned that he was the beneficiary of the latest shakeup in the Soviet hierarchy. The Prague Spring of 1968 had strengthened Brezhnev's leadership position and he had purged many whom he considered threats. The first secretary had been introduced to Strankov once many years before, and the former Motherland director was saved from exile based solely on having a firm, dry handshake.

But it was no longer the 1950s and Ivan Strankov was not the man he once was.

A cursory moment's introspection would have revealed that Strankov's first loyalty had always been to himself, but Strankov the self-proclaimed genius, Strankov the master manipulator of the Soviet system, was incapable of self-examination. In his mind, Russia had betrayed him. He therefore no longer owed loyalty to the USSR.

The Red Menace was long gone. This he learned his first day returned to Moscow. The masked figure had disappeared sometime in 1960. Several Iron Curtain services had claimed credit for his death, but no body was ever produced.

Strankov accepted his new assignment in Cuba, and there he marinated in his bitterness for two long years.

The former Motherland director oversaw completion of the secret

Soviet base. The plans were drawn up well before the Cuban Missile Crisis, so all Strankov had to do was stand back and let the men under his command do their jobs.

He never gained back much of the weight he had lost in the gulag, and when after twenty-five months he started mysteriously losing what little he'd regained, he returned to Moscow from Havana. There he learned that the cancer that had been secretly gnawing away at him from within was already well advanced. There were no treatment options. At most, the doctors gave him three months to live.

The death sentence became the most liberating force in his entire life. Despite the advice of his Soviet doctors, Strankov returned to Cuba.

He became a man possessed.

By an amazing stroke of luck, Dr. Oleg Plassko had been teaching botany at Universidad de Habana for the better part of the Sixties, and Strankov had already brought the old Motherland scientist back into the fold.

"They have clipped my wings, Comrade Colonel Strankov. Clipped my wings!"

Plassko had slurred drunkenly while nursing his daily vodka bottle in the tiny office from which the Cubans had forced him to work at the university.

Plassko was delighted with the freedom Colonel Strankov gave him on the Soviet base and, his genius finally properly financed, was only too happy to keep his great work secret from the Cubans and KGB.

Certain modifications were made to the Soviet missiles under Strankov's command. Engineers who learned early on to fear their base commander followed his orders unquestioningly, no matter how strange or dangerous.

Ivan Strankov's work became his life, and his single-mindedness extended that life a month, then two, then a year beyond the best-case projections of his doctors.

Captain Ivan Strankov had his own dying wish to fulfill.

The Red Menace was gone but the nation he still loved was still there.

But no one and nothing lived forever.

13

Captain Ivan Strankov felt the familiar little twinge of euphoria that stirred in his belly every time he awoke to the creeping realization that he had not died in his sleep.

Every day was a gift; a new step towards the greatest act of vengeance in the history of the human race. He had been dreaming about his grandparents, about his career, his exile in Siberia, his recent years in Cuba. And, for some reason, the Red Menace.

That was strange. His old enemy was long gone and Strankov had successfully banished him from his mind long ago. So why was the Red Menace so prominent in his thoughts right now? And why, for that matter, was Strankov sleeping sitting up and why could he not move his arms?

Strankov's eyes slowly fluttered open. He found that he was staring directly into the eyes of a waking nightmare.

"Well it's about time, Comrade Crapski," said the Red Menace. "For a minute there I thought you were going to sleep straight through Judgment Day. Which for you, incidentally, is about twenty seconds from now."

The Menace had drawn up a folding chair and was knee to knee with Strankov in the small supply closet. He was leaning forward so that their faces were two feet apart, and was smiling placidly beneath his glowing red mask.

Strankov lunged, straining at his bonds, but all he managed to do was tip his chair forward. The Red Menace tapped his chest and sent all four chair legs back to the floor. Strankov launched a wild foot forward, but the Menace grabbed the leg by the ankle and shoved the Soviet captain's foot back down under the wooden folding chair.

"Only girls and commies kick, Strankov," the Menace instructed.

The Russian captain bellowed for help but all that passed his purple lips was a pathetic squeak. The Red Menace held up his index finger and Strankov saw the tiny barb that extended from the tip of the gauntlet.

"Light dose. Just the vocal chords," the Menace said. "You can talk, you just can't yell. So what should we two old buddies chat about? Hey, I know. How 'bout you tell me everything about these nukes you've parked ninety miles from Florida?"

Strankov bared yellow fangs, as if by sheer will he could rip out the masked man's throat. "You Americans are so prosaic."

"I'd probably be insulted if I knew what that meant," said the Red Menace.

"The MIC agent. Wilson. He is the reason you are here." Strankov shuffled his feet beneath his chair. The Menace expected him to kick out again, but the fight had apparently drained from his legs. The Russian pulled them together, boot heels nearly touching. "I never thought MIC would be threat any longer. I certainly did not imagine that they would bring you from retirement. I should have been more careful."

"And if wishes were horses, beggars would ride. You were always lousy at the spy stuff, Strankov. The only guy on the planet who didn't know you were a complete bust was you. Now, if we could move this along? The nukes?"

A soft growl rumbled in the Russian's throat. "In a way I am actually glad to see you. For years I was in gulag my hatred of you kept me alive. Then I get out to find you are gone. Poof. Vanished. But now you are here at end. Is fitting. Before now I think only that I will wipe out America and only hope to get you. Now I know you die too."

"Okay, let's back up, Charlie," the Menace said. "First, you've got maybe four missiles here, tops."

"Three."

"Fine. Three. No way you're wiping out America with three nukes. Second, you're assuming I'm not going to pull the plug on them which, for the record, I am. Third, don't you find all this talk about killing in bad taste? No offense, and I don't know if you've seen a mirror lately but, pal, you look like death warmed over."

The yellow fangs returned, this time as part of a triumphant grin.

"That, as you Americans say, makes two of us."

The Menace heard a soft scraping sound, like two pieces of sandpaper being rubbed together. Too late he realized he should have bound the Russian's feet.

The brilliant white flash came from Strankov's boots. Something hidden in the heels.

In that strange split-second before an explosion, when time seems to slow to an impossible crawl, the Red Menace had a sudden burst of memory: schematics stolen from a Sarajevo apartment. A Motherland device secreted in a boot heel. A small explosive charge triggering a canister of poison gas.

The world suddenly tripped back to normal speed just as the explosive gas cloud blew out from below the chair in every direction.

Instinct kicked in. The Menace grabbed Strankov by the lapels the instant he saw the flash of light. Before the soft pop of the small explosion even registered in his ears, he was yanking the Russian forward. The gas exploded from Strankov's heels beneath the chair, but the Red Menace and the Russian captain were already flying away from the blast zone, away from the poisonous cloud.

The Menace hit the door hard just above the lock with the meaty part of his right shoulder. The doorknob shattered, ripping chunks of metal and concrete from the frame.

The Menace tumbled back into the hallway dragging Strankov with him. The two men landed in a tangled heap on the hallway floor. The chair to which Strankov was tied shattered on impact and chunks of brittle wood scattered crazily in every direction.

The poison gas cloud hissed harmlessly from the closet and dissipated along the high ceiling of the long corridor.

One broken chair leg slid end-over-end across the cement. It stopped only when it tapped the toe of a military boot that belonged to neither Strankov nor the Red Menace.

"Aw, crap," said the Red Menace, flat on his back, when he saw the two shocked Cuban soldiers standing three feet away.

"Kill hi—!" Strankov gasped, his voice a hoarse whisper.

"Hold that thought," the Menace said, and rabbit-punched the Russian sharply in the nose. Strankov's head bounced hard against the concrete floor, rivers of blood spurted from both nostrils, and his bloodshot eyes fluttered shut. The Menace shrugged up to the two new arrivals. "C'mon, I can't be the only one who was getting sick of that guy. Show of hands?"

The dumbfounded Cubans quickly gathered their wits. Both men grabbed for the rifles slung over their shoulders.

The soldiers were fast. The Red Menace was faster.

A foot shot out and caught one Cuban in the knee. There was a satisfying crunch of bone, and the man dropped to the floor, howling in pain and grabbing at his broken kneecap. One down.

The second soldier had his rifle free and was swinging it around, but in the time it took to grab his weapon, the Menace had already sprung to his feet.

The Red Menace grabbed the rifle in both hands, barrel and butt. The furious soldier expected the masked man to try to wrest the gun from his hands and he braced both feet firmly for the titanic struggle. But rather than tug on the gun, the Red Menace pushed; hard. The gun launched forward into the soldier's face, the stock slammed the man in the forehead and the Cuban's hands automatically sprang open.

The Menace swung the rifle around fast, slamming the butt into the woozy soldier's temple, and the man obligingly dropped to the floor in an unconscious heap.

The victory was short lived. The Red Menace heard the heavy footfalls of running reinforcements before he could fling the gun away.

Five more soldiers raced into view far down the corridor. They had arrived on the scene with great urgency, summoned by the crashing door and sounds of a fight, but the men stopped dead when they saw the rifle clattering across the floor as if thrown by a ghost. Nearby was Soviet Colonel Strankov and two Cuban conscripts, all lying on the floor amidst the ruins of the closet door and a shattered folding chair. A thin cloud of mist slipped from the open supply room door.

Down the hall, the Red Menace stood stock-still.

Had they seen him? The hallway lights were weak, but he was standing almost directly under one of the caged bulbs. They were far enough that they wouldn't see red, but in the light he'd likely be an indistinct black blob, a ghostly apparition.

Confusion. Shouts in Spanish. At the Menace's feet, the man cradling his broken knee screamed something the Red Menace did not understand. Up the hallway, hesitation vanished. The men leveled their guns and ran toward their fallen comrades.

The Red Menace turned and ran. He flew into the shadows at the hallway's edge and kept his head low as he raced for all he was worth in the direction opposite the soldiers. Gone were thoughts of age and mortality, of mental and physical weakness. The trip to the base had been exhausting, but in the heat of battle adrenaline kicked in.

A single gunshot rang out and he felt the bullet whiz past his ear. The Menace's own gun was out, instinct took aim and he fired back as he ran. The shot took a charging soldier square in the chest and he collapsed to floor, tripping two of his running comrades. The men fell flat and their scattering guns bounced off the walls.

As the Red Menace raced around the corner he got a glimpse of Strankov. The Russian might be dead. The Soviet colonel lay unmoving on the floor in front of the closet, twin streams of blood dribbling down his ghastly purple face. He'd needed more time with Strankov. Another five minutes would have been enough.

No matter. Strankov was finished. He'd given the Russian ample warning at their last meeting. As he ran, the Menace took aim at Strankov's chest.

A barrage of sudden gunfire from the two running soldiers forced his gun back beneath his flapping cape.

The two tripped soldiers scrambled to snatch up their dropped weapons.

The fresh salvo ripped chunks out of cinderblock in his wake as he raced around the corner and bounded up the stairs, furious that he hadn't had the chance to finish off Strankov once and for all. He burst like an angry wraith into the missile control room.

The room was still empty. He slammed the door shut and grabbed for a deadbolt. Not only was there no deadbolt, there was no lock at all on the steel door.

"Why are Russkies always so blasted trusting?" he grumbled.

The Menace flung a chair up under the door handle one-handed and with the thumb of his free hand he flipped the notch on the butt of his gun.

Two soft gas pops were echoed by nearly simultaneous splats on the long, low window that overlooked the missile silos. As soon as he'd fired his gun, the Menace was diving for cover behind the main console in the center of the room.

Behind him, footsteps pounded up the bunker stairs. An angry rattle shook the door handle. The door popped open and the chair lurched on its castors, zipping across the room and slamming violently into another chair, toppling it to the floor.

The steel door swung back to reveal three soldiers. The instant the door opened, a wild twirling caught their eyes and one let loose a panicked barrage of automatic weapons fire. Pockmarks riddled the overturned chair, sending the shredded piece of furniture skittering insanely across the room.

A shout in Spanish. A cry of discovery.

One of them had spotted the Red Menace. Three guns took aim at the lurking shadow behind the central console. In the instant before the men could pepper the crouching body with bullets, the delayed charges on the window clicked. Two tiny little pops…and a typhoon of fire and glass engulfed the small control room.

The blast launched shards of heavy plastic in every direction. Chunks of window became sharpened spears piercing soft flesh. The three soldiers were blown back into the hall and the Menace heard one tumbling down the stairs. More shouting. The fourth, missing soldier? More voices? It did not matter. Many more would be coming.

As if on cue, the base klaxon sounded. The persistent *"Ahn-ahn! Ahn-ahn!"* hummed through the concrete like a living presence.

The Menace jumped from his hiding spot behind the console and flew to the open window. Up and over, he rolled across the secondary console and through the chips of shattered glass, acutely aware that in his youth he would simply have dived through. He knew the instant before he hit the soft ground outside that he had landed wrong. He had misjudged the unevenness of the surface. A funny angle, just barely an incline; a horrible crunch in his left knee.

The Menace sucked in a tortured gasp even as he hobbled off, the crunch of plastic under his feet giving way to the soft blanket of jungle.

The knee wasn't broken. That much he knew or he would not be able to move at all. It was cold comfort, for the pain was excruciating.

He sucked up the pain and limped off into the night.

Behind him, soldiers appeared at the broken window. A few shouts in Spanish and suddenly there were flashes of light accompanied by the steady pop of automatic weapons fire. Bullets zinged blindly out into the night.

Screams from the direction of the missile silos. Lights flicked on all around the base to reveal frantic Cuban guards flinging themselves to the ground and covering their heads as their comrades in the bunker fired blindly outside.

The Red Menace hugged the wall of the bunker and ran as fast as injury would allow to the southeast.

Men yelled. Spanish shouts were joined by raised Russians voices. He strained his ears, but the Red Menace did not hear Strankov among them.

More lights. Click-click-click. One after another switched on until the entire area was washed warm in mock daylight.

Shadow was good enough most times, but complete darkness was best for his costume to work perfectly. He had neither now, and in direct light the Red Menace became visible. An indistinct black blob, yes, but a visible target nonetheless.

Into the jungle. A Russian soldier suddenly appearing out of nowhere through the overgrowth; startled at first, then grabbing for his sidearm.

The Menace's weapon already in hand. A quick shot to the throat and the Russian was down in silence, a crimson stain blossoming across his uniform blouse.

The Red Menace jumped over the body and felt a stab like a knife in his knee accompanied by a strobe light flash of pain behind his eyes. Still, he ran.

The jungle was alive with stomping boots and angry shouts. Military discipline for the Cubans seemed to entail blundering around through the brush with no direction, with occasional burps of automatic weapons fire to relieve the tension. A band of soldiers came within five yards of the Red Menace but a volley of friendly fire from a rampaging mob of Cuban conscripts mowed most of the gang down.

More screaming, more stampeding boots.

The Red Menace skirted the scene of bloodshed. He ran.

There was no way to get back down the hill. There was now only one route of escape. The salty spray of the sea and the roar of water crashing on rocks directed his feet. He burst from the jungle into a grassy clearing.

Few lights dotted the shores of the bay. He could not judge the distance to the bottom, could not see how far the rocks extended into the blackness.

In the distance he heard a rumble and looked up to see the ominous outline of a plane against night sky. They had scrambled fast. Helicopters would be next.

Dogs barking from the jungle. The wild gunfire had stopped as had the unfocussed crashing around in the underbrush. The soft sounds of controlled voices and the hiss and click of walkie-talkies. The Russians had taken charge.

For the Red Menace, there was no other choice.

He took a running jump and flung himself as far out from cliff's edge as humanly possible. He became a black smear in an endless black night before vanishing with nary a sigh off the same precipice where, unbeknownst to the Red Menace, his old friend Jeb Wilson had been pitched to his doom.

14

Dr. Thaddeus Wainwright sat at a rusting wrought iron table on the balcony of the Revolucion Grande Hotel and watched the darkness slowly bleed from the sky above Havana. Wainwright's legs were crossed and he picked a speck of lint from the knee of his sharply creased white slacks.

Wainwright had not slept since finishing the Becket Security proposal for Castro's mansion. His inability to sleep had nothing to do with restlessness over the mission or worrying about his friend Patrick Becket's idiotic impulse to run off on this last foolhardy adventure. Wainwright simply did not sleep. Not any longer. At this point in his very long life, Thaddeus Wainwright could no longer remember the last time he'd had even an hour's sleep. He knew it had been a very long time and that permanently lost sleep was one of the earliest side effects of his special treatments.

Days were not so bad. Daytime was when the whole world was alive and he could throw himself completely into one distraction or another and be lost for hours. Yet even deep in some South American jungle, high on some desolate Asian mountain or lost in an African desert, Wainwright was on some level always aware of the sun crawling remorselessly across the sky towards the horizon. Once it dropped from sight and the small lights high up in the heavens and far below on Earth flickered on, Wainwright felt the long pull of the endless gray twilight. Later, when the full veil of night drew across the land and the earthly lights flicked out one by one as the waking world at last went to sleep, Thaddeus Wainwright was left a solitary man cursed to suffer in silence in an endless black night of his own making.

"The price of self-medicating," he sighed to the still slumbering city.

Wainwright blew a long, thoughtful cloud of smoke at the dying night and flicked his cigarette butt over the balcony railing.

The sleeping night had not been totally silent. At about two o'clock Wainwright had heard a sudden commotion of sirens, planes and helicopters to the northeast. With the lights out in his hotel room and only the orange glow of his cigarette floating before him, he watched a trickle of military vehicles taking the northeast roads out of town.

But that had been hours ago. Now a pink cotton candy smudge had been dragged across the low rim of the horizon and the morning birds were just starting their serenade squawk as harbingers of the sticky new day. The world was beginning anew and as always it was greeted by the lonely man who could only ever sit on the outside looking in.

Wainwright was pushing thoughts of Podge from his mind and wondering if it was too early for the hotel staff to scrape up breakfast when he heard the rustle of fabric and felt the change of air pressure of a body dropping onto the balcony behind him.

Wainwright knew something was wrong even before he jumped to his feet — the awful grunt, the inelegant landing that shook the balcony like an earthquake and rattled the glass top of the patio table — but he was in no way prepared for the human wreck in cape and mask that collapsed in his arms the instant he turned.

"My God, what have you done to yourself?" the doctor gasped.

He grabbed the Red Menace up under the arms and all but dragged the near-dead man into the hotel living room. Once inside, the Red Menace tore weakly at his mask and gauntlets and dropped them to the floor. Podge's face was glistening with sweat and his matted hair was pasted to his sopping wet scalp.

"Are you injured?" Wainwright demanded. "Bullets? Bones? Your leg. What's wrong with your leg?"

Podge was limping heavily and favoring his left leg. Wainwright guided him to the sofa and he collapsed back into the worn cushions.

"I'm fine, doc," Podge said. "Just blew out my left knee. You're gonna have to do something with it."

He was gritting his teeth and with his left hand was squeezing his left leg just above the knee. Wainwright could see the grotesque swelling through the pant leg.

"This was a terrible idea, Patrick," Wainwright tut-tutted as he hustled into his bedroom. He reappeared in the suite's common room a moment later carrying his black doctor bag. "You're middle-aged now. For God's sake, you realize that, don't you? And should I even ask why you're wearing a Cuban Army uniform?"

Podge pulled at the blouse of the khaki military garb he now wore.

"This? I joined up with all the other kids. They had a real convincing 'Uncle Fidel Wants You' poster at the neighborhood recruitment center. Plus, if I stay in for twenty years, I get a free pineapple and a half-price casket with my execution."

Wainwright grunted disapproval even as he sliced up the length of the pant leg with a pair of sharp scissors retrieved from his bag. The uniform was damp and smelled of salt water. The doctor did not even bother to question why.

Podge's knee was the color of an overripe plum and swollen to twice its normal size. "Well you've done it, haven't you?" Wainwright complained. He probed the knee with expert fingertips. "The thing's the size of a grapefruit."

"Just so long as it's a good American grapefruit from Florida and not one of those crummy little banana republic ones."

"Would you please shut up and let me work?" Wainwright snapped.

Podge leaned obediently back on the sofa and awaited the verdict.

When Wainwright at last completed his exam, he sat back on the coffee table and began rooting around in his bag. "Well it isn't broken. That's the good news. The bad news is that it's attached to a complete imbecile."

Podge did not see the tonic the doctor mixed for him. With eyes squeezed shut he only heard metal fasteners opening, tiny clinks of glass and Wainwright's shifting weight on the creaking coffee table as the doctor worked. As he waited, Podge ground his molars and let out tiny snorts of air through his nostrils.

After what seemed like an eternity, he felt Wainwright's hand grip his leg. The pain was so great that he did not feel the small prick of the needle. He only knew he'd been injected when he looked down and saw Wainwright withdraw the syringe.

The doctor wore a deeply displeased expression as he wordlessly gathered up various small bottles, envelopes, leather pouches and a small mortar and pestle and replaced them with practiced efficiency in his black bag.

Podge expected fast relief from the agony, but if anything the horrific pain had gotten worse. It was as if his knee were suddenly on fire.

"It's not working, doc," Podge gasped.

"Yes," Wainwright droned, somehow managing to deliver the word in five syllables and with a tone of unreserved condescension. His eyes were flat as his hands continued to angrily stash items away in the depths of his bag.

The pain reached an agonizing crescendo…and was gone.

The horrific fire became a soothing, numbing warmth that spread from the point of the injection throughout the inflamed knee. Podge let out a relieved gasp, the tension drained from his limbs and his head dropped back against the sofa cushion.

"You don't know how close you just came to being fired as my doctor." His face relaxed, at last liberated from hours of excruciating pain. For the first time he realized that his jaw ached from clenching it so tightly.

Wainwright scowled. "This isn't aspirin and warm milk, Patrick. I'm not sure the long-term effects all this could have on your system. We could be toying with fire here."

"It hasn't hurt you any."

"First off, I have never needed to take the mixture I just gave you. I'm not running around like I'm eighteen. Second, what I did take I no longer need to. That damage was done long before you were born. Third, the formula is unique to my body chemistry. You know better than anyone that the damnable stuff only works perfectly on me."

"That's not entirely true, doc."

He regretted the words as soon as he uttered them. A constricted look like that of a man in deep physical pain crossed the older man's face. As quickly as it appeared, the injured expression vanished and Wainwright returned to his work.

"I'm sorry, doc," Podge said.

Wainwright was not even looking at his patient as he flung the used syringe inside his case and snapped the bag shut. "I only hope this wasn't a complete waste and that whatever you uncovered gallivanting around all night was worth all of this, Patrick."

In reply, a handful of plastic vials scattered across the coffee table.

"Samples from the dead zone. Samples from the plants around the dead zone. Samples of the stuff I think they used to kill everything within the dead zone. You should see the greenhouse they've got buried out there, doc. It's even bigger than yours, the one that East German bastard Deitrich torched on you in back in '57. Does the name Oleg Plassko mean anything to you?"

"I'm sure it doesn't." Despite his anger, Wainwright could not mask his curiosity. He held one of the vials up to the light. Through two protective layers of glass and plastic he watched the thick green liquid ooze from one end of the tube to the other.

"He's an old Motherland scientist," Podge said, and pressed on through Wainwright's disdainful sneer. "MIC didn't think much of him, at least not back then. The lab is his baby. Strankov must have brought him out here to make that gunk. But that's the least of our worries. Thaddeus, they've smuggled nukes onto the island."

Wainwright's head snapped up. "Good God. You're sure?"

Podge nodded. "I confirmed three silos on my way out. And that base is not under construction. Those birds are in the nest and are ready to fly. And as long as I'm the bearer of glad tidings, I met our old pal Strankov. The bad news is I'm not sure if he's dead. The really bad news is that if he's not dead he's probably going to be incredibly cheesed off right now. The really, really bad news is that he's got an even bigger grudge against me and America than ever, and by the looks of it he's so close to shuffling off this mortal coil that he wouldn't give two figs if he started World War Three on his way to Hell's waiting room." He shut his eyes. "That's it. I'm wiped. I've got to get some sleep. Oh, one other thing. I might have breathed in some Motherland poison."

The announcement was greeted with silence and Podge only knew that Wainwright had heard him when a moment later he felt a needle slip into his arm.

"Geez, that hurt," Podge groused.

"Consider yourself lucky that you're well enough to whine, you reckless fool," Wainwright said. The doctor withdrew a blood sample and taped a square of gauze treated with an oily substance over the wound. "I'll check this to see if you have to start planning your funeral. In the meantime, change out of that ridiculous uniform and leave it outside your bedroom door. I'll dispose of it."

Podge dragged himself reluctantly to his feet and pulled off his cape, fully exposing the Cuban Army private uniform he wore beneath.

Podge tested his knee. At first the pain was still a memory, but when he put a little pressure on the left leg there was a sharp stinging ache in his knee.

"You'll need a few hours rest for it to work," Wainwright said. "*If* it works. Stay off it. Right now I'm going to somehow have to get all this information to Kirk's boy in Washington. Hopefully D.C. will still be there when you wake up," he added, more to himself than to Podge. "One miracle at a time, I suppose."

"No sweat. Already done," Podge said matter-of-factly. He was clearly pleased by the surprised look on his old friend's face. "What, you didn't think I was dancing the cha-cha at the Club Babalu all night, did you?"

At this, the doctor said nothing. He snatched the dropped mask and gloves from the floor and stuffed them in Podge's hands. "Hide them," he commanded. "And don't forget that uniform. I haven't lived this long only to get killed due to your sloppiness."

Without another word, Wainwright disappeared into his bedroom, black doctor bag and Podge's blood sample in hand. The door clicked quietly shut behind him.

15

Falling ... falling ... A speck with arms and legs tumbling through the damp night air; the froth-churned waves racing up to meet him.

Saved at the last minute by starlight glinting off the water. In the weak light he was able to orient himself, to control the angle of the dive. He knifed into the waves with a barely audible splash and disappeared beneath the surface.

A long moment during which all that could be heard was sea crashing on rock.

Then a dark figure bobbing to the surface; choking, spitting water. The cape dragged him toward the jagged rocks and he reeled it desperately in, up under one arm, swimming one-handed.

The infernal cape had nearly killed him. It was a dripping lump under his arm when he at last dragged himself up on shore and collapsed face-first in the white sand.

He lay there for a long moment, panting. Barely alive. The sounds of activity were a distant thing. Planes circling, spotlights scanning wilderness from the bellies of swooping helicopters. All activity high up the cliff face and a good half-mile away.

Ten minutes, twenty ... he had no idea how long he lingered on the beach. Too long. He finally dragged himself to his feet but as soon as he tried to walk his left leg buckled and he collapsed back to the sand.

He could not stay any longer. The dogs would eventually pick up his scent, the Russians would soon realize he'd jumped into the bay. The helicopters and troops would soon come. By sheer force of will he hauled himself back to his feet.

The whop-whop-whop of approaching rotor blades sliced the warm night air.

The chopper dropped down the cliff face and raced across the waters of the bay. A single light played wildly across the dark waves.

Hobbling, staggering, he made it to the overgrowth that lined the sand and collapsed to the ground, dragging his wet cape over his body.

The helicopter raced to the shore but came up a quarter mile away. It hovered over the beach for less than a minute, floodlight splashing artificial daylight on sand, water and flora. Palm fronds whipped crazily in the hurricane winds.

For a few distressing seconds the chopper slid through the air in his direction, but at the last moment it shifted inland and with a roar of mechanized thunder it was gone. The helicopter raced up the dirt road that ran parallel to the beach, crested a hill and vanished. The thrum that shook the earth faded into the night.

Seconds later, the helicopter reappeared over the cliff a mile out and headed back up to the plateau to join the other aircraft.

Most of the activity was still focused up near the missile complex. The lone chopper was only an attempt to cover all bases. They did not yet know where he'd gone.

Feeling a wash of relief, he got back to his feet. A fatal mistake.

The roar of the helicopter and crashing surf had masked the sound of the Cuban Army jeep that was parked at the shoulder of the road.

The private was on routine patrol and unaware of the crisis on the Russian base above the bluff. He was drawn to the beach by the hovering helicopter and had crept down to the shore on foot. The young man was watching the activity high above when the incandescent figure in red suddenly rose up from the bushes two feet away from where he was standing.

The soldier wheeled and in the starlight the Red Menace saw the automatic in the young man's hand. The Menace lurched forward and grabbed the soldier's wrist purely by instinct, simultaneously launching an elbow back into the man's face. The soldier grunted in pain but did not release the gun. Another elbow to the nose, then another, and another in rapid succession until the man's nose was shattered and his face a mass of blood and stringy flesh.

A single sharp report screamed through the night, but the barrel was aimed downward and the bullet sank into the soft sand.

The Red Menace did not release his grip on the man's wrist. As they wrestled for the weapon, he launched a final vicious blow. There was a horrible, lethal crack of bone and the Menace knew the deed was done.

Bone shards launched back into brain and the dead man fell to the sand.

The Red Menace wavered above the body for an instant, the private's handgun now in his own gloved hand. He had forgotten his own injury in the heat of battle, but all at once the white hot pain returned in fury to his knee, exploding brightly behind both eyes. His leg buckled and he dropped to his backside on the ground next to the corpse.

Panting for only a moment; forcing the fresh shock of pain away.

A few shabby hovels dotted the dark landscape yet no lights had flickered on at the sound of either the helicopter or the gunshot. In a land where only Castro's goons carried guns, the unarmed civilians of Cuba knew enough to keep their noses out of anything that might lead to prison or worse. If anyone was awakened by the commotion on the beach, none dared come out to investigate. Still, it would not do to linger.

The Red Menace got to one knee, holding his left leg out stiffly to one side, and rolled the body over. The soldier's face was an unrecognizable pulp. He scanned the body quickly and determined that it was about the right build.

The Red Menace reached inside the folds of his cape and withdrew a dark piece of fabric. When he shook it open, a second mask and pair of gloves fell to the sand.

The material was flimsier than that of his own costume. Although he had carried the spare outfit for years in case he needed to confuse an enemy, he never had cause to use it before. He quickly changed clothes with the soldier and put his own costume back on over the Cuban Army uniform.

There was nothing special about the black pants and shirt he had worn under his cape; no store tags, monograms or other markings that would lead the Cubans back to Patrick Becket. Once the soldier was dressed in his black clothes, the Red Menace quickly put the spare cape, mask and gloves on the body.

His injured knee prevented him from carrying the corpse to the water. Instead, he dragged the body through the sand and out several yards into the surf where he threw it facedown on top of an outcropping of slimy, seaweed-strewn rock.

"Sorry about this, buddy," he said.

He grabbed a handful of mask on the back of the man's head and proceeded to bash the dead soldier's face repeatedly against the rock. Bone cracked audibly and though it was largely unseen in shadow and behind the cheap mask, he could feel the face collapse with every break until it was a flattened soft mass of bone and oozing tissue.

The Red Menace felt like a ghoul as he left the desecrated body on the rocks and waded back to shore wearing the dead man's uniform under his cape.

With his foot, he scuffed out the heel marks the dragged corpse had made in the damp sand. "Oh, swell," he said suddenly.

He quickly patted his pockets and was relieved to find the keys to the jeep in his borrowed trousers. He made a mental note never to tell Wainwright he had forgotten to check for them when he'd switched clothes. The doctor would be furious at his absentmindedness and claim he was getting sloppy in his old age.

The Menace drove the jeep on back roads into Havana.

The city was wide open to him this early in the morning. Those soldiers who had not been called northeast to search around the missile base were patrolling main roads.

The Red Menace had been in Cuba twice before and had made a few friends. But that was in the days of Batista, before Castro's revolution. He was not sure if the old baker would still be alive, let alone still be in business.

He was relieved when he smelled the aroma of freshly baked bread as he pulled the jeep into the alley behind the row of small shops.

The threat of dawn brushed the rim of the gray heavens as he tucked the jeep in the shadows beneath a row of ragged palms and limped over to the gated rear door.

Before he could even knock, the door opened and a short, stocky man came out bearing an armload of heavy baking trays. The sweating man was startled at first to see a stranger in the alley, but the shock lasted only a fleeting moment before his face lit up.

"Senor Rojo!" he cried. He dropped the trays with a horrible clatter that was enough to wake the hounds of hell and grabbed the Red Menace in a massive bear hug.

The Red Menace was quietly bothered when he realized that this man who he had considered old thirteen years ago was not much more than sixty. In 1959, when they last met, the bread maker would not have been much older than the Menace's current age. The realization somehow made worse the pain in his left knee.

"Miguel, my friend," the Red Menace said, disentangling from the hug. "I'm sorry I don't have time for a proper reunion, but I need your help."

"*Si, si.* Anything."

The Menace produced a hardened plastic capsule from the folds of his cape. "You remember that mail route you helped me with? The one we never got a chance to use? You think you can still get a message through?"

"Si," the bread maker said, nodding. "Fernandez, he still is here. I drop by with an order at least twice a week. All these years later we still keep up the act, just as you told us, even though it has been a long time since we hear from you."

The Red Menace handed over the capsule. "The mail must go through."

The bread maker puffed out his chest. "I promise," he insisted. "But, senor, you are injured. Quickly, come inside."

"I can't. I've got to get moving. But there's one more thing." The Menace nodded back to the jeep, which was slowly growing visible as dawn crept remorselessly over the horizon. "I need you to get rid of my ride. No traces. And fast. Understand?"

"My son is a mechanic now," the old man said. "It will be parts within the hour."

"*Gracias*," the Red Menace said.

The masked man turned, his cape billowing in his wake, and disappeared so quickly into the shadows of the alley that for a moment the baker thought his eyes were failing him. Then he remembered that this amazing vanishing act was normal procedure for the mysterious masked figure.

"You are here now," the old man said softly to himself. "It can only mean that Castro's days are numbered. *Madre de Dios, gracias.*"

He hustled inside his bakery, careful to close and lock the alley door behind him. The kitchen was like entering a blast furnace. An old woman and a young boy toiled at the ovens.

"Out, get out," the baker said, shooing the elderly woman from the small back room. "See to the shop out front. Sweep the floor, clean the windows, I do not care."

The young boy, he sent on an errand. "My son, Julio. Get him here quickly, quickly." The boy nodded and raced on bare feet from the bakery.

Once he was alone, the baker gathered a lump of sticky bread dough onto the scarred and floured cutting board. He prepared the dough as he normally would, but at the very end he placed the capsule the Red Menace had given him inside the kneaded lump and folded the dough over it.

Ten minutes later, the boy returned with the baker's twenty year old mechanic son in tow. The baker gave Julio some rapid, hushed instructions and his son nodded understanding and hustled back into the alley.

Over the next hour and a half, the baker chased the curious old woman from the kitchen door twice as he proofed and baked the single special loaf of bread. Forty-five minutes in, Julio returned to inform him that the Army jeep was no more.

When the bread was finished, the baker made a tiny nick in the rich brown crust and placed it along with two loaves baked earlier that day in a basket on the handlebars of an old bicycle near the door. By now there were customers lining up outside the bakery, they were far behind the daily routine, and the poor old woman was frantic.

She became even more panicked when the baker turned his shop over to her and the young boy and set off on his bicycle.

Carlos Fernandez was a truck driver who made a daily trip to the sugar cane fields to the east. The baker was relieved to find that Fernandez had not yet left his home. He delivered the three loaves of bread with special instructions for the loaf with the tiny nick in the crust. His part finished, the baker got back on his bike and peddled away.

Fernandez took the bread in his cab and drove his old Ford along the south coastal roads to a small fishing village beyond Santiago de Cuba. There he delivered the marked loaf of bread to an eccentric artist whose small yard was a collection of junk smeared with splotches of brightly colored paint. Fernandez was driving away in a cloud of dust as the artist hustled into his studio and drew tight the tattered curtains.

He slipped behind a pile of junk to a hidden trapdoor and a ladder that led down to a dark cavern that the ocean had carved into the solid rock. The artist lit a torch, tucked the loaf of bread up under his arm and hustled off through the adjoining secret tunnels which snaked off in the direction of the Guantanamo Bay Naval Base.

DIRECTOR SIMON KIRK was in a meeting in the Washington, D.C. headquarters of MIC when the special Pentagon courier arrived with the package from Guantanamo Bay.

For a brief moment Kirk thought that the young lieutenant was bursting in on the meeting to inform him that MIC was being shut down. It was an understandable mistake, and Kirk forgave himself for making the logical assumption. The shadow of termination constantly hovered over the impoverished agency, and this was the first time in his five years as director that Kirk received an emergency government communique.

The MIC director dismissed his staff and brought the thick envelope back to his private office. He tore open the envelope and shook the contents out onto his blotter.

The capsule inside was hard plastic and it took him a moment to figure out how to open it, since it did not have a conventional lid. The paper inside was folded tightly and Kirk opened it up and tried to smooth out the wrinkles with the side of his hand. Halfway through reading the message, his hand froze in place and he stopped attempting to flatten out the paper. By the time he was finished reading, his hand was shaking, his mouth had gone dry and the color had drained from his face.

It took him three attempts to hold his hand steady enough to press the button on his intercom.

"Call the White House," he commanded when his secretary answered. "I need a meeting with the President."

"Yes, sir. And when should I schedule—"

"Now! Right now! Tell them I'm on my way!" he snapped.

Kirk grabbed up the paper and folded it once up the middle. He felt lightheaded and had to rest his knuckles on the edge of his desk for a moment to collect his thoughts and his breath. When the room at last stopped spinning, he straightened up.

In his top desk drawer he removed the file he had brought with him to Patrick Becket's Hawaiian estate two weeks before and stuffed the folded sheet of paper inside.

File in hand, he marched out of his office. His secretary was just hanging up the phone.

"They say the earliest he can see you is tomorrow morning," the woman said. She wore a bright green skirt and matching sleeveless top and the white plastic rims of her small prescription glasses curled up to little swooping peaks.

"Get back on with them and tell them this is a national emergency, that I'm on my way and I will be there in five minutes," Kirk barked.

The woman was startled by the intensity in her employer's voice and was fumbling the receiver from the cradle as Kirk hurried from the room.

Manpower and Intelligence Coordination was headquartered in a subbasement in the Treasury Building on Pennsylvania Avenue and 15th Street. In the decade after its creation, MIC had controlled the entire level and half the rooms on the next floor up, but as MIC's influence waned Treasury had reclaimed much of the space. Original MIC director Harmon Kirk had watched his agency and influence shrink to the point of near uselessness. He never gave up hope for the country he loved, just over the agency he led. He finally abandoned MIC to move on to other special projects, turning the reins of MIC over to the only man he thought might be able to save it: Simon Kirk, his eldest son.

"Don't sweat blood over her, Simon," Harmon Kirk had said on his last day as director. "She's seen better days and maybe her time has passed. That's up to the pencil-pushers to decide. Just do your best and you'll do me proud."

Kirk was not worried about making his father proud as he marched through the basement hallways of the Treasury Building. His main concern was that Washington not become a radioactive crater by week's end.

At the end of the hall stood a lone sentry.

The Marine on duty did not express surprise when Director Kirk appeared before him, even though this was the first time the MIC head had approached his station in the nearly two years he had been assigned this post. He merely checked the young MIC director's security pass and let him through.

The tunnel led under East Executive Avenue and into another subbasement. More Marines as well as Secret Service checked his credentials.

Were he the director of the CIA or FBI or much of the rest of the alphabet soup of government agencies, he would have been waved through without question. Instead, the men studied his MIC credentials as if he had printed them on a Xerox machine in his basement and offered them with ink-smeared fingers. While Kirk fumed in place, a senior Secret Service agent placed a call upstairs on a black wall phone. It was all Kirk could do to keep from shoving past the men and racing for the elevator. He tapped his toe and checked his watch as he waited.

"For heaven's sake, would you hurry?" he finally snapped.

What seemed like an eternity was only six minutes. A Secret Service agent accompanied him on the elevator. Kirk forced thoughts of mushroom clouds over the National Mall from his mind as they rode up in the small car.

The President's secretary was waiting for him when he stepped out on the first floor of the White House.

"I apologize for the miscommunication with your secretary, Mr. Kirk," the woman said. In contrast to his own secretary, the woman was older, wore a simple blue dress and her hair was pulled up into an efficient gray bun. "She wouldn't say why you needed to see the President, but apparently you think this is a matter of some urgency. Of course I can squeeze you in now rather than tomorrow."

The woman subtly stressed the patronizing phrases "you think" and "squeeze you in." On matters of national emergency, the director of MIC was supposed to have direct, twenty-four access to the President of the United States. It was clear the attitude of the rest of official Washington towards MIC was shared by the President's secretary.

Show me some more of this attitude when your Georgetown duplex is a radioactive cinder, lady, Kirk thought. But he held his tongue.

The woman ushered Kirk through the beehive of activity that was the West Wing of the Presidential mansion, through her own busy office, and opened the door to the most famous room in the world. "Director Kirk to see you, Mr. President."

The President of the United States was sitting at his desk, the hint of an angry brow pressing like a threatening thundercloud over his eyes.

Richard Milhous Nixon gave Simon Kirk an inexplicable uneasy feeling these days, but this had not always been the case.

In 1960, when Kirk was a lad of eighteen and able to vote in his first presidential race, he happily pulled the lever for Ike's former VP. But in the intervening years something seemed to have changed in the man. Kirk could not place his finger on it, but the President seemed twitchier now, almost paranoid. Kirk had not voted for him in '68 and would not do so this fall. Not that the candidate the Democrats were running was any better. The ramifications of a George McGovern presidency were too horrifying to even consider, and if the South Dakota senator were elected Simon Kirk would consider using the last of his power as director of MIC to hitch a one-way ride on NASA's December Apollo flight to the moon.

"What's so important the Secret Service had to drag me off Marine One, Kirk?" the President demanded as his secretary backed from the Oval and closed the door. "My daughter's here for a few days and I was meeting her and Pat at Camp David."

"You might want to get them out of this area, Mr. President," Kirk said briskly. Ignoring the trappings of the famous room and the obvious irritation of the most powerful man on Earth, he walked over to a sofa and opened his manila envelope. One-by-one he began arranging papers and photos on the coffee table.

"I've just received some disturbing intelligence—" Kirk paused, glancing up at the still-seated President. "Please, sir, this is urgent." He looked back across his paperwork, rearranging some photos. "Some disturbing intelligence from Cuba."

President Nixon was clearly annoyed that someone so young was not intimidated by his surroundings. He certainly should have been, for it was not as if Simon Kirk was regularly invited to the White House. The

President's first term in office was nearly over and he could only remember meeting the MIC director twice in nearly four years.

The President scowled as he got up from his desk and joined Kirk on the sofa.

"The situation started about a month ago with a report from one of our field agents," Kirk began. "That man has since been killed."

From there, Kirk quickly gave the President the full rundown of information, essentially the same briefing he had supplied Podge Becket in Hawaii but augmented with data collected from spy planes in the intervening weeks. The President's aggravation dissipated as it became clear the young MIC director was not wasting his time.

"Why haven't I heard about this damned Russian base?" Nixon demanded. He was flipping through aerial photographs of the Cuban military complex.

"Vietnam, the Soviets and domestic troubles have apparently distracted every other agency. This fell through the cracks and into my lap. As it is, I could barely get the Air Force to get my reconnaissance photographs. The existence of a hitherto unknown Russian base in this hemisphere and the murder of my man was troubling enough that I ordered further investigation. Mr. President, I have just found out that it's nuclear."

The word hung for a moment in the silent air between them and Kirk swore he could see the President's face pale behind his five o'clock shadow.

"Are you sure?" Nixon asked.

Kirk nodded. "The man I sent in is one hundred percent reliable. If he says there are nuclear missiles in Cuba, they're there. In light of that fact, even more disturbing is the presence of this man." Kirk found an old photograph he'd included in the file which he'd retrieved from MIC's records room. "Ivan Strankov. He was a power player back in the Fifties, and I've done some checking since I found out he was involved. The guy is dying. Cancer. According to my man in Cuba, we should be deeply worried what a dying Ivan Strankov might do with those missiles under his command."

The President's eyes shifted back and forth across the table, as if trying to take in all the information at once. There were aerial photos, pictures taken from the ground, typed reports, and an old surveillance photo of Ivan Strankov taken in Budapest in 1955.

"What is this dead-looking area?" Nixon asked.

"We're not sure. Probably the accidental release of a defoliant. That's our best guess. We're lucky it happened because that's what revealed the base, but whatever killed the plants is, frankly, less relevant than those three missile silos."

"Okay, so help me here, Kirk. What are our options?"

"I'm not an advisor, Mr. President. I'm just the messenger. If MIC uncovers information we pass it on to relevant agencies. In this case, I'll inform the CIA."

"But, dammit, the base is already there, Kirk," the President snapped. "What good can the CIA do about it now?"

"I don't know, sir. Probably not much. But I thought you should know first because of the potential imminent nuclear threat. Strankov is a very bitter man with nothing to lose. On a personal level and not as an advisor, I hope you and your family get out of town, at least until we have confirmation of Colonel Strankov's death. It'll be horrifying enough if nuclear Armageddon comes to Washington. America doesn't need a presidential succession crisis on its hands as it's trying to pick up the pieces."

"Strankov's death? So your agent is taking him out?"

"I meant Colonel Strankov's *natural* death. It could come any day now. The man should have been dead months ago. And just so we're clear here, technically my man down there isn't an MIC agent. He's more a freelancer."

"But he's on the ground now, Kirk," Nixon said. "The CIA will take too long to mobilize. Will he try to do something about those damned missiles?"

Kirk ran his hand through his thinning blond hair. "Maybe. I don't know. According to his report, there are three silos. I don't know how one man does anything about that. Well, two men, actually. But the second is more support than a field agent. For all I know they could be getting out of Cuba already, since destroying the nukes wasn't part of the original plan."

The President sat back and crumpled a black and white photograph in one angry hand. "The goddamn reds tried pulling this horseshit under Kennedy. You think they got them built within the past four years? Ah, hell, what does it matter if it was under Johnson? If it leaks out now it'll be my fault. Every other damn thing is." He flung the photo to the coffee table and leaned back against the sofa cushions, pressing the palms of his hands against both eyes. "That's it. We're going to have to live with nukes in Cuba. I can't invade. Can you just imagine the antiwar protests if I did? Goddamn hippies are already camped outside all day and night over Vietnam. I sure as hell can't nuke Havana. It'll be World War Three with the Russians jumping in for Castro. There's no way the spooks at Langley can do anything now. Even if we can get in and disable them they'll just repair them. And according to you they've put a mad dog dying Russkie in charge of the pantry who could launch a strike just 'cause his ass itches."

The President got up, kicked the leg of the coffee table and wandered back over to his desk. He stood at the window, his back to the room, as Kirk began gathering up his paperwork. "I suggest you convene your security people right away, Mr. President," the director of MIC said softly. "They always have options for every scenario."

"Not for this, Kirk. There are only two options: We leave the nukes on our doorstep or we pick up the pieces when your crazy Russian pushes the button."

Simon Kirk silently agreed that these were the two likeliest outcomes. The first was ugly, the second unthinkable. Yet there was a third unlikely, unspoken possibility that the MIC director dared not mention.

It was as if the President had read Kirk's mind. The MIC director had his folder tucked under his arm and was nearly to the door when America's chief executive spoke.

"Your man on the scene," President Nixon said. "How good is he? I mean, is it possible he could do something about those nukes?"

Kirk pursed his lips and took a deep breath. "I can't answer that question with any kind of certainty, sir. He's never worked for me before. He actually was retired. From what I understand, he probably would have tried to in the old days. But he's ten years older now and might not be up to the challenge. We should consider ourselves lucky he managed to find out that which no other intelligence service had discovered so far."

"Retired," Nixon moaned. "America's fate is in the hands of damn senior citizen?" He leaned his knuckles on the windowsill and hunched his shoulders. "I'm sorry, I'm not blaming you, Kirk. Who knew you were the only damn one around here who knows which end of the baby to wipe? Whatever your budget is, we never should have slashed it. If Washington lives through this, I'll double it. Now do me a favor and tell my secretary to get in here."

Kirk glanced back from the open door. Sunlight streamed around the silhouette of the President as he stood at the Oval Office window. The weight of the free world was on the shoulders of the round shouldered man in need of a shave. No matter what Simon Kirk thought of any sitting President — and he had cared little for most who had served in his lifetime — President of the United States was not a position he envied.

Leaving the solitary figure at the window, Kirk backed from the room and closed the door to the Oval Office with a gentle click.

16

Podge Becket went to sleep with a dull ache in his knee and a throbbing headache forming behind his temples. He awoke with a knee free of any pain and a persistent pounding at his closed bedroom door.

"Mister Patrick Becket, you will wake up now."

The voice was flat, with a hint of irritation. It was not Wainwright. Major Ameriga Blanco called out his name again and continued to knock on the door.

"Yeah, just a sec, Lupe Velez," he called, clearing his throat. The persistent knocking ceased. He grabbed his Cartier watch on the nightstand and when he saw that it was only nine in the morning he frowned and gave it a shake. The hands continued to tick along and he had to reluctantly accept that it was only four hours since he'd crawled into bed. Either that or he'd slept straight through to the next day.

Podge expected he would have to drag himself out of bed, but he was pleased to find his muscles and joints surprisingly free of pain. He checked his left knee. The swelling was completely gone, as was nearly all the bruising. If there was any trace of the injury he'd suffered it was a barely visible redness around the kneecap. Even the mark of the needle was gone, aided by the greasy gauze Wainwright had applied.

Podge stood and the knee took his weight. He lifted his right leg and hopped a few times on his left foot. Nothing. It was as if the injury had never happened.

"Your tonic's getting better with age, doc," he muttered.

Podge grabbed his silk robe and was looping the belt as he opened the door.

Major Ameriga Blanco was worrying a hole in the carpet just outside his bedroom. An army private with a rifle stood beside her.

Across the room, Wainwright lounged on the sofa. A thin curl of smoke snaked from the tip of a cigarette clipped between the doctor's long fingers. Another Cuban soldier stood at attention behind Thaddeus Wainwright.

"If we're being shot would you mind if I brush my teeth first?" Podge asked Ameriga. "I don't want to offend the undertaker."

"I was sent to escort you to your meeting with el Jefe," Ameriga said.

"Yes, did you forget, Patrick, that we have an appointment this morning with His Royal Fuzziness?" Wainwright said, punctuating his words by flicking cigarette ash into a tacky beanbag ashtray on the coffee table. "Here's your security report." The doctor picked up a file from the sofa cushion beside him and tossed it to a stuffed chair.

"What's with the added muscle?" Podge asked, nodding to the two soldiers. "We didn't need chaperones on our first date."

"It is of no concern to you," Ameriga said.

"Apparently there was some sort of trouble during the night," Wainwright explained. "Don't bother to press them. My friend here didn't have any details."

Ameriga shot a withering look at the private standing behind Wainwright. The soldier had arrived at the suite a few minutes before Ameriga. The young man stood more rigidly at attention and studied the faded wallpaper.

"I'll be a few minutes," Podge said. "While you're waiting, call up some caviar and an ice ax and bill it to Mr. L. Trotsky in 12A."

Podge showered and dressed quickly, and he and Wainwright were hustled down to a waiting jeep. Twenty minutes later they arrived with their army escort at the Cuban capitol building. They were told to leave Podge's security proposal in the jeep.

"I can't help but notice we're not at Papa Fidel's casa," Podge said.

"You have been invited to breakfast with other foreign visitors to Cuba," Ameriga explained. "It is a great honor that you are even permitted to be here."

"Yes, Patrick," Wainwright said. "Be grateful they allowed us in through the front door to a dining room and aren't dragging us out the back door to an unmarked grave."

Podge expected a torrent of angry Spanish from Ameriga or at the very least a silent sneer. Instead, the major's face was bland as she led them to the table.

The dining room was a throwback to the ostentatious splendor of a free Cuba. There were large crystal chandeliers, high-backed chairs with upholstered seats and a long table similar to but much larger than that of Idi Amin. Podge was at least thankful to see that this table, unlike the Ugandan dictator's, was not loaded with trays of human legs and tureens filled with bobbing human eyeballs. Still, given the slavery conditions under which the people of Cuba lived, the bodies were there even if only metaphorically.

About a hundred people still milled about the room, chatting and laughing nervously. Podge got the impression that he and Dr. Wainwright were not the only people there to whom this impromptu breakfast was a surprise.

Fidel Castro entered in grand fashion a few minutes after Podge, flanked by several generals whose uniforms apparently were issued with scowls along with the standard berets, boots and sidearms. There were Russians among them, and although Podge subtly scanned the room for a sickly purple face, he did not see Ivan Strankov; neither with Castro nor mingling with the rest of the assembled crowd. With luck, the Russian colonel's remains were on a plane back to Moscow.

"Good morning, mi amigos! Friends, all my good, good friends!" Castro called.

The dictator waved his arms high over his head like a Hollywood starlet acknowledging the crowd from the red carpet on Oscar night. He singled a few men out for special attention with a wink or a punctuating poke at the air with his omnipresent cigar. Podge smiled tightly and nodded when the cigar stabbed the air in his direction.

"Furry prat," Wainwright groused under his breath.

Servers in drab army uniforms hurried to wrangle the guests into seats. Podge and Wainwright were seated together three quarters of the way up to Castro, who took his place at the head of the table. To Wainwright's left was a fat little bald man with a fringe of yellow hair whose face Podge could not see. To Podge's right sat Major Blanco.

"You sure you want to sit there?" Podge asked her. "I might sneeze and get capitalism on you."

"How easy a system it must be for one like yourself," Ameriga said. "Your wealth is inherited and the workers supply you with all your creature comforts. You are like a prince in the United States with not a care like the common men you exploit, no?"

Podge nodded thoughtfully, as if the major's point had given him contemplative pause. "You have large honkers," he suggested.

He glanced to his left for Wainwright's approval but, irritatingly, found the doctor deep in conversation with the balding man one seat up. That was odd. Wainwright rarely took to strangers. Podge turned back to Major Blanco for some more hostile sparring, but the food had arrived on plain clay platters carried by frightened waiters, and Ameriga was no longer paying any attention to him.

Podge frowned. "Nobody wants to play with me," he complained.

Podge was disturbed by the large number of Americans in the group. His was the only acceptable business any American should have in Cuba, yet judging by the accents of many of the happy chattering voices, many of his countrymen did not share his view.

The breakfast, it became clear, was the method by which Cuban state security had decided to observe and question in one room a large group of recent foreign arrivals. No doubt this impromptu meal was an attempt by the government to uncover information that would lead them to the Red Menace, whose appearance on the island nation coincided with the arrival of these men. Podge was surprised by the delicacy of the scheme. He had assumed that questioning in every communist country began with bamboo under the fingernails and ended with a bullet to the back of the head. What's more, Podge did not get the impression that the Cubans were concerned. At the head of the table Castro was laughing as he chatted with a Belgian banker.

Podge soon learned why the atmosphere was so relaxed.

When Major Blanco and the other security officials were momentarily summoned to a whispered conference at Castro's end of the table, the diner across from Podge, an emaciated French hotelier who had arrived later than all the rest, leaned forward.

"There was some trouble last night," the man confided to everyone within earshot. "Attempted sabotage at a Cuban hospital in the hills. They say the Americans." He snorted a little superior snort and rolled his eyes. "But, *of course*, the Americans. But, you see, the spy's body has washed up on the shore. I saw it with my own eyes not ten minutes ago. A crazy man in a mask and cape. I suppose they could have called this off, but you were all already here, so..." The Frenchman shrugged and brushed both ends of his pencil thin mustache with a smart swipe of his index finger.

"You hear that, doc?" Podge said. "Pepe le Pew with the halitosis says America is sending spies to blow up Cuban hospitals. Isn't that interesting? And here I thought we were saving all our ammo for Vietnamese widows and orphans."

Wainwright ignored him and continued his intense conversation with the diner to his left. Podge finally got a good look at the man's face.

The cheeks were a little fleshier and the neck sagged a bit more than it had in his old MIC file photos, but it was the same face that had been next to Strankov's in several of Jeb Wilson's surveillance pictures. Dr. Oleg Plassko's glasses were even thicker than they had been in the Fifties and the Russian botanist looked like a squinting mole at the far end of two round prisms. In the old days, MIC would have identified Plassko as the man in Wilson's photos before the mission even started, but Podge couldn't fault Simon Kirk's people. Podge himself had missed the boat on that one. The scientist had fallen off the map after Motherland had gone belly-up in the Fifties.

Wainwright was smiling and nodding and hanging on Plassko's every word far too eagerly for Podge's comfort. Patrick Becket's good friend was a hostile, eager-to-offend jackass, not this happy, agreeable imposter.

"It is not just matter of selective breeding," Plassko was saying in a thick Russian accent. The fat scientist talked energetically, punctuating nearly every word with wild, two-handed gestures. "Not selective breeding, no, not that at all. One can actually enter cell chemically and alter makeup from within. Alter, change it. Is new organism."

"So by affecting change at the cellular level you don't have to wait generations," Wainwright replied, bobbing his head appreciatively. "And you say you get the results you desire in a single generation. Fascinating, doctor. So you actually program a cell like these people program computers?"

That was it. Wainwright never called anyone "doctor." As far as he was concerned, every physician or scientist who wasn't him was an idiot, quack or fraud.

"Did someone spike your Quisp?" Podge whispered.

"Shut up, Patrick," Wainwright hissed over his shoulder, irritated.

"I do not know much things about computers," Plassko said. The fat hands waved Wainwright's analogy from the air like a distracting mosquito. "Those calculators, they are having no business in real science."

"No, of course not," Wainwright wholeheartedly agreed.

Podge, whose main field was computers, actually anticipated an age when computers would be in every laboratory in the world aiding every field of science, but as Wainwright had apparently gone utterly insane there was no sense pointing this out.

The hushed conference near the head of the table was finishing up. The Russians who had accompanied Castro into the dining room filed out through a side door leaving nothing but Cuban officials. It was only when the crowd of Communists thinned that Podge recognized a face in the crowd.

Captain Esteban Suarez was laughing at some joke Castro had made. The silver front tooth of Jeb Wilson's murderer glinted in the chandelier light.

Podge poked Wainwright and, before the doctor could complain again, nodded to the head of the table. Podge could tell from the single raised eyebrow that Wainwright, too, recognized Suarez from the photos Kirk had supplied them as mission prep.

"Yes, of course, I see," Wainwright said to Plassko, slipping a hand into his pocket as he spoke. "Your work is brilliant, doctor. Simply brilliant."

Wainwright fumbled with his hankie before wiping his nose and replacing the handkerchief in his side jacket pocket.

Podge slipped his napkin over the little white pill Wainwright had dropped on the table while pretending to drop his hankie. He drew the pill in and pocketed it.

Ameriga returned to her seat, as did the other Cubans. Podge made a note of Suarez's location at the far end, away from Castro.

"Were you guys fighting over who's paying the tab?" Podge asked Ameriga. "Because I forgot my wallet in a Ugandan whorehouse."

"The presidente is going to grace us with a few words," Ameriga replied.

At the head of the table, Castro rose to his feet and cleared his throat. A hush fell over those assembled. For his part, Podge looked longingly toward the exit and wondered how convincingly he could fake an epileptic seizure.

It was worse than he anticipated. Podge found the little despot even more odious than the previous day. Castro acted as if all the strangers in the room were old friends, and there were only two ways the dumpy man in baggy camouflage treated his old friends: Death by firing squad or fifteen hour sermons on the glories of communism. By the end of their interminable breakfast, Podge longed for the humane bullets of the former over the collectivist gasbaggery of the latter.

At the end, there were hugs and cigars and kisses to the cheek as the dictator traveled down his line of guests like a bride visiting tables at a wedding reception. Up close, Castro's beard looked like a tumbleweed and smelled like a litterbox.

"We will meet tomorrow, rather than today, Senor Becket," Castro assured Podge when he reached him. "Today is—" He waved his cigar. "*Loco*. Is crazy. Tomorrow."

Castro left him with a slap on the back and continued down the line.

"I'm glad to see my time is so valuable to him," Podge said, flinging his napkin to the table in annoyance. "Oh, don't look at me like that," he said to Ameriga, irritated. "My time is money. I know that's hard for a brainwashed communist to get, but it's a fact. He just added another twenty grand to the bill."

"You truly are diseased," Ameriga said. "Money is an illness with you."

"It makes the world go 'round, baby," Podge said. "Even commie

Cuba, even if you don't get that. In the meantime, I hope you people haven't had all the toilets shot,

because I have to go to the little capitalist's room. Want to guard the door?"

Major Blanco said not a word as she led Podge past Castro's party down toward the main entrance. Podge was not sure what Wainwright would use as a distraction. He simply knew to expect something when he reached Captain Suarez. The doctor did not disappoint. As Podge passed Suarez's seat, there was a sudden great crash from behind and all heads swiveled up towards the head of the table.

A waiter lay prostrate on the floor amid a pile of broken dishes and scattered cutlery. A protective circle had formed around Fidel Castro and several soldiers had drawn sidearms. None but Podge saw Wainwright's leg slip back from where he'd tripped the young man. None but Wainwright saw Podge use the opportunity to snake his hand behind Captain Esteban Suarez and drop the pill Wainwright had given him into the milky coffee Suarez had just ordered.

"Come, it is nothing," Ameriga announced, releasing the butt of her gun. The room was returning to normal as she ushered him into the grand hallway.

Podge lingered in the men's room for what he considered to be a respectable amount of time and when he and Ameriga returned to the dining room they found Castro gone along with his entourage and Captain Suarez flapping on the floor like a salmon in a Grizzly's mouth. The crowd was aghast. Those close cowered away from the convulsing man; those on the other side of the table leaned forward for a better look. Only one man hustled down the length of the table, pushing diners aside as he went.

"Stand back," Wainwright commanded. "Everybody, back. I'm a doctor."

Wainwright flung Suarez's chair out of the way, deliberately spilling the remainder of the captain's coffee in the process.

"You," Wainwright snapped at Podge and Ameriga. "Hold him down."

They did as they were told, aided by two nearby soldiers.

Wainwright checked pulse, carotid and pupils. Captain Suarez's eyes were wide and he continued to spasm even as the men and Ameriga pinned his limbs to the floor. The wild twitching crossed his torso like a wave and found sudden focus on the left side of his body. Left arm and leg suddenly went slack and the left side of his face drooped.

"This man's had a stroke," Wainwright pronounced. "Do you have aspirin? Of course not. This is Cuba. If you hadn't made me leave my bag in the jeep... Where are your blasted medical attendants?"

As if on cue, men in white coats hustled into the dining hall drawing a stretcher behind them. Wainwright supervised the loading of his patient onto the gurney and wore a grave expression as the captain was wheeled out of the big room.

"Will he survive, doctor?" Ameriga asked.

Wainwright shook his head. "I doubt he'll make it to the hospital. You do still have those here in Cuba, don't you? Either way, the poor fool's last minutes on Earth are going to be utter agony. A friend of yours?"

Ameriga shook her head. A Cuban colonel with a huge mustache and bugging, beetle-black eyes was gesturing to her from near the door as the stretcher passed by on its way into the main hallway. "No," she replied. "Please wait here." She abandoned the two men and went to confer with her superior.

"Will they be able to find out it was poison?" Podge asked from the corner of his mouth once they were alone. Wainwright gave him a withering look, and Podge said, "I'll take that as a no. Well, it wasn't as hands-on as I'd've liked, but we got them back for Wilson. Bully for us." His pinched brow matched his darkly unsatisfied tone.

"Be pleased with the victory, Patrick. It might be your only one here. By the way, I haven't had a chance to tell you, but I tested your blood. There's no trace of poison."

"Maybe your new best friend Plassko dropped something untraceable in my Corn Flakes and I'll drop dead of a phony stroke at the batting cages three weeks from now. And what was Strankov's Dr. Frankenstein doing here anyway?"

"By the sounds of it, he was teaching botany at the university before Strankov even got out of Siberia," Wainwright said. He filched the last sugary roll from a tray on the table and peeled away bits of it as he spoke, tossing them into his mouth. "Kismet put these two back together. His Russian handler got called here for this impromptu affair, and Plassko was dragged along for the ride. They came and collected him while you were in the bathroom. It actually might be our one stroke of luck. I let him think he's brilliant, I let him *know* that I was brilliant, and I managed to wrangle an invitation for supper. He wants to talk shop. He feels like he's dying here amongst all these lesser minds. It might open a door for us. We'll see. Why is that idiot grin plastered across your face?"

"I'm just picturing you being forced to pretend someone other than you is brilliant for another whole meal. If breakfast didn't kill you, dinner will finish you off."

Wainwright's face was deadly serious. "Don't underestimate this one, Patrick. He's dangerous. I tested the samples you brought me as best I could. Had to use leaf clippings from plants in the lobby. We should be *very* worried. It's a bacteria. A mutated version of one that attacks tomatoes, peppers and other plants. Plassko has given it a limitless appetite. It is vicious and it does not discriminate. It no longer is restricted to a few plants, it will attack *any* plant life, and fast. The original bacteria lives in soil and in colder climates might die over the winter, but in warm areas it will not die."

"What exactly does that mean for a tropical island like Cuba?"

Wainwright tossed the last uneaten bit of breakfast roll to the table and dusted the crumbs from his hands.

"It means, Patrick, that if the bacteria had not been stopped after it was accidentally released up at that base — and we now have to assume that was accidental — this island would by now look like a baked rock."

"And if they figure out a way to release it in the U.S.?"

"I'm guessing that the Midwest would have weeks, depending on the method of dispersal. I assume that's where they'd strike first, in America's breadbasket. It'd maybe be a few months before the entire continent was wiped clean of all vegetation. Maybe we could crack the code of the antibacterial substance before half the country was devastated. As it is, I was unable to figure out the chemical composition of the stuff they sprayed to stop it. There are only traces on the living plants you brought me. I could use some of the undiluted substance."

The party was breaking up. Men filed for the exits, many accompanied by Cuban state security. Major Ameriga Blanco signaled for them by the door and Podge and Wainwright began picking their way through the departing crowd toward her.

Podge knew that the smartest course of action would be to hightail it out of Cuba as soon as possible. He had accomplished his mission. He had found out what was on the Russian base, he had smuggled the information off the island and it was hopefully in Simon Kirk's hands by now. And he had avenged Wilson's murder.

Wainwright could see the gears turning in his friend's mind and instantly understood what was troubling Podge. "Smart thing to do would be to leave," the doctor pointed out. "Regrettably, Patrick, it's not in your nature to do the smart thing."

"Maybe it is this time, doc. I barely got out of that place in one piece last night. Security's going to be even more beefed up now. Costume won't work in full light, and they're bound to have them all switched on now. On the other hand, they think the Red Menace is dead. I maybe bought some breathing room for us there. I don't know. Those missiles should be disabled or destroyed. And Kirk doesn't even know about this bacteria the reds have their mitts on. Even if Strankov is dead, we can't just leave them with that stuff. If they figure out a delivery system for it, we can say bye-bye to the fruited plains. You and I might be America's last line of defense." The last words he whispered quickly under his breath for they were nearly upon Ameriga.

"And what's new about that?" Wainwright said. "Ah, my dear."

Wainwright nodded to the Cuban major and took her right hand in both of his. She seemed surprised by the gesture but allowed the doctor to guide her into the stream of guests exiting the dining room.

"Welcome, wife number lucky thirteen," Podge grumbled.

Podge fell in with the departing crowd, knowing that he and Wainwright — and, most chillingly, possibly all of North America — were dead in the water unless a game-changer presented itself. And soon.

17

THE Ukranian physician who was assigned to the small hospital on the Russian missile base had strongly objected when his patient refused to stay in bed, but Colonel Ivan Strankov insisted that his wounds were superficial.

"You could have a concussion," the doctor said. "And your nose is broken."

"I am riddled with cancer and you want to keep me in hospital for a bump on the head?" Strankov snarled.

This doctor opened his mouth to argue but, realizing that his dying patient was not wrong, screwed his lips together and went about his other duties.

Strankov sat on the edge of the cot and pulled on his boots. The cotton gauze plugging his nostrils made it difficult to breath, so he pulled the two wads out. The blood was brown on the near ends and had coagulated to gooey red on the far ends. Fresh blood failed to pour from his nostrils and so he threw the discolored gauze to the floor.

Strankov had learned when he had awakened in the infirmary twenty minutes before that the search for the masked intruder had ended with a surprising twist, and so he was waiting in full uniform, nose shattered and eyes blackened like a raccoon's mask, when the body was carried into the hospital on a makeshift wooden stretcher.

The masked man had washed up onshore. His clothes were sopping wet, and when he was placed on the examining table water ran in rivulets to the floor.

As he stooped to examine the body stretched out on the table, Strankov could not help but wonder how long before he would be lying dead on a cold slab with interested eyes peering down at him. It would happen here, no doubt. He did not have much time left, that much he knew. Would they fly him back to Moscow or would they burn his body in Havana? Would he receive a hero's burial, or would they spit in his face? None of that really mattered to him. What he had planned, he did for no one but himself.

"Did you do this to him?" Strankov demanded of the major in command of the Cuban troops that had found the body. He pointed at the mangled face.

"No, comrade colonel," replied Major Grynko. "He was dead when we found him. They say he likely died jumping from the cliff. He must have struck his face when he hit the rocks. No one could survive that fall. Fool American."

Strankov was not as sure of the dead man's nationality, and he offered only a noncommittal grunt to his subordinate.

The skin was pale, but that happened in death. A shark had taken off most of the lower right leg, draining the body of nearly every drop of blood.

Strankov showed no emotion as he passed the bloody leg stump.

The age was difficult to tell. The man Strankov saw the previous night still seemed quite fit. But all he had ever seen of the Red Menace was the chin and mouth, and that would not have changed much on a healthy man in fourteen years. No matter either way. This man's face was smashed, his bones pulped, teeth missing.

"If only he could have been made to suffer for the murder of Comrade Colonel Petr Bolgevik," Major Grynko offered.

This was the only blessing in the unexpected reappearance of Strankov's old enemy. The Red Menace was being blamed for the body of the KGB officer found shot to death in Strankov's bunker office. At least Colonel Strankov did not have to invent a feeble lie to cover for Bolgevik's murder.

Strankov's eyes were growing watery and he blinked hard to clear them. Immediately he felt fresh, sharp pain in his broken nose and a trickle of warm blood from his nostrils. Spine becoming rigid, he demanded fresh gauze from the Ukranian doctor. When the physician was not fast enough, Strankov wrenched the box from his hands, yanked out a package of gauze and tore open the paper himself. He turned his back on the soldiers and medical staff and pinched the gauze to his nose.

Colonel Ivan Strankov made the entire room wait five minutes for his bloody nose to stop running. When the gauze was soggy crimson and no more blood flowed from his nostrils, he let the damp mess drop from his hand and turned back to those gathered.

"Give me those," he commanded, as if no time had passed since he last spoke.

The major handed him the cape, mask and gloves that had been stripped from the body. The mask and gauntlets Strankov dropped to the table.

The cape felt flimsy, the material cheap. And the color. It had always turned red close up, but this cape was still black.

"Perhaps the trick is body heat," he mused. He drew the cape around his own shoulders and waited for it to change color. It remained black.

Strankov's body was cold. It was always cold these days, even deep in Cuba's dense jungle. The soldiers around him were freely perspiring, as usual.

"You. Put this on."

A sweating young private dutifully put down his rifle and pulled on the cape. Strankov studied the material with squinting eyes, yet the cape remained black.

"Turn off the lights. Go across the room, into that corner."

The hospital lights were doused and the soldier retreated to the corner of the infirmary. Although daylight streamed through the windows, Strankov had encountered the Red Menace enough times to know that the shadows in the corners were deep enough. The Red Menace would have vanished, yet the soldier remained clearly visible and looking like a complete fool draped in the cheap black cape.

"Lights on."

The hospital lights flickered on and the soldier returned the cape, which still failed to turn red as he crossed back over to Strankov.

It was possible that the cape worked only on the Red Menace's body. It seemed farfetched, but Strankov knew enough not to underestimate American ingenuity.

The body on the table could be the Red Menace. Or not.

"Increase the patrols," he ordered. "Get more dogs from the Cubans." He gathered cape, gloves and mask. "Get me the autopsy results as soon as you are finished," he ordered the doctor on duty.

Strankov checked his watch and hurried from the infirmary. Outside was like stepping into a kiln and he stopped dead against the push of tropical air.

The Russian leaned against the infirmary wall. He felt dizzy, and though his stomach was not churning and he had not eaten in hours, he felt as though he would vomit. How many days had he vomited up what little he could swallow, and when there was nothing left how many hours had he spent dry-heaving?

Though the air was warm and the sun was hot, his limbs remained cold.

The door to the infirmary suddenly opened. The soldiers who had carried in the mangled body were surprised to see the colonel loitering outside.

"Is everything well, comrade Colonel Strankov?" Major Grynko asked.

Strankov growled. Wordlessly he straightened up and marched across the compound towards the bunker.

Sympathy from his subordinates. God, how he hated everything about this world. He had thought exile in Siberia to be the worst of all punishments but this modern world was hell of a whole other magnitude. But it would not be for much longer.

Who cared if the body in the infirmary was not that of the Red Menace? In two days he would destroy the Red Menace's home, and if the ancient thorn in Ivan Strankov's side still lived he would have no place to go home to.

And if as a result of Strankov's dying actions here in Cuba the entire world burned in nuclear fire? If Ivan Strankov lived long enough, he would do a joyful dance of death as the fallout rained hell from the sky.

With a strength he had not felt in years, Strankov ripped the bunker door open and disappeared inside. Behind him, the metal door slammed shut like a coffin lid.

18

CLAPP HOPPER tried his level best not to shift the old feather mattress or squeak the boxspring as he slipped out from under the old comforter. Despite his best efforts, the lump next to him under the covers stirred and moaned.

"I'll be down in a few minutes, Pa," said the vaguely human shape to which he had been married for the past thirty-eight years.

"Sorry, Ma," he said, and patted the biggest mound in the pile. His wife emitted an exhausted purr when he smacked her rump and the pile of bedcovers rearranged itself.

Clapp slipped out of the room, tiptoeing around the noisiest of the bare floorboards on his way to the bathroom.

There were two other bedrooms off the narrow second floor hall. Both doors were open and the rooms beyond were dark.

Bill and Jason were long gone. Both men had wives and children of their own now, and Jason didn't even live in Kansas any longer. He was clear off on the East Coast, living in New York and working in publishing. Bill was still instate, but had opted for life as an insurance agent amid the bright lights and hurly-burly of Omaha.

Gladys had turned the room at the end of the hall which the two older boys had shared growing up into her sewing room. In front of the window, Clapp could just make out the silhouette of the flea market Singer sewing machine perched on the old Formica kitchen table which he'd hauled up from storage in the barn.

His youngest son, Walter, was ten years younger than his closest sibling and had just left for college in California.

All three of his sons were scholars; the first men in the family to further their education beyond high school. Clapp felt a swell of pride mixed with sadness as he passed Walter's room. When he tugged the pull chain on the ceiling light, the light splashed out of the bathroom and illuminated Walt's neatly folded-down bedcovers and his highboy, which was empty of nearly everything but some bare wooden hangers and a few pairs of shoes and slacks his youngest had outgrown, due either to size or style.

Clapp shaved with the same straight razor his father had gifted him on his fourteenth birthday and dressed in the clothes he had laid out in the bathtub the previous night. He had been laying out the clothes like that for almost four decades of marriage, consideration for a wife who did not need to get up at the crack of dawn. Yet, like every other day for the previous thirty-years, he need not have bothered.

Before Clapp was finished with his morning routine he could smell the enticing aroma of freshly brewed coffee.

When he got downstairs, Gladys was already dressed and hustling around the kitchen. The toast and coffee were already laid out for him, and she was pouring a glass of orange juice. A single fried egg and two slices of bacon were splattering the stovetop.

"Paper's not here," Gladys said. "I'll call Lucy MacLeren about that John of hers again. Only time that boy's on time is Christmastime, and that's just for the tips."

Ma had a bowl of oatmeal and Pa had his bacon and eggs and, once the dishes were washed and put away, the two of them began their long day on the farm.

Clapp tended to the cows while Gladys saw to the chickens.

When Clapp exited the barn forty-five minutes later, the first rays of sunlight were splashing over dew-brushed fields.

Clapp did not often stop to watch the sunrise, but on some days it was simply too spectacular a thing to ignore. The backdrop of the late summer sun rising brilliant white over the postcard-perfect image of Clapp's golden fields of gently swaying wheat brought a tear to his eye that surprised even Clapp. He brushed it away.

"Dang hay fever," he muttered, lest the passing early bird of legend mistakenly think the ordinarily reserved Clapp Emmett Hopper had developed some kind of hippie poet's sensitivity in his old age.

It was not so much the present sunrise witnessed, but the future sunrises missed that touched Clapp's soul. It pained Clapp to think that there would come a day when he'd have to retire. Clapp figured he had fifteen years left at best — and probably more like ten — during which he could squeeze the last strength of youth out of his rapidly aging body before he'd have to sell the place. Even more it grieved him to know that there would soon be no Hoppers left willing to work the farm.

Not that he was not proud of his boys; he was. No father could be prouder.

No, it was just one of life's realities that he had to live with. The boys had their lives to lead and if they could make their way without having to get up before dawn and work until after dark every day, then good on them. He'd raised three bright sons.

Anyway, the end was a long ways off for Clapp Hopper. For now Clapp had a high school kid from town who helped out around the place weekends, Walt still pitched in at planting time between semesters, and Clapp had lots of daily chores to keep himself busy. Too busy to get weepy over the millionth sun he'd seen crawl up over the horizon since he'd inherited the place from his dad.

Clapp headed back to the old farmhouse. He'd sprung for some fancy siding a decade ago and the yellow aluminum glinted in the early morning sunlight. Gladys was tending the vegetable garden next to the rear porch.

An old tent from the Army Navy store was tossed over the old Hoyt-Clagwell next to the garden. Fortunately the tractor had held out through planting season, but the right rear wheel had given up the ghost after he'd gotten the very last seed in the ground and Clapp was waiting on a replacement. It was supposed to be in this week, and he'd have to remember to call Burt Handley in town at lunchtime to see if it had arrived.

"Ma, remind me to give Burt a call on that wheel this afternoon," Clapp said.

"I'll put a note on your placemat when I go in," Gladys promised.

Clapp's wife was chipping a hoe through the row of staked tomato plants, tilling rich brown soil. Gladys was proud of her little garden, proud of the crop yield she managed to get out of such a little plot of land every year. Clapp and the three boys had full bellies for many winters thanks in large part to the various vegetables Mrs. Hopper so diligently canned come autumn. Although most of the jars were empty and covered in dust on cellar shelves lately, since Gladys didn't need to fill quite so many these days.

When Clapp was a buck of eighteen, Gladys had been the most beautiful girl he had ever laid eyes on. She was forty pounds heavier now and about as many years older, yet in that early morning sunlight, in a threadbare apron and worn cloth skirt and wearing a pair of Clapp's dirty work boots, she was the still the prettiest girl in the Midwest to one old farmer's tired eyes.

Gladys paused to wipe her brow with the hem of her apron and suddenly noticed her husband leaning on the fence next to her vegetable garden, a smile on his weathered face. "Why are you staring a hole through my head, Clapp Hopper?" she asked.

"Just wondering how the Almighty didn't notice an angel had dropped from His Heaven into my backyard."

"Oh, saints preserve us. Get back to work, you old fool," Gladys said. She struggled to subdue a grin as she returned to her labors.

Clapp's earlier thoughts of retirement were well banished as he headed for his workshop.

Clapp Hopper could not possibly know that at that very moment, in a jungle thousands of miles away, men were working feverishly to hasten Clapp and America to an early retirement. And if all went according to plan, one day hence it would not be a heavenly angel but an object decidedly more hellish and terrestrial dropping from the sky.

At the door to his work shop, Clapp looked back at Gladys and, unknowingly, at ground zero: The little vegetable and herb plot next to the Hoppers' back porch which his dumpy wife in the sad cloth dress was tending, an oblivious smile on her careworn face.

19

COLONEL Ivan Strankov held the corroded iron railing in a two-handed death grip as he glared down at the team of scientists. The men barked angry orders and questions at one another as they tinkered with wrenches and screwdrivers inside the open compartment below the nosecone of the Russian missile.

The steel plated doors that sealed the silo off from the world were closed tightly above Strankov's head. Soon, light would stream down through the opening. Soon, the rocket would rise on a plume of screaming flame. Soon, hell would be unleashed.

Strankov rapped his knuckles on the iron railing. Bits of rust broke away and fell like orange snowflakes to the floor far below.

"Work faster," Strankov commanded. "They will all three be ready to fly in hours, not days, or I will have all your heads."

He had issued the same order half-a-dozen times already in the past hour. The faces of the scientists glistened with sweat and their underarms and the backs of their coats were stained dark. Most made a point of not looking up at the voice that bellowed down at them. The two most senior engineers nodded anxiously up at the angry colonel who hovered over them all like some sickly predatory bird.

The wall of the Soviet missile silo was a tube of smooth concrete sunk deep in the jungle floor. At various levels up the shaft were retractable metal platforms that allowed access to the Shevchenko II missile and its nuclear payload.

The nuclear warhead had been removed during the night and for a few hours the missile had been as impotent as a neutered dog.

The original targeting of the three missiles would have, Moscow hoped, dropped one warhead on New York City and two on Washington, D.C. However, Russian missile guidance systems were as primitive as abaci and it was possible that the New York City missile might drift too far north and land in upstate New York, Connecticut or Rhode Island. This was the reason for the redundancy on the D.C. missiles. New York City was important, but Washington was the real prize, and it was unlikely that both Soviet missiles would wander off course into the heart of Pennsylvania or, worse, several miles out in the Atlantic. Almost certainly one would strike its intended target.

At least, that was the case before Strankov had ordered the missiles retargeted.

Colonel Strankov snapped his fingers. "The map," he demanded.

A scientist in a white lab coat hustled forward and rolled open onto the railing a thick map of the United States.

"This one will strike in northern Kansas," the scientist explained, nodding to the missile on which the others worked and which was currently programmed to come down directly on Gladys Hopper's Kansas vegetable patch. "The others, here and here."

There were three red circles on the map. The first in Kansas, one in eastern Kentucky and the last in central Utah.

The circles were wide, allowing for the missiles to stray a hundred miles or more in any direction. The spread was not so crucial, only the fact that all three missiles struck the North American continent. Plassko had insisted that one missile was sufficient, and that a single detonation would merely mean a slower amount of time until complete devastation. But Strankov did not have time. Every day he felt the tug of death at his hem. All three missiles would be ready to fly by dawn.

Strankov brushed a hand across the circles on the map. First Kentucky, then Kansas, then Utah. He closed his eyes and pictured the news stories the next day. At the start they would have no idea. Duds, they would say. Then would come the horror of realization. Then it would escalate. To where, Strankov knew not. Nor did he care.

Ivan Strankov opened his eyes and the beautiful visions of blackened

American farmland vanished from his mind's eye. He rolled up the map clumsily and shoved it back into the hands of the nearby engineer.

"Where is Plassko?" Strankov demanded.

"Comrade Doctor Plassko still has not arrived. The university said he went out to supper after his last botany class. Your men are looking for him."

The groan of struggling gears sounded from below, and Strankov and the engineer looked down.

A small elevator was fixed to the wall and was used to raise men and materials to the various platform levels. From a door at the lowest level, two new men had entered the silo hauling a barrel-shaped object. When the elevator reached them, they rolled the item onto the lift on a hand cart and settled it carefully between them. With a jolt, the small elevator began to rise up the side of the missile.

Strankov watched with eager fascination as the elevator came level with and stopped beside the group of men working on the open side of the missile. The others came forward and helped the two new arrivals roll the object off the elevator.

The cylinder was large, the size of a trash can. Top and bottom were solid stainless steel disks, and five strips of steel spaced around the sides of the cylinder acted as support between lid and base. The tube itself was thick, clear plastic. Although the exterior was slightly scratched, the contents of the cylinder were visible.

Gallons of thick green liquid sat like lime Jello inside the tube.

The team of scientists grunted and swore as they hauled the cylinder off the hand cart. With the barrel held high between them, they took awkward baby steps across the platform until they reached the open side of the missile.

It did not insert properly on the first attempt. The bottom stainless steel disk missed the corresponding track inside the rocket and the stumbling men nearly dropped their precious cargo. On the second try, the cylinder caught the grooves in the track and slid neatly inside the open cargo area.

The men laughed and a few applauded. One of the youngest did that which he had not dared do before. He looked up to Strankov, finally expecting approval from the base commander. Ivan Strankov was a gargoyle baring yellow teeth.

The engineer blanched and tapped the nearest scientist on the arm. One by one, the men looked up and the cheering died in their throats. The silo fell silent.

"Finish here," Strankov commanded. "You have two more to convert."

The colonel turned sharply on his heel and marched off the platform, disappearing through an open door above. Rust rained down on the upturned faces below.

PODGE AND WAINWRIGHT spent the afternoon poolside at the Revolucion Grande Hotel as they waited for night to fall. For Podge, the waiting was interminable.

Wainwright at least had his supper with Dr. Oleg Plassko to focus on. Nothing was likely to come of it, but the rendezvous was at least something. Podge had only a hidden cape and mask and no game plan.

Podge glanced over the tops of his sunglasses at the window of his corner suite eight stories up. Inside was hidden perhaps America's last chance to avoid a full-scale nuclear war. The look was not lost on Wainwright.

"It would be suicide, Patrick, to make a run for that base tonight," the doctor warned. "Perhaps we should have left Cuba after all. There isn't much we can do."

"We've got to try, doc."

"And we will, I suppose, do something idiotic, and I suppose we'll both die in the process. But even you'll admit there's nothing either of us can do for the time being. Put it from your mind. Take a nap. Take a swim. Or if you must do something to annoy the communists, pester that amorphous Marxist blob over there some more."

One of Major Blanco's men, a hulking plainclothes Cuban named Ramon, made no attempt to blend in with the bathing trunks and bikinis. The large man sat sweating on a stool beneath the awning of the bar on the hotel side of the pool. He was wearing a cheap black business suit, shiny black tie and a felt hat pulled down over one eye.

Russian Politburo members and other high ranking party officials often stayed at the Revolucion Grande and, consequently, it was stocked with all manner of exotic items unavailable to the average peasant back in Russia. This included cleanish linen, tepid running water and enough imported booze to float the U.S.S. Kennedy up the Volga.

Ramon steadfastly refused the drinks Podge had been regularly sending him all afternoon. Podge summoned a waiter and ordered up another, this one served in a hollowed out coconut with a little fizzing sparkler spearing two pineapple slices.

When the drink was placed before him, Ramon pinched the sparkler out between thumb and forefinger and glared daggers at Podge.

"You haven't lost your knack for making friends, Patrick," Wainwright observed.

"Excuse me, what did you say?" Podge said. "I couldn't hear you over that throng of admirers that's always surrounding you for autographs everywhere you go. Hey, you think maybe he doesn't like pineapple? Hey, el Fatso," he called, "what does stinkbutt Marx have against pineapple?"

Wainwright suppressed a chuckle and closed his eyes on the sun.

When Major Ameriga Blanco arrived in the late afternoon, the counter in front of Ramon was littered with a dozen warm pink, green and red concoctions, all jutting straws and umbrellas, and each looking like happy hour's answer to Sputnik.

"Get those out of here," Ameriga ordered the bartender. The man quickly obliged the uniformed woman and the untouched drinks disappeared behind the bar.

Ramon shifted his great weight on his stool but Ameriga waved him to stay. The hulk remained in place as she crossed the patio over to Podge and Wainwright.

There was only a handful of guests lounging around the pool so late in the afternoon, none of them Cubans. The Revolucion Grande seemed to have cornered the market on overweight European men whose skin went from bleached white to sunburned scarlet, depending on the number of days they had beached themselves poolside. Skinny young mistresses in bikinis cooed or overweight, middle-aged wives in one-pieces hectored as they applied imported Noxema to acres of sun-abused Eurotrash flesh.

Podge and Wainwright had found a private corner away from the other guests. Privacy was a rare commodity in a public hotel in a communist nation, especially for a pair of Americans. Podge had managed this amazing feat when they first arrived at the pool by waving a mittful of pesos in the air, shouting "Andale, you Speedy Gonzalezes!" and offering a tip big enough to build a four lane bridge to Miami to the first hotel employee to get rid of the other five chairs that were crammed in the corner.

When the Cuban major's shadow fell across them, both men saw Ameriga note through hooded eyes the marks where the wooden legs of the missing chairs had stained the patio, but she made no mention of her observation.

"Dr. Wainwright, this was waiting for you at the desk," she said, handing over a scrap of paper.

"And I'm sure you didn't read it, so there's no way you could simply tell me what it says," Wainwright droned.

"Dr. Plassko wants you to come to the Universidad de la Habana half an hour earlier than you had planned," she replied.

Eyes flat, Wainwright crumpled the note without reading it, checked his wristwatch and quickly climbed out of his lounge chair. "This is why communism will eventually dominate the world, my dear. Efficiency over privacy. The West wastes millions on mailboxes while the totalitarians simply have their secret police goons read you your gas bill over the phone. I'll see you later, Patrick. Be good."

Wainwright left them poolside and headed to the hotel. A nod from Major Blanco and the massive bulk of Ramon unstuck himself from his barstool and fell in the doctor's wake. Wainwright took note of his lumbering shadow with an impatient sigh.

"That communist bilge about sharing doesn't fly with me," Wainwright called over his shoulder to Ramon as he headed inside the hotel. "You're hiring your own taxi."

Ramon ducked his head below the doorframe and the glass door swung shut behind the two men.

"Your meeting with el Jefe has been rescheduled to tomorrow morning at ten o'clock," Ameriga informed Podge once Wainwright was gone.

"Just let him know if he bumps it off another day he's going to have to dip even deeper into the Cuban treasury. By the time I'm done adding zeroes to his bill, you slaves'll be in hock up to your eyeballs until Cinco de Mayo 1997."

Ameriga scarcely acknowledged his words with a nod. She was peering through narrowed eyes at Podge's bare torso. Podge raised a bland eyebrow.

"Kitten, unless you plan on slipping out of those fatigues and into a camouflage bikini so we're on even footing, kindly remember that my eyes are up here."

Ameriga was not deterred. "This was a bad wound," she observed.

"Oh," Podge said, suddenly wishing he'd stayed in his suite. His fingers brushed the ancient white scar on the left of his chest. "Yachting accident. I scuppered the capstan when I should have bimmied the Jack Tar."

"I do not know what those words mean, but I suspect this is the — how you say it? — the bullshits."

Podge laughed. "It's a crying shame you're a commie babe," he said, slapping his hands to his thighs. "You're too damned smart to buy into all this pinko crapola." He hopped lightly to his feet and grabbed his towel and a white terrycloth pool shirt which were hanging over the back of his chair. He shrugged on the shirt, covering his scar. "I'm going out for supper tonight, if that's okay with state security. You can either join me inside the restaurant or sit in the car outside with a pair of binoculars. Ladies choice. Either way, I'll be ready in twenty."

He was humming "South of the Border" as he left the pool area.

Major Ameriga Blanco glanced around the pool and saw only the last of the dying day's straggling fat tourists and their indulgent women. No Cuban or Russian security personnel other than Ameriga were present. Of course, they could be observing from any of the hotel windows or other rooftops around the area.

If Ameriga was being watched it was not by her men, for she had given the team that had been observing the American Patrick Becket the evening off. It was Major Blanco's belief that they had botched their job the previous evening. If so, she would know for certain by evening's end.

One way or another, by night's end Mr. Patrick Becket — or whatever name he preferred to call himself — would tell her the truth.

20

Dr. Oleg Plassko stumbled through the doorway in the dark, bumping his knee on a wastebasket as he fumbled for the light.

"This!" he announced, pausing only to expel a loud, despairing belch. "This is where genius in Russia lands you."

Dr. Thaddeus Wainwright stood in the doorway and peeked around the corner.

The massive shape of Ramon, his Cuban security minder, loomed in the hall behind him.

Plassko's Universidad de la Habana office looked as if it had once been a closet. Pipes wrapped in asbestos and painted ugly yellow ran up one wall and across the ceiling. There was scarcely room for a desk, certainly not adequate room for the one that had somehow been wedged in the small office. Wainwright assumed they had gotten it through the door in pieces and reassembled it inside. The only other furniture was a single tall wooden filing cabinet. Students who visited Plassko's office were forced to stand, as there was no room for extra chairs.

The only seat in the room was Plassko's and, as Wainwright watched, the fat little man wedged himself between the wall and desk to demonstrate just one of his many daily indignities. Plassko threw his stubby arms out wide, nearly touching wall on both sides.

"See?" he announced, blinking desperately behind his thick glasses. "See? I do not have room to — what you Americans say? — I have no room even to be thinking here."

"Has that ever been a problem for a Russian?" Wainwright asked.

"Yes, yes!" Plassko insisted, completely missing the sarcasm. "Is problem for me all the time. Well, not *all* the time." He winked broadly and belched once more.

"Yes," Wainwright glanced over his shoulder at Ramon.

The hallway was dark, the only light spilling in came from one distant window. The security man was silent; a three hundred pound cigar store Indian.

Wainwright was not certain how much English the Cuban secret policeman understood. It was not as if English speaking was uncommon in Cuba, and Wainwright got the impression the young man understood more than he let on. If Ramon was intelligent, as Wainwright suspected he might be, the beast wore the perfect disguise. And it would make the evening problematic.

Wainwright had met Plassko at the university and they had eaten at a nearby small restaurant patronized by faculty and students. Plassko was delighted to find that lunch was not a fluke and that Wainwright was clearly a man of superlative intellect with a deeply sympathetic ear. As the meal progressed and the imported vodka flowed, Plassko's tongue began to loosen.

There was very little that pleased the Russian about his work at the university. He considered his exile to Cuba as bad as any forced labor camp. Plassko had hinted darkly at some government work that had gotten his superiors in trouble years before, but did not come right out and mention Motherland or Colonel Strankov. Only recently, he had whispered over dinner, had his genius been allowed to blossom fully again.

In his office at the university, Plassko collapsed in his chair and waved a fat hand around his head. "Do you notice something, eh? I am botanist, remember."

"No plants, no windows," Wainwright said. "I would think that the office of a botanist, particularly a brilliant botanist, would have plants and windows."

"Yes! Yes! But this! This is what they care about." Plassko flipped a pile of papers on his desk and sent them scattering to the floor. "Paperwork. Is only being dead trees. I will show them dead trees. I will be having parade in my honor. Hic!"

Wainwright found this loathsome toad of a man unbearable. Still, he kept his tongue in check. "You were going to show me something," Wainwright said.

The light flicked on in Plassko's eyes and he dived into one of his desk drawers with both hands, producing a notebook which he handed over to Wainwright. "You will see. Genius." He thumped a fist proudly against his own chest.

Wainwright scanned the notebook. It was filled with Plassko's handwritten notes, as well as many sketches. What Wainwright read made his blood run cold, yet years of practiced stoicism helped him to keep his face bland and his voice level.

"I don't understand much of this," he lied.

Plassko's face fell. "You say you read Russian."

"I do. But this... I'm sorry, and please take no offense, Dr. Plassko. I can see you are obviously quite brilliant and decades ahead of your time. It's just that I have a hard time reading your handwriting." Wainwright forced an apologetic smile.

A deep furrow formed in Plassko's brow. "Is bad, my writing?"

"It's certainly my fault," Wainwright said. "But it would help me immeasurably in my appreciation of your work if I could actually see what you describe in here."

Plassko twisted his mouth in concentration and ran one hand over his bald scalp, gripping the stringy yellow hair at the back of his head.

"Yes, yes," he said at last, nodding. "You are friend of Castro, after all."

"Most assuredly. Dear old friends are we," Wainwright said, making a mental note to convert to Catholicism at the first opportunity so that he could go to confession.

"Let us go for drive, then!" Plassko said, jumping to his feet. He had a woozy moment during which he grabbed the edge of the desk for support.

"One moment first. You say this notebook is the only evidence of your work here?"

"Yes. I keep just to make notes while I am at university."

"Nothing at your quarters on campus? No notes, backup journals, anything?"

"No, no, no! Is all in there," Plassko said. "And here." He tapped a pale finger against his own temple, weaved a little in place, then snatched the notebook and flung it back inside his desk. "We go now!" Plassko marched from the office and nearly plowed into the security mammoth Ramon. "Out of my way, large Cuban man."

Plassko was halfway down the darkened hallway when he realized he was alone. He paused and leaned against the wall for support as he looked back.

Wainwright was attempting to close the door to the botanist's office.

"Is wrong something is?" Plassko called.

"No. Trouble with the door. Tricky. Swollen in the humidity. It's fine now."

Plassko nodded, turned away, and once more began marching down the corridor.

The Russian had not noticed that Ramon had suddenly gone missing. *Mostly* missing.

Wainwright gave an angry kick at Ramon's lifeless leg, which was sticking out into the hallway. The security man's size sixteen foot hopped out of the way and the doctor was finally able to tightly shut the office door.

Wainwright returned his ballpoint pen to his inner sport jacket pocket, which was already swollen with Plassko's notebook. The pen contained the same paralytic as the Red Menace's glove barb. The dose he had jabbed into Ramon's arm was enough to keep the security man out of action for seventy-two hours. After that?

After that it would not matter if Ramon woke up and sang of all that had happened this evening. Wainwright and Podge would either be out of Cuba or, if what Plassko had hinted at over dinner came to pass, there would be no America for them to return to.

Wishing there was a way he could contact Patrick Becket, Thaddeus Wainwright hustled down the dark university hallway.

PODGE DINED at a busy restaurant on Havana's bustling Alameda de Paula promenade. There were Russians there, in uniform and in street clothes, as well Cuban officials, both military and civilian. Podge recognized two of the officers who were with Castro when the dictator had arrived for breakfast at the capitol building that morning. One side of the restaurant was a balcony surrounded by vine-covered trellises on which a raucous party for a Cuban general was taking place. Tables were mounded with more food than Cuba's poor saw in a year, and men laughed heartily while they sloshed glasses of liquor high in the air for toast after toast. At the head of the table beamed the fat little hero of the hour. The rest of the restaurant was subdued in the shadow of the general's party. The native Cubans seemed most fearful, as if afraid a single dropped fork might be seen as disruptive or, worse, counterrevolutionary.

"Nice to see the peasants know their place," Podge commented on the funereal pall the general's festivities had cast over the rest of the diners.

Across the table from Podge, Ameriga said nothing.

Major Blanco did not eat. She sat with her back to the wall and her arms crossed as Podge sampled roasted pork, rice and black beans and yucca con mojo. The Cuban major noted that he did not fill his belly but seemed merely to eat enough for sustenance.

"Are you not hungry, Senor Becket?" she asked.

"I had a big breakfast," Podge explained. "Plus it doesn't help my appetite to have you sitting there staring at me the whole time."

"Many of the men here are my superiors. How would it appear for me to eat with the man I am supposed to be guarding?"

"With the bash Generalissimo Fatass is throwing, who'd notice?" Podge said.

He finished his meal and refused coffee and a cigar, asking the waiter for the check which he quickly paid. They were leaving the restaurant as the wait staff backed out of the kitchen with a large birthday cake covered in pink frosting and a dozen candles. As the door closed, Podge glanced back to see the waiters wheel the cake on a serving cart out onto the veranda amid cries of delight from the general's party.

It was still early in the evening and Podge had yet to decide what he was going to do later that night. Wainwright had insisted multiple times that day that any attempt by the Red Menace to return to the base was doomed to fail. But the more he considered his options, the more he understood how limited they were.

He would have to go back. He'd at least have to try. America would send no troops to Cuba. Not with the mess still going on in Vietnam. Nuclear weapons were out of the question ninety miles from Florida. No, in the current world political climate, Washington would accept the missiles in Cuba, with perhaps a little empty bleating at the United Nations that would only serve the ego of the Soviets. The Red Menace would have to do something, whether or not it turned out to be his final act.

"You are deep in thought this evening," Major Blanco observed. They were wandering the block outside the restaurant. Podge had not even been paying attention to where they were walking, allowing Ameriga to direct his path. He realized when he looked up that they had strayed from the bright lights of the promenade and had taken a winding cobblestone path that ran beside an ancient tumbledown fortress wall.

"May I ask you something?" Ameriga said, pressing on before he could speak. She urged him with an extended hand to precede her down a staircase hewn from rock. "I do not understand this Dr. Wainwright. He is your physician, no?"

"He is my physician, yes."

"And he also is employed by your security company, not as a physician."

"If you call what he does for me work. I sometimes don't see him for years at a time. He's more like a freelance pain-in-the-ass with full benefits."

"This is what I do not understand. If he is your subordinate, why does he dare speak so freely to his employer?"

"It's the American way, baby," Podge said, glancing back. Her face had soured, and he smiled. "Thaddeus Wainwright is a very old friend. He was actually a friend of my grandfather years ago, but don't tell him I told you that. He's sensitive about his age. So, no, the kid in the mailroom can't talk to me like Wainwright does."

"I see," Ameriga droned.

Podge was not sure how she managed it, but in those two tiny words was condemnation of the entire American republican form of government.

Their path took them down to an isolated beach that was walled on three sides. Far above, well hidden from view, the general's party thundered along unseen.

"Hey, senorita, don't knock America until you've tried it. You might not think much of me, but remember we have John Wayne and Gary Cooper."

"We have el Jefe and Che," she replied.

"And despite that, I still gave you a chance, darlin'."

"You do not like our heroes, Mr. Becket, but you think even less of your own. You are here to help Fidel Castro, an enemy of your nation, enhance his security. What would your John Wayne think of that?"

The instant he heard the click of the hammer behind him, Podge knew he'd been played for a fool. It was his own fault. He should have known better. No matter how great was Ameriga's beauty, she was still a member of Fidel Castro's goon squad. Podge had been so lost in thought that he had allowed an armed Cuban soldier to nudge him to a secluded beach and he went along like a sheep to slaughter.

Podge turned around very slowly.

Ameriga's holster was empty and her automatic was clutched in a hand that did not waver an inch. The gun was pointed squarely at his stomach.

"Whoa, lady," Podge said, backing up. "I can learn to love Che. Yo amor el bloodthirsty murderer. See?"

"You left your hotel room last night," Ameriga said, her voice suddenly very cold and professional. She stepped forward, gun level. "Where did you go?"

"What? I went to bed. Geez, what the hell is this?"

Ameriga clearly did not approve of the lie. She shoved the gun barrel hard into his belly.

"Do not tell stories to me. Dr. Wainwright, your friend and employee with the large mouth, left your suite at one o'clock and went to the lobby for eighteen minutes to smoke a cigarette. While he was gone, I personally searched your room. You were not there. And so I ask again: Where did you go?" She twisted the gun barrel in emphasis.

Podge made some rapid calculations for his chances of getting off the beach in one piece, none of them good. Fortunately, luck was on his side.

High above, the general's wild birthday celebration suddenly kicked into high gear. A ranking diplomat had brought fireworks and chose that precise moment to begin lighting them. When twin streaks of green flame whistled off the veranda, Ameriga glanced instinctively up and Podge made his move.

He dug his heel into the sand, slapped the gun with one hand and pivoted out of the way when, by accident or deliberately, Ameriga's finger pulled back the trigger.

The gunshot cracked loudly through the warm night air but was drowned out by another spiraling rocket, this one flaming red, that screamed off the restaurant balcony and whizzed through the air after the first pair of green fireworks. Ameriga's bullet struck the soft sand of the beach as the partygoers screamed and applauded with delight.

Even as the fireworks were twirling off over the water, trailing hissing streams of sparks in their wake, Podge was snatching Ameriga's gun and snapping her wrist down against his knee. Her hand sprung open and before she even knew she'd been disarmed, Podge was popping out the magazine. He skimmed it out into the dark water.

"I'll just hold onto this for safekeeping, shall I?" he said, tucking the gun into his waistband.

The next rocket to soar from the veranda was like a wayward comet and flashed a streak of white over the secluded beach. The brief light revealed a wild fury in Ameriga's eyes, fury that any man, let alone this particular American, had so easily disarmed her.

"You are not what you pretend to be," she insisted. "This man in red whom everyone searched for. He appeared last night during the time you were missing from your hotel room. I suspect that I did not search your room as well as I should have."

"Lady, I have no idea what you're even talking about. I'm here at the invitation of your fearless leader. For Pete's sake, you're the one who flew over and picked me up in Africa, remember? I was only happy to stay there with my cannibal buddy Idi."

"I believe you were in Africa under false pretenses. I believe that you were there to trick Castro into inviting you to Cuba. I believe you are the man this Russian Colonel Strankov fears, this Red Menace. Now give back my gun to me, you fool," Ameriga snapped, holding out her hand. "Before someone comes along and shoots you."

"Oh, well, since you put it that way," said Podge, nodding very reasonably. He heaved the gun into the ocean where it made a little far-off splash.

"Idiot American," she snarled. She tried to slap him across the face, but he caught her by the wrist and replaced her hand at her side.

Ameriga allowed him to hold her wrist a fraction of a second longer than she should have, and when she finally pulled away it lacked her usual forcefulness. He smiled down at her, their faces now mere inches away.

"I'm a big fan of flattery," Podge said.

She was perspiring, and it had nothing to do with her anger or the warm night air.

Her chest heaved as she gulped air and her face was flushed. She pushed him away, but the shove was almost gentle, and she took a step back.

"We are on the same side. Did it not occur to you that I could have reported everything I just told you to my superiors at any time today? If I had, they would be torturing you for the truth right now. Although your torturer would have to be someone other than Captain Suarez, since you somehow poisoned him this morning."

Clearly Podge had underestimated the young major's intelligence. He knew with certainly that she had not seen him poison Suarez's coffee at breakfast, but still she had managed to deduce it. The same went for her figuring out his real reason for helping Idi Amin in Africa. And it was true that a loyal Cuban major would have had him dragged to one of Castro's torture chambers if they even suspected the true identity of the Red Menace. Since the truth would have eventually come out of him under torture, there was a better than fifty percent chance she was telling the truth. Still…

"So you're not a loyal Castroite," he said. "So what does that make you?"

Her face was deeply shadowed, and she glanced around as if the very air might hear. When she spoke, she kept her voice so low Podge could scarcely hear her over the pounding of the surf behind and the party above.

"My tio, my uncle, was Juan Carlos Pena, a friend of this Red Menace from many years ago. He raised me for a time after my parents died. He was murdered a month ago. I do not know why they killed him. The records were closed even to someone with my security clearance."

Podge remembered Juan Carlos well from several visits the Red Menace had made to the island nation back in the Fifties. He did not know that Juan Carlos had been killed. But the timing was right. He had probably aided Jeb Wilson and MIC, and wound up with a bullet in the brain for his trouble. "So, you love America now, just like that? I knew it. No one can be as hostile as you pretend to be without harboring some deep-seated lust. What got you? Our purple mountain majesties? The Liberty Bell's curves?"

"*America*," she snarled. A glob of spit rose in her throat and she expelled it into the sand. "My uncle was nearly killed because of America's betrayal at the Bay of Pigs. I have no love for your country, make no mistake." Her chest puffed out proudly, nearly bursting the buttons on her tight-fitting uniform. "I love Cuba. I love her people. And for that, I hate Castro and his filthy Russian allies and all they have done to bring her to ruin. Still, I am only one. I cannot hope to make the change for better. Until I find out this Red Menace, this great shadow of death my uncle spoke of, has returned to Cuba. "

"That's going to be a problem for you, sister, since I heard from a guy at breakfast that this spy you must be talking about was killed. Drowned or something."

"So my superiors they think," she replied. "They have called off the search for him, but we are still meant to be looking for the allies."

Podge thought of Wainwright. The doctor was out somewhere right now trying to wheedle information out of Strankov's favorite mad scientist. He was probably safe wherever he was. Whatever Plassko was playing at with that bacteria, it was a side issue. The greatest threat right now was the nukes. Besides, Wainwright would be subtle in his questioning of Plassko and knew enough not to draw the attention of Cuban authorities. On the other hand, Wainwright would be furious at Podge for that which the younger man was contemplating.

 Wainwright would say Podge was crazy for trusting the girl. His old friend would surely bring up Vegas, Olga Cherblonya, and the massive scar on Podge's torso. But Podge also knew that Major Ameriga Blanco was probably his only chance of getting back onto the Russian missile complex. In the end, reward outweighed risk.

"So the Cubans think the Red Menace is dead," he said. "What about the Russians?"

"That I do not know. They still have the body. Up there, with Strankov. The Russian is demented. I am afraid what he will do with those missiles. Yes, do not pretend you do not know about the missiles," she snarled. "If he fires them at the United States, this could be the end of Cuba, of my home."

Another round of fireworks shot off the balcony, whizzing crazy circles through the star-flecked sky. The light illuminated hot tears in Ameriga's eyes.

Podge nodded. "Okay, if the Red Menace is alive, he'd probably want help getting up there. Think you can do that?"

Ameriga sniffled and nodded. "Si."

Podge rubbed his palms together. "Well, what are we waiting for? Let's *vaya con dios*, darlin'"

STRANKOV WAS marching aimlessly down one of the many underground corridors that crisscrossed beneath the Cuban jungle. While this indolence aggravated him, Ivan Strankov was a logical creature. He understood that there was nothing he could do at this stage but wait for the scientists to finish their work.

Of course, there was the matter of Oleg Plassko. The irritating little fat man had gone missing at a crucial time. Oh, his work on the bacteria was finished, and engineers were responsible for constructing the encasements for his great creation, but Plassko still should have been at the base. Strankov would deal with the scientist once the rockets were on their way to the United States. If it had not been for the absentminded fool's accidental release of the bacteria a month ago, the Red Menace would have remained in retirement. Not that it mattered much now. The shark-eaten body that had been discovered was surely that of Strankov's old nemesis. As the hours passed and the end drew near, it had been easy for Strankov to convince himself this was the case. Yes, the Red Menace was gone. Soon, too, would be the nation he had loved so dearly. And then Strankov himself would follow into the abyss.

Strankov had decided only in the last hour that these would be the last hours of his life. There would be no parades in his honor. Moscow would not understand. Nor would he wait for the cancer to claim him. If Russia survived after the unprovoked attack on America, he would not allow the Politburo to dispatch their Cuban lackeys to clap him in irons. No, Strankov's end would come at his own hand.

He felt the weight of his automatic against his thigh as he walked. One bullet, through the roof of the mouth. Oblivion.

Strankov kept his hands clasped behind his back as he walked. He liked the cool, windowless subterranean corridors. It was almost like strolling through his own tomb.

The colonel allowed himself a rare smile, which vanished when the voice chimed in behind him.

"Comrade Colonel Strankov!" The Ukranian base physician was red-faced and sweating as he ran up to the base commander. He clutched a single sheet of paper in his sweating hand. "My autopsy findings on the body the Cubans discovered. I knew you would want to see this as soon as possible, comrade colonel."

Strankov snatched the paper. When he scanned it, the ghastly purple flesh of his face paled. "Are you absolutely certain?" he demanded.

The physician nodded. "He was no older than twenty-six. I have checked with my counterparts in the Cuban military, and they say a young soldier of that age disappeared last night while on patrol. He and his jeep, both vanished."

Strankov crumpled the paper and pressed it against the doctor's chest. He was beyond rage, beyond fear. Yellowed eyes twitched back and forth, looking at everything and seeing nothing.

He thought of the missiles, only one so far ready for launch. Of the bullet in the chamber of his automatic. In whose brain would that bullet now end up?

Strankov turned wordlessly. The Ukranian physician watched the base commander hustle away down the hallway. As the doctor smoothed the crumpled autopsy report, he made a mental prediction. One week. Ten days at most, and it would be the sickly old former Motherland director lying on his autopsy table.

The doctor pocketed the report and listened to Strankov's footfalls fade in the distance.

21

WAINWRIGHT drove Plassko's car to the foot of the jungle hills. They were stopped twice by Cuban military patrols. Fortunately, Wainwright's Russian was good enough for the Russian speaking Cuban soldier in the first instance and his phony Russian accent was good enough for the English speaking Cuban soldier the second. Plassko dozed much of the ride in the passenger seat with his face pressed against the window. He became alert only long enough to growl at the soldiers and wave his credentials.

"Uneducated witnits," he said to Wainwright the second time before passing out in the puddle of drool that stained his necktie.

The beefed up patrols confirmed Wainwright's earlier fears. It would be next to impossible for the Red Menace to sneak back onto the base this night.

Before the first Soviet checkpoint, Wainwright fished in his black bag and produced a small vial of liquid. The contents had an acrid, minty odor. He waved the bottle under Plassko's nose and the Russian's eyes popped open wide.

"What is—?" He blinked the drowsiness away and glanced around. "Ah, yes, yes. Very good, very good."

"I think it would be better if you drive the rest of the way," Wainwright suggested.

"Of course, of course," Plassko agreed. The scientist was quick and alert as he darted around the car and hopped happily behind the wheel.

Wainwright corked the vial and slipped it back in his bag. The special smelling salts were not bottled sobriety. The Russian's brain would be greatly stimulated for only half an hour, and after that the liquor crash would be fast and severe. He hoped it would be enough time.

At the Russian checkpoints, no one questioned Wainwright's presence in the car. Plassko was waved through almost without having to slow down.

It was clear to Wainwright that Plassko was expected at the base, and since all the guards appeared to be aware of the fact, and none were willing to stop Plassko even for a minute to search his car or question his passenger, Wainwright could only assume that he was wanted at the top. Strankov.

The fat little scientist was thankfully oblivious to the fact that his presence was required by the base commander. He parked near his quarters and rushed Wainwright over to the bunker.

"Come along, hurry, hurry!" he insisted, waddling between the two sentries at the door. "Ignore them." The scientist's general urgency and the fact that he was hustling his guest along in Russian was enough to allay any suspicions of guards who had no desire to interfere with Colonel Ivan Strankov's orders.

The stairs and the hallway were blessedly free of Russian or Cuban military all the way to the door of Plassko's lab. Florescent lights flickered on, revealing a large subterranean pair of connected rooms.

Plassko hustled his guest through the main room with its flourishing tanks of plants to a long back greenhouse made bright with artificial light. There were tables here to work on, and cabinets and shelves spaced evenly all around. The workspace was a far cry from Plassko's cramped office at the university.

Many of the tanks were sealed tightly and contained wilted stubs of plants, the results of Plassko's experiments.

As Wainwright passed a table on which was carefully arranged dozens of tools, he slipped an object into his palm unseen and continued on after the Russian scientist.

"Have you ever grown tomatoes?"

"Yes," Wainwright said, a hint of impatience in his voice. He placed his black bag on a workbench. "And not without difficulty, since they weren't eaten in my time."

Plassko frowned. "What you mean? Man, he has been eating the tomatoes for centuries."

"A numskull with a fat yap by the name of John Gerard convinced everyone they were poisonous." Wainwright waved a hand in the air and glanced back into the outer room and the hallway door. "Forget it. Immaterial. And, frankly, I have neither the time nor the energy to pretend to find you scintillating any longer, you execrable communist globoid. Strankov's thugs could be looking for you at any moment."

Plassko was not certain, but he thought he might have just been insulted. And how did this American know of Colonel Strankov? He was going to ask, even got so far as to open his mouth, when the tall man who had been so friendly all day long suddenly did something that could only be interpreted as very unfriendly indeed.

Wainwright grabbed the fat little scientist and spun him around, pinning his ample belly against the workbench. Before Plassko could protest, Wainwright clamped one strong hand over the Russian's mouth. Something silver flashed in the doctor's free hand, the object he had surreptitiously picked up from the outer room. Up and sharply down, the blades of the pruning shears impaled the back of Plassko's hand, pinning the scientist to the bench. He screamed but the sound was muffled by Wainwright's hand.

"That is only a little pain," Wainwright whispered in the Russian's ear. "I can deliver you from this little pain, or I can increase it." He twisted the shears and the Russian gasped as his watering eyes widened like saucers. "I'm going to let you speak now. If you call for help, someone may come. If they do, I will kill you before they can save you. If no one hears you, I will punish you for shouting. Either way, shouting will make things worse for you. Do you understand?" Plassko nodded desperately. "Good." Wainwright released his grip on the scientist's mouth. "You drooled on my hand," he said, wiping his palm on the back of the botanist's jacket. "Godless savages."

"What do you want?" Plassko whispered hoarsely.

"I know you've weaponized the bacteria. I know it attacks every living plant and I know you're loading it onto the missiles here to launch at the United States."

"How—"

"You're a loquacious drunk — a boring one at that — and *I* am a genius," Wainwright explained. "Where is the bacteria stored?"

"Here. In lab. Over there." He pointed to a series of ordinary General Electric refrigerators which were lined against the wall.

Wainwright hustled over and popped one of the doors. There were dozens of vials of the green goo that the Red Menace had brought to the Revolucion Grande in the early hours that morning. "No more back in Russia? Nowhere else in the world?"

"No. Here alone. Two small refrigerators out front. This is all."

Wainwright opened the doors on the next three fridges. The shelves and freezer compartments had been removed to free up space within them. Two of the fridges contained barrel-sized containers of the green substance. The third was empty. Wainwright spun to Plassko and stabbed an angry thumb at the empty fridge.

"They must have loaded up in first missile already," the Russian said, rapidly replying to Wainwright's unasked question. He had tried to pull his hand free when Wainwright's back was turned, but the pain was too great. There was blood all over the workbench. Plassko detested the sight of blood. His eyes welled with tears.

"How soon until Strankov launches the missiles?"

"Hours, if first one is all set to go. Work on other two, this is quickly done. Quickly. By dawn, surely." Plassko was practically balling. "Please let me go. I only do what Strankov tells me to do. I am just man of science, like you."

Wainwright's lip curled in disgust. He was grateful at that moment that he was not armed, for he might not have been able to stop himself from putting a bullet between the eyes of the blubbering Russian botanist. As it was, he marched over to Plassko in three big strides, grabbed the cowering scientist by the lapels and hauled him to his tiptoes until the two men were nose-to-nose. Wainwright's jaw was clenched and he glared fury down at the trembling Oleg Plassko.

"Tell me how I kill the bacteria," Wainwright snarled, "and it is just possible that I might — and I stress *might* — not kill you along with it."

And as much as he had always feared Colonel Ivan Strankov, Dr. Oleg Plassko realized that he had finally met a man far more frightening, and that maybe, just maybe, he should have found happiness after all in his tiny office at the Universidad de Habana.

AMERIGA HAD little trouble driving the supply truck up through the checkpoints and onto the Soviet missile base. Her security clearance was high and the Russians on the base viewed the native Cubans as an unworthy servant caste. Her presence in the cab was scarcely acknowledged and the bed and undercarriage given perfunctory searches each time she was waved further along up the hillside.

Only one guard dog at the last blockade sniffed the air and growled and she held her breath and thought they had been found out, but when the Russians searched the truck they found only food, lumber and tools.

At the missile base she found an isolated area beside the supply depot. She backed the truck under a canopy of camouflage netting and cut the lights and engine.

The back of the truck was covered by a tough canvas roof. If the Russians had inspected more closely, they might have seen the extra bulge in the center of the canvas.

Ameriga grabbed hold of the upholstery in the far corner near the cab and yanked hard. Silver snappers tore away one-by-one revealing a second layer of canvas. Sandwiched in between was a masked figure.

The Red Menace swung down from the steel crossbars where he had been silently perched since Ameriga had sealed him inside in Havana.

The visible part of his face glistened with sweat and his limbs were sore and stiff. For what seemed like the hundredth time in the past two days, he reminded himself that his muscles would not have been so slow to respond in the old days.

"Are you not well?" Ameriga whispered, taking his elbow as if he were an elderly patient in an old folks home.

"Oh, yeah, thanks," the Menace said dryly, shaking her hand loose. "That just helps one whole whoopee of a lot."

The blood flowed back and the pins and needles fled. The Menace shrugged his shoulders and, satisfied that his arms and legs were fine, crept to the back of the truck and dropped quietly to the ground. Ameriga grunted as she climbed down the squeaking bumper. He shot her a silencing glare and held a gloved finger to his lips.

Luck was on their side. Security was greatest at the checkpoints outside the base. Inside was no worse than it had been the previous night. The dead Cuban soldier he had left in the water had done his job. Strankov must have fallen for the Red Menace's ruse, or at least the Menace had cast enough doubt that the Russian colonel had relaxed just a hair too much. Age and ill health had not diminished the great arrogance of Colonel Ivan Strankov.

The chainsaws had fallen silent and the steady streams of trucks that had been hauling brush onto the base had stopped, this despite the fact that Plassko's circle of dead jungle remained only partly covered. Strankov was no longer worried about camouflage which, the Menace knew, could only mean there was little time left before the three missiles were sent screaming from their silos.

As the Red Menace had feared, the base lights were all burning brightly. Swarms of insects crazily attacked the air around post-mounted spotlights, and floodlights on every corner of every building bathed the entire hilltop in amber.

Foot patrols, some with German shepherds, marched around the perimeter of light, their gazes directed outward to the jungle. They did not see the masked man already in their midst as he stole across the ground, darting from building to building, until he reached the edge of the missile field.

In the jungle it was midnight, but at the silos it might well have been noon. Every light in the area was directed across the three silos. All the netting and harvested foliage had been stripped away and dumped in clumsy piles around the field. There was nothing above the three silos but the clear sky and the vast panoply of Caribbean stars.

"There," the Red Menace whispered to Ameriga.

Their backs were pressed against the side wall of a corrugated metal outbuilding.

The Cuban major was panting heavily and seemed irritated that the Menace was not.

When she peeked around the corner of the shed, she saw a lonely Cuban soldier guarding what looked like the opening of a concrete culvert.

"What is it?" she asked.

"A vent for a missile," he explained as he slipped his gun from its holster. "More importantly, it's our way inside."

Before he could take aim at the soldier, she grabbed his hand and shook her head fiercely. "That man has done nothing wrong," she hissed. "I will not kill a Cuban innocent and I will not permit you to do so unless absolutely necessary."

The Red Menace frowned. "See, this is what happens when you let girls into the treehouse." He reset the dial on his gun, insisted with a silent nod that she could trust him, and took aim at the unsuspecting guard.

The soft pop was audible only to Ameriga and the Menace. Near the concrete vent, the shocked Cuban soldier grabbed his chest and doubled over. Over at the shed, the Red Menace holstered his gun and grabbed Ameriga's hand. They were darting across the open space as the unconscious soldier collapsed to the ground.

The vent was sharply angled, with iron rods embedded in the concrete to form a ladder. Ameriga went in first and the Menace followed, dragging the young Cuban conscript after him. He hooked the unconscious soldier to one of the rods just out of eyesight of anyone who might be peering down from above.

The air grew colder the deeper they climbed and they exited into semidarkness at the back of a large chamber. As Ameriga climbed from the vent, the soft echo of her scuffling feet signaled a very high ceiling.

There was enough ambient light entering the cylindrical room from various points of entry for the Red Menace to see the shadowy shape of the Shevchenko II rocket. The exterior was a series of gray panels accessed by a stairs and catwalks. The nosecone with its nuclear payload and the silo doors far above were obscured by shadows.

"We are lucky they were not here," Ameriga whispered.

"Luck had nothing to do with it," the Menace said, his tone businesslike as he hustled to the metal stairs. "They're working on the second missile now. They're already finished with the first."

"How do you know?"

"You've got eyes, haven't you?" he whispered back as he mounted the stairs. Ameriga stole up swiftly behind him. "Silo doors were partly open on the first missile, but not much activity around it. They're done with that one and it's ready to go. Silo doors were still closed on the second and lots of activity. They're working on that one right now. Nothing happening around this one, so they haven't gotten this far yet. We still have time to stop at least one."

They were on the first platform at the side of the missile. The Menace ran his glove across the smooth surface. He found a panel and popped it open. Inside was an overstuffed Crayon box of colored wires, both fat and thin.

"Do you know how to disarm a nuclear missile?" Ameriga asked.

"Sure thing," the Menace said. "I've done it a couple of times before. It's pretty easy once you've got the knack for it."

He reached in with both gloves and proceeded to rip out colored wires, dumping them like half-cooked spaghetti on the metal grate at his feet.

He ordered Ameriga to gather up every last scrap of wire, and she drew it all into her arms as quickly as he yanked it from the missile. Once he was finished, he shut the panel and found another. More wires spilled to the platform and Ameriga dutifully gathered up every piece. He moved up a level and started work again.

"This bird is grounded," he finally whispered when he finished with a fourth panel, clicking it shut. "It'll take them weeks to fix it. Knowing the Russkies, it could be decades. After all, they just discovered the wheel last Thursday. Maybe Washington can put some pressure on Moscow before then."

Ameriga sneered behind her bundles of wires. "Washington."

"Hey, don't blame me, lady. I only work here. Besides, with two birds still ready for liftoff there might not be a Washington after tomorrow. And I guarantee you that all the spineless, sniping whingers who've made a career of grousing about us are suddenly going to realize how much they miss D.C. when it's gone."

They made their stealthy way back down the metal stairs and into the hallway. Ameriga was stepping into a corridor when the Red Menace suddenly grabbed her by the arm and yanked her back into the shadows, flinging his cape over her head.

Before she could ask, Ameriga heard the soft shuffle of approaching boots. She held her breath as the patrol grew closer.

She had made a pouch from her untucked shirttails in order to carry the wires, and from her vantage point she could see that one of the wires had fallen to the floor. The thin blue wire with the shiny copper ends sat in the full light of the main corridor, directly in the path of the approaching boots. Ameriga made a move to collect the wire, but a strong hand held her firmly in place. A voice in her ear was less than a whisper. One word: "Wait."

The Red Menace slowly slipped his gun from its holster.

The two soldiers appeared. Russians. Eyes locked ahead as they marched along. They passed over the bit of wire without seeing it and continued down the hall. The Red Menace released Ameriga and slid his gun back in its holster.

She hustled out and retrieved the wire. "We need to get rid of these."

The Red Menace found a side corridor with a lone office at the dead end. He guarded the door as Ameriga dumped the wires in the trash basket under the desk.

"Now comes the tricky part," he said.

The Red Menace took the lead, and the two intruders stole back out to the main hallway. Sliding along single file, the unlikely allies that were Cuba's Major Ameriga Blanco and America's Red Menace crept off in the direction of the second missile silo.

OLEG PLASSKO directed Dr. Wainwright to a wall of cupboards in which was stored many white plastic drums. The sloshing liquid inside was clear. When he popped the lid, he noted that the liquid smelled faintly of what could only be described as pungent, medicinal chocolate.

"Is substance I create to destroy bacteria. Only other thing I have luck with is irradiating bacteria in lab. Killed bacteria, but dosage needed also killed plants as well. That is safe. Kills bacteria and is safe for plants. Is good, da?"

"Is good we shall see," Wainwright droned.

Wainwright quickly poured some of the liquid into a large stainless steel container from his bag. With luck, he would be able to figure out what was in it and mass-produce the substance in the United States, should the nightmare come to that.

Once he was finished and the large container was safely stashed in the recesses of his black bag, Wainwright loaded some more of the clear substance into a spray bottle. He smashed one of the small vials from the first fridge onto the cement floor and pumped the clear chocolate liquid on the puddle of bacterial goo. The instant the spray hit the Jello-like substance, the puddle changed from ominous green to crusty brown.

"Is fast to be working," Dr. Plassko volunteered.

Wainwright became like a madman. Racing back and forth, he smashed vial after vial of the green substance, spraying the antibacterial liquid on the growing smear of brown on the floor. The two large containers for the missiles were impossible for him to move alone. He managed to pry the stainless steel lids open and dumped bottles of the killer medicinal chocolate directly into the containers. The liquid moved through the thick bacteria like drain cleaner through a clog, clearing it to transparent for a brief moment before transforming the contents of each tube an ugly brown.

"More out there, you say?"

"The last of it. Last in world," Plassko lamented. He was weeping openly again, but not for his injured hand. His tears had only gotten worse as he watched his life's work, his baby, poured out and murdered on the floor before his very eyes.

Wainwright found the two little fridges from which the Red Menace had taken his specimen. He wheeled them back into the rear greenhouse.

The doctor noted on his return that some of the plants on the shelves and in open tanks had begun to wither. The bacteria not only traveled from plant to plant, it was carried through air as well.

"You are insane," he snarled at Plassko. With renewed vigor he attacked the last of the bacteria in the Russian's lab. "How long would it have taken for this monstrous substance to wipe out the United States?"

The stimulant Wainwright had given Plassko at the base of the hill had begun to wear off. Plassko was lapsing once more into a boozy fog. "With tanks in three missiles, and missiles spaced across North American continent, I estimate no more than three weeks before American heartland dead of crops," the Russian slurred. "Now that you destroy large containers meant to go in missiles, Strankov, he has only one rocket left. Still, not to worry. If it lands in center of continent, it will reach coasts and destroy small vegetation by month three or four. Larger specimens like trees will die at slower rate as bacteria works into deep roots. Plants at higher elevations could last longer. Sequoias, large trees, they will take more time. But all will be dead in eight months, perhaps one year. By the time large trees die, America will already be starving, beggar nation." Plassko seemed to notice for the first time the shears that harpooned his chubby hand. "Oh, my. Is bad," he said, giggling.

"Heaven deliver us," Wainwright muttered.

He was finished. The concentrated bacteria was destroyed. Yet some had been released into the air in the room. The plants in all the nearer tanks had withered to brown, and the invisible killer was moving rapidly from tank to tank. If it escaped from this room and into the jungle outside, it could mean the end to Cuba.

Fortunately, there was a sprinkler system installed in the ceiling to care for the larger plants. Wainwright hooked the tanks of antibacterial liquid directly into the pipe that fed up to the crisscrossed network of tubes and nozzles.

"You knew what he had planned all along and still helped Strankov," the doctor said as he worked.

"Oh, yes, yes," Plassko said. "A hero of the Revolution. Back from exile." He was having a hard time standing on his feet and he sank woozily down onto his fat rear end, his arm and pinned hand extended above his head. Blood trickled from his wrist down to his armpit. "Ahhh, is good," he sighed, relaxing on the floor.

Wainwright turned a nozzle on the wall and a fine mist of antibacterial formula diluted in water rained down on the lab. He peered intently at the plants that had been visibly wilting in the open tanks. Where the mist landed, the wilting stopped. Once he was convinced the room was clean, he shut off the sprinklers.

Wainwright's clothes were lightly damp, as from a heavy fog, as he crossed back over to Plassko.

The Russian was still sitting on the now wet floor, seemingly oblivious to everything that had just transpired in the room. Plassko was singing an old Russian folk song when Wainwright pulled the gardening shears out of his hand.

"Oh," Plassko said, smiling at his bloody hand. "Thank you, kind sir." He lapsed back into oblivious song.

"I took an oath a long time ago to do no harm," Wainwright said, more to himself than to the humming Russian at his feet. "But almost as long ago I realized that there are men who would do the entire world harm if given a chance. Back then they did not have the means to do so. But now…"

Wainwright took a deep breath, locked eyes with the drunken man on the floor, and plunged the bloody shears deep into Plassko's heart. The botanist gasped, blood spitting from between his lips. He grabbed feebly at the handles of the shears but at first could not seem to find them, and when he finally reached them his fingers no longer had strength to grab on. And then he suddenly no longer seemed to care. Plassko's face went blank in death and he pitched forward onto the floor.

Wainwright felt nothing for the dead man who would have murdered an entire continent of people, possibly annihilate the population of the entire world. He had a more urgent matter with which to deal. How to destroy the last drum of the bacterial weapon and stop this ultimate evil from being unleashed on the world.

He grabbed up a large bottle of the antibacterial liquid and stuffed it in his bag. The bottle was too large and he could not fasten the snaps.

How the devil he was going to get through a hundred Russian and Cuban troops to a Soviet nuclear missile silo and somehow dose Colonel Ivan Strankov's makeshift warhead with a bottle of Ovaltine was, it pained Wainwright to admit, beyond him.

At least he could thank the Almighty that he'd probably be killed long before he had to admit this limitation to Patrick Becket.

Wainwright realized the instant he opened the door to the laboratory that his end would likely come much sooner than even he had anticipated.

He pulled the handle only a little so that he could peer out the narrowest of cracks for approaching enemies in the hall. Wainwright had not anticipated that at that very moment there were three soldiers standing just outside the lab door.

The Russian soldier who had been pushing the handle nearly stumbled into the room when the door was unexpectedly pulled open. The Red Army man's eyes grew wide when he spotted the stranger, and wider still when he saw the ruined lab and the distant body of Oleg Plassko lying in a pool of blood.

"Sukin sin!" the Russian swore, grabbing for his sidearm.

Wainwright yanked the door further open and thrust it back again sharply, cracking it hard into the side of the young man's head. The woozy soldier stumbled back and dropped to one knee in the hall and Wainwright slammed the door shut.

In that fraction of an instant when the door was open he had seen the other two soldiers wrenching guns from holsters.

There was no lock on the lab door. Wainwright had no gun of his own. Nothing convenient with which to block the door.

A shouted grunt outside and the door popped open an inch. Wainwright threw his back against it, slamming it shut. Pounding on the door. More shouting. The door hopped and jumped like a bucking bronco as the soldiers tried to force their way in.

Wainwright thrust his hand into his bag, digging desperately beyond the big bottle of antibacterial liquid. His hand clutched at a round object fastened to the corner of the bag and he wrenched it loose. It was small, only as big as a change purse.

The gas bomb would kill the Russians, surely. Wainwright was immune to the poison, and indeed to most every poison. But Dr. Thaddeus Wainwright was not immune to bullets, and the gas was not so fast-working that all three soldiers would succumb before they all managed to squeeze off a dozen shots.

The door stopped hopping behind him. They were uniting for a final assault. He could not hope to hold them out. Still, Wainwright braced his shoulders hard against the door and set his feet firmly on the floor, gas bomb at the ready.

A pop from the hallway. Then another, and another.

Gunfire. They were trying to shoot their way in. But if that was the case, why did he not feel the vibrations of the bullets through the metal door?

Shouts in Russian. Panic. Fear.

Wainwright did not hear that which silenced the Russians. He only heard the three automatics become two, then one, then none.

Then silence for an infinitely long moment.

An instant later, an urgent rap on the laboratory door.

"Ding-dong, Avon calling," a muffled voice called from outside.

Wainwright could not believe his ears. He spun around, grabbing the handle.

He tore the lab door open and for the briefest moment a look of uncharacteristic shock passed the doctor's face, for in the hallway he found standing amid the three fallen Russian soldiers not only the familiar masked figure in brilliant red, but also the quite unexpected sight of Major Ameriga Isabella Blanca.

"Do I have to explain?" the Red Menace asked, nodding to Ameriga as he hurriedly dragged a dead Russian soldier into the room.

"Would I prefer if you didn't?" Wainwright asked, frowning.

"Pretty much, yeah," said the Red Menace. "And it'd free up time for Shemp and me to hide these moldy bodies in the dumbwaiter. We're kind of at a dead end here, doc, so maybe no one heard the gunshots. I think they'd be here by now if they had."

"Get out of way," Ameriga commanded. She already had the second Russian corpse by the wrists and she dragged it roughly past Wainwright into the lab.

The Red Menace hurried out and pulled the third dead man into the room and Wainwright quickly shut the door behind them. He clipped the gas bomb back into the corner of his bag as the others dragged the bodies behind a lab table.

"Lucky we stumbled on you when we did," the Red Menace said, trotting back over to the door. He pulled it open and glanced up and down the hall. It was clear.

Ameriga hustled over and wordlessly slapped into Wainwright's hand one of the guns she had liberated from a dead Russian soldier. He rolled his eyes heavenward. "I should have stayed in Ceylon," the doctor sighed.

The Menace ignored him. "We'd been following those Russkies at a distance," he said, pulling his head back into the room. "They weren't in a hurry. Looks like they were just looking for Plassko, so I don't think we've been found out yet. Still, we'd better get a move on, just in case. What's with the Clorox bottle?" He nodded to the plastic jug jutting from the top of Wainwright's bag.

"For the missile," Wainwright explained, patting the side of his satchel.

"I don't think we need to bother washing them, doc," the Menace droned. "Radiation tends to kill most household germs."

The doctor gave a patronizing little sigh. "So you still think it's *only* nuclear weapons we're dealing with here, do you?"

Wainwright clucked his tongue and was shaking his head pityingly as he ducked out into the hall. Ameriga slipped out behind him, gun drawn and dark eyes alert to any movement up or down the long corridor.

Alone in the lab, the Red Menace shook his head. He had been trying so many times in recent days to convince himself that things had changed in the decade since he had last donned his costume, but the truth was this was exactly how he remembered it.

"He was an insufferable pain in the neck back then too," he muttered to himself.

The Red Menace snapped the wall switch, dousing the main lab lights, and hustled out into the hallway after Ameriga and Dr. Wainwright.

22

Colonel Ivan Strankov was calm by the time he reached his office. The autopsy report had rattled him, but the fact that the Red Menace had pulled a switch with the body fished from the bay was irrelevant. There was no sneaking onto the base. The jungle was loaded with soldiers, the cliff face down to the sea was now awash in floodlight beams and there were armed checkpoints all along the only road up to the base.

So, the Red Menace was alive. It would not matter. The missiles would not be stopped. By morning Strankov would strike America and the nation the Red Menace loved so dearly would begin a months-long decay that would inevitably end in death. Perhaps it was a good thing the Red Menace would live to see the United States die. How painful a thing would it be to him to watch the nation rot and its people starve.

Strankov snapped on the lights in his office and strode behind his desk, snatching up the bulky black phone and stabbing out a three-digit base code.

"Major Grynko, Colonel Strankov. I want all of your men on duty." As he listened to the major's reply, Strankov stuffed the phone between his shoulder and ear and took a fresh pack of cigarettes from his desk drawer. "Yes, wake the men off duty. I said I want them all, major. There were several in the infirmary earlier." A pause to listen as he peeled the cellophane from around the pack and tapped one cigarette loose. "I do not care, get them out of bed and back to work," he said as he stuck a cigarette between his purplish lips. "The American terrorist who attacked us last night is still alive and I want every man available with a gun in his hand and on patrol at once. Concentrate on the perimeter. Contact the Cubans for reinforcements, troops who are familiar with the terrain." A struck match and the unfiltered cigarette flamed to life. "We launch by dawn and he must not be allowed—" Strankov paused.

He had reached to stuff the cellophane and dead match in the trash can under his desk, but the small wastebasket was already full.

"Colonel? Comrade Colonel Strankov?" the small voice of Major Grynko called from out the phone receiver.

Strankov fished around blindly in the wastebasket and threw the mysterious trash onto his blotter. His jaw dropped when he saw the multicolored wires. Strankov flung the phone down, pulled the wastebasket up onto the desk. It was filled practically to overflowing with wires. Eyes wild, Strankov grabbed the phone.

"Pull your men back from the perimeter! He is here! The Red Menace is here!"

Strankov slammed down the phone and leapt to his feet, drawing his sidearm. There was more than one bullet now in the clip. Before he buried a round in his own brain, fate had given Strankov one final opportunity to kill his hated enemy. He would not miss that chance.

Feeling a surge of vindictive energy, Ivan Strankov raced out his office door.

23

THE Red Menace stood at the corner in Strankov's subterranean maze and peered at the quartet of soldiers lounging around an open door halfway down the corridor.

Wainwright and Ameriga held back around the corner and out of Russian eyesight. The Menace's cape and mask shielded him in shadow at a distance, but the others would be sitting ducks if the soldiers spotted them.

"We must find another way around," Ameriga hissed.

"Either we go around or we go through, but we can't linger," Wainwright whispered. "I elect we go through."

The Red Menace shook his head firmly. "Not through." His gun had been in his gloved hand, but he holstered it and turned his back on the soldiers, shooing Wainwright and Ameriga back in the direction from which they had come.

Wainwright sensed what was troubling his friend and stopped dead. "You can't worry about us," the doctor insisted. "You can get through those four easily. Hell, I probably can. Those missiles are of paramount importance. They cannot be allowed to take off."

Ameriga nodded firmly. "It would be the end of Cuba," she said.

"Because of course *that* would be the great tragedy in all this," Wainwright whispered. "I mean, where would all the really good bananas come from?"

Whatever angry retort she might have made which would have risked drawing the attention of every nearby soldier was forgotten in the sudden howling noise that screamed in their ears and seemed to shake the entire missile base.

Ahn-ahn! Ahn-ahn! Ahn-ahn!

Swirling lights high on the walls blazed to life all along the corridor before and behind them, flashing in time with the bellowing klaxon.

"Strankov knows we're here," the Red Menace snapped.

His gun was back in his hand.

Echoing footsteps pounded up the hallway from the direction of Plassko's lab. Many more soldiers behind than there were in front. No choice but to go forward.

The Red Menace flew up the hall and around the corner.

The four Russian soldiers who had been standing near the open door were startled by the sudden appearance of the masked figure. Three were slow, one was fast.

Bursts of fire erupted from the barrel of a single Kalashnikov rifle. Fortunately, although the Russian was quick on the draw, he was lousy with his aim. Deadly missiles tore chunks of concrete from the ceiling, sending stone dust hail scattering wildly all around the corridor. A flashing light shattered in its cage and a blaring speaker became a sparking ganglia of bullet-riddled wires.

The hail of bullets whizzed like angry hornets above the Red Menace's head, and even as he sprinted forward he felt the slugs draw closer. Ahead, the rifle bounced frantically and several bullets zipped past his right ear.

Arm up, firing as he ran. The Menace took a single shot and the wild shooter's forehead snapped back, a crimson dot at its center.

The remaining three had found their weapons. Before the others could fire, there came a loud pop, this time from behind the Menace. Up ahead a stream of red erupted from the throat of one Russian and he threw down his gun and fell to the floor.

From the corner of his eye, the Red Menace caught a glimpse of raven hair and a curl of smoke from Ameriga's pistol as she ran to keep pace with him. Wainwright sprinted along in her wake.

The two remaining Russians dove behind the open metal door. Gun barrels peered out, firing blindly up the hallway. Wainwright and Ameriga threw themselves to their bellies and the bullets screamed above their heads, chewing away at walls and ceiling.

Screaming in Spanish from around the corner at their back. The Cuban troops that had run up from the direction of Plassko's lab had reached the bend in the hallway and were caught dead by the panicked firing of the Russians. Crazed slugs chopped away at the walls.

On the floor, Wainwright jammed a hand inside his bag and tore out a poison gas bomb. His thumb flicked loose a tiny pin and he sent the round bomb rolling like a billiard ball up the hallway. It caromed off the right wall and shot at a ninety degree angle into the unseen crowd of Cuban soldiers.

Above, the Red Menace threw himself against the wall, flicked the dial on his gun and pulled the trigger. A single soft pop and he threw himself down to the floor.

The pellet smacked the iron door and the ensuing explosion wrenched the door from its hinges and sent it screaming into the Russians cowering behind it. The Red Army soldiers were lifted up and thrown back in a cloud of fire and smoke.

As the door exploded in front of them, the gas pellet detonated behind.

A cloud of noxious smoke vomited from the bend in the corridor. Cuban soldiers staggered into view, clutching their throats and falling to the floor.

Wainwright was already scrambling to his feet, already running for the ruins of the door and the dead Russians beyond.

"Go!" the doctor snapped.

From out of the cloud ran two soldiers, guns blazing. Ameriga was halfway to her feet, automatic at the ready, but when she saw the men she froze.

The soldiers were coughing, oozing sweat, yet stumbling forward. With his last dying gasps, one drew a bead on Ameriga.

A gloved hand appeared above her shoulder. Two rapid-fire shots took out the pair of charging Cuban soldiers. They tripped over each other's feet, skidded to a stop and were still in sudden, terrible death.

All around, lights still flashed and klaxons blared. A Russian voice came on the loudspeakers and barked out commands to the base.

The Red Menace snatched Ameriga's hand and yanked her to her feet, grabbing her by both shoulders.

"They would have killed you!" he snarled, giving her an angry shake.

She wrenched free of his hands. "I told you, I will not shoot Cubans."

"Lady, that kind of fuzzy-headed sentimentalism's gonna get you—"

He was interrupted by a shouted voice calling out from up ahead.

"Here! Hurry!"

Wainwright was halfway up the hall and desperately motioning for them to join him. He was crouched over one of the men thrown back by the explosion. Wainwright had dragged the twisted wreckage of the door off the soldier and was working around the body. When the Red Menace and Ameriga reached the doctor's side, they found the injured Russian was still alive.

"He says the remaining two missiles, the ones you didn't disable, are too well guarded for us to get to," Wainwright said.

"He's lying," the Red Menace replied. "There's got to be a way."

Wainwright held up a small clear vial that contained a yellow liquid. "He is *definitely* not lying," he insisted. He flung the vial and a syringe inside his bag.

"Doc, one of those missiles is loaded with that bacteria. You said we had to kill it or it'd wipe out the entire United States."

"And Canada, Mexico and eventually Central and South America. Possibly the entire world."

"So we've got to stop it. We've got to at least try. Wait a minute. The nukes.

They would have had to take out the warheads in order to install that gunk, right?"

The light flashed on in Wainwright's eyes. He spun to the dying Russian and

asked a few sharp questions in the man's native language. The battered soldier answered, pointing a feeble finger down the hallway.

Ameriga was glancing anxiously around. A voice in Spanish which had followed the Russian on the loudspeaker system was announcing that there were intruders on the base, warning that the masked man had accomplices this time, and commanding that any strangers be shot on sight.

"They know you are not alone," she told the Red Menace.

"I've got ears," he told her. To Wainwright he said. "You know where they are?"

Wainwright held up a staying finger as the Russian feebly answered his questions. "Wait...yes. Yes. I've got it."

Wainwright hopped to his feet and grabbed up his bag. The two men skipped around the wreckage and bodies and had gotten no more than a few feet when there came a loud report behind them. When they turned, they saw Ameriga stepping over the body of the man Wainwright had questioned. The soldier had a fresh bullet wound in his forehead and his mouth and eyes were wide open in death.

"He could not be permitted to tell where we are going," she insisted.

Chin held high, she stepped between the two men and headed up the hallway.

"You sure know how to pick them," Wainwright grumbled.

"What was that? I couldn't hear you over the noise of your latest divorce."

Alarms screaming a furious chorus all around, the two men sprinted up the hall after Major Ameriga Blanco.

STRANKOV STOOD on the silo's floor and glared furiously up at the men above. The panels had been opened on the Shevchenko II and the damaged wiring exposed.

"We cannot repair it in time, comrade colonel," an engineer called down.

Ivan Strankov's gun was clenched in his hand so tightly that his purple skin was white. Bony knuckles strained taut flesh.

"Red Menace," Strankov growled. His eyes burned with deep pools of fiery hate as he spun on his heel and marched from the missile silo.

One missile gone. Only two available to strike the United States. Already the
    timetable for the West's destruction had been thrown back by a third

and the Red Menace had only been back for a day.

Strankov could not delay the launch. The KGB would soon be sending a replacement for Colonel Petr Bolgevik. Strankov could not murder him too. Every second Strankov delayed risked intervention by his superiors. The KGB had many spies in Washington. Moscow must have found out by now that the Americans were aware of the base. It was all coming undone. He would have to settle for two missiles.

Plassko had prepared the other two canisters. They were ready to be loaded in place of the nuclear payloads. One more along with the missile already upgraded with a bacterial warhead would have to suffice.

Strankov's stride as he pushed himself along the hall was almost that of his younger self, yet he could feel the cold cloud of death creeping into his lungs, freezing his joints. He forged ahead, hatred warming his blood, quickening his stride.

Plassko would have to calculate the best locations for only two bacteria-laden missiles to strike the United States.

One of the engineers had heard from a guard that the botanist had returned to the base, but Plassko had not checked in.

Strankov reached Oleg Plassko's lab and his fingers were brushing the door handle when he noticed the stains on the hallway floor.

He squatted down and pressed his fingertips to one of the dark pools. They came back smeared with blood.

"No," he said, his voice a barely audible whisper.

His heart was pounding as he opened the door a crack and reached in darkness to find the light switch.

Strankov trusted his senses, and they were telling him that there was no one alive inside. Still, he stayed low and kept his gun at the ready as he crept into the room.

Blood trails on the floor led to a pile of three bodies. In the back greenhouse he found Dr. Oleg Plassko, a pair of pruning shears jutting from his chest. Nearby, the entire supply of superbacteria was a glob of jiggling brown on the cement floor. When he saw that the two large canisters which were to be loaded on his missiles were stained brown as well, Strankov released a howl of feral rage.

"Idiot! Traitor!" he screamed, pumping two rounds into Plassko's face. The seated corpse lurched to one side and tipped to the floor.

Only one missile loaded with bacteria. Only one chance remaining.

The Americans might now find a way to stop the bacteria's spread. They were infuriatingly resourceful, and they now had the time. America just might have a chance. But there was a day of reckoning for one particular American coming before that of his countrymen. For the Red Menace, there would be no tomorrow.

Weapon in hand, Strankov ran from the lab.

BULLETS PINGED off the generator and ricocheted crazily all around the corridor. Concrete dust filled the air and choked their lungs.

They had nearly reached their destination when the ambush came. Fifteen Cuban soldiers lying in wait; more seemed to spring out when the shooting started. The Red Menace and the others barely had time to dive for cover.

The bellow of the klaxon had been silenced around the base, but the warning lights continued to flash all around.

The Menace, Wainwright and Ameriga hunkered down behind the metal unit and felt the hum of steady gunfire which caused the generator to vibrate like a plucked violin string. Ameriga squatted on her haunches and pressed her hands to her ears. Her gun remained useless in its holster.

"Cover me, doc!" the Menace shouted over the din.

Wainwright stuck his gun around the concrete base of the generator and squeezed off a few rounds. The instant the doctor fired, the Red Menace was up and blasting away, scanning the hallway even as he pulled the trigger.

It was difficult to see over the dust and the flashes of gunfire. Two Cubans fell as the Red Menace's bullets found their marks. There were three other bodies already on the floor. All this and more did he see in the split second he made himself visible before he dropped back down behind the generator.

"It'd help if you pitched in," the Menace snapped at Ameriga.

"No! I am a traitor to the communists, not to Cuba!"

"I'll put that on your headstone."

"Forget her!" Thaddeus Wainwright snarled. "If you've got some bit of derring-do planned, the time would be now." As he spoke, Wainwright raised his automatic over his head and fired blindly down the hall. The doctor detested using guns, even though espionage work frequently placed one in his hand. But he especially hated using one clumsily. He preferred the scalpel to the ax.

A grunt of pain and a shout in Spanish. One of Wainwright's wild bullets had struck a Cuban soldier.

For a brief moment there was a lull in the gunfire and in that instant the Red Menace hopped up, braced his hand on top of the generator and squeezed off two quick rounds in rapid succession. Twin pops of compressed air and a pair of fat projectiles soared down the hallway. The Menace collapsed back to the floor as the firing resumed.

Through a grate in the generator's side, Wainwright saw two Cuban soldiers suddenly stop firing. The men were struggling with the hand grenades on their belts, and Wainwright could just make out the sticky black dots that the Menace had shot at both men. In a brilliant flash of yellow, the explosives in the charges detonated, the grenades to which they were attached burst apart in twin blazes of white flame and the hallway was consumed by a wave of fire, smoke and dust.

Shards of concrete clattered like hail and gruesome chunks of meat splattered down around the generator. The gunfire abruptly ceased.

"Lucky shot," Wainwright sniffed.

"Never luck, doc. Panache."

They were up and running, through the field of fallen soldiers, around a chunk of collapsed ceiling and into the a room on the right of the hall.

It was a lab, with quarters for the technicians and engineers. As the dying Russian had promised, in a chamber to one side of the laboratory they found the pair of nuclear warheads that had been harvested from two of the missiles. The Menace pulled two small objects, each the size of a deck of playing cards, from the folds of his cape and slapped the first to the casing of the warhead.

"You're sure this will do it?" he asked as he poked a few buttons.

"Plassko said low doses of radiation killed the bacteria. A high dose should take care of the last canister they've got out in that missile, and you'll get no higher than this."

"Only trick now is keeping that one poisoned bird from flying," the

Red Menace muttered. "One catastrophe at a time, I suppose."

He fastened the second object to the next warhead and entered in another code.

The items were the latest gadget from Becket Security, Inc. A small electronic brain inside the device counted down the time in Roman numerals on a small screen embedded in the side. When the clock reached zero, explosives inside would detonate, in this case triggering the nuclear warheads. The Menace set the mini-bombs to go off simultaneously in six hours, which would give them all time to get off the base and, in his and Wainwright's case, time to get off the island. It would be cutting it close, but he dared not give it more time. As it was, any moment his bombs might be discovered. He only hoped that the soldiers and civilians on the base would be so preoccupied that the charges attached to the nukes would remain undiscovered.

"You are sure those will work?" Ameriga asked, crinkling her nose suspiciously.

"Welcome to the future," the Red Menace said, winking broadly.

He shut the door on the storage room and the three of them made their way back out to the hallway.

The smoke was still thick and the slowly bulging ceiling groaned under the weight of the jungle trying to force its way down into the tunnel. Clods of wet earth fell to the corridor floor and dangling roots reached down like beggars' arms.

They would not be heading back that way.

"Only one way out," the Red Menace said.

They headed in the direction opposite the collapsing tunnel. They had taken but a few steps when the report of a single gunshot echoed through the hall. The Red Menace and Wainwright whirled as one, each man with a gun in his hand, both firing at once.

One of the Cuban soldiers had survived the explosion. The bloodied figure lay amid the ruins, propped up on a pile of jagged concrete blocks, a smoking pistol in his hand. The Menace and Wainwright's bullets caught him in the chest and the soldier hissed a final sigh of air, dropped his gun and was still.

Nearby, Ameriga wore an expression of utter bafflement. Her hand was pressed to her belly. When she removed it, her palm was slick with blood. She looked up at the Red Menace and seemed to want to say something but the words would not come, just tiny gulps of air. She collapsed. He caught her before she hit the floor.

"Doc!" the Menace yelled.

Wainwright hustled over and examined the injury. The bullet had caught Ameriga in the back, just to the right of her spine. The exit wound in the front was large beneath her torn shirt. Blood flowed freely from both sides of the wound.

Wainwright glanced somberly at the Menace and shook his head.

Wordlessly, the Red Menace picked Ameriga up in both arms and carried her down the hall. He found the stairs that led up to the control room from which he had escaped into the jungle the previous night, and once he and the others were inside he set Ameriga carefully down on the floor.

Her eyes rolled as she fought to remain conscious and her head lolled on her chest.

"I do...I do for Cuba..." she managed to breathe.

"You're a hero of the *real* revolution," the Red Menace said. He kissed her on the top of her raven hair and she flashed a weak, radiant smile.

Wainwright was across the room studying the missile controls. "Yes. Yes, it can be done." He began frantically entering commands into the computerized system.

"Hurry up, doc," the Red Menace said. "We've got to get out of here."

The window through which he had made his escape the night before had not been replaced. He was wondering how he would get Ameriga out and down the hillside.

There would be no saving her life, but he would not leave her to die alone.

Wainwright was hastily adding data into the primitive Russian computers. An urgency seemed to thrill through the grounds outside, and the Red Menace looked out the hole in the wall toward the missile field. The silo doors over the only rocket to contain a bacteria canister were slowly closing. The Red Menace heard the hard metal clunk reverberate across the wide open area. Wainwright worked feverishly at the controls and the Menace heard shouting from outside. A moment later he saw twin spouts of fire shoot out from a pair of hidden vents. Trees at the jungle's edge burst into flame.

"Not too much, remember," the Menace warned.

The plan was to close the silo doors if possible and burn off fuel in a controlled burst while the missile was still trapped below. With the silo doors closed, the missile would not achieve liftoff, and even if the Russians were able to refuel they would not be able to do so before the nukes went off, taking out the remaining bacteria and the rest of the base. It was a plan that they had rapidly cobbled together on their way through the underground maze. They had thought of everything, except for the cold voice that abruptly shouted out at them from the open control room door.

"Stop!"

It was his own fault. The Red Menace had allowed himself to be distracted by Wainwright's work and Ameriga's deteriorating condition. Seated on the floor, the Cuban major coughed a mouthful of crimson onto the front of her blouse.

"Hands off the controls. Now!" the tall figure at the door commanded. Ivan Strankov took a step into the room as Wainwright reluctantly raised his hands. "Whatever you have done you will undo or I will shoot your masked companion."

Strankov glanced at Ameriga and lifted his nose. Just another injured Cuban soldier, another Red Menace victim not worthy of Colonel Ivan Strankov's time.

"You'll shoot him no matter what I do," Wainwright suggested.

"Yes, I will," Strankov said. "Eventually. But one bullet can be merciful. Several, at multiple points, can make for most delightful torture. I assure you I know about torture. I have the scars from a Siberian exile to prove it." These last words he spoke not to Wainwright but to his great enemy, the Red Menace.

"I warned you, Strankov," the Red Menace said. "I gave you the option to keep out of this. To stay in Russia. To die an old man there. You chose to come back."

"As did you, my old...*friend*. Now throw your gun away and remove mask."

"Gee whiz, I'd love to, Boris, but it's kind of chilly in here. I don't want to catch my death." The Red Menace strained to keep eye contact with the Russian colonel, lest he telegraph that he had caught movement from the corner of his eye. On the floor, Ameriga had regained consciousness. The Cuban major was dragging her gun feebly from its holster.

Rage twisted Strankov's mouth. The Red Menace's spine grew more rigid, for an instant not knowing who would fire first, Ameriga or Colonel Strankov.

Sadly, it was Ivan Strankov.

Strankov's nose seemed to sniff the air and his eyes grew sharp. In an instant, the old soldier's instinct abruptly kicked in. If it was a soft sound or a small movement spied with Strankov's peripheral vision, the Red Menace would never know. He only knew that in one moment the Russian's gun was leveled on his chest, and in the next Strankov was wheeling on Ameriga and firing. The bullet smacked hard into her chest and she snapped back against the wall, her own gun slipping from slender fingers. She left a smeared blood trail on the cracked concrete as she slid lifeless to the floor.

Strankov's instinct for imminent danger had served him well, but only briefly. When he saw the flash of brilliant red beside him, Strankov realized he had made a grave miscalculation, that he was much slower than he once had been. His gun was wrenched from his fingers before he could fire a second shot and he felt a deep scratch on the back of his hand. Eyes growing wide, Ivan Strankov fell paralyzed to the floor.

Across the room, Wainwright stood bored, arms crossed. "Are we finished?"

"Restart that rocket, doc," the Red Menace ordered.

Wainwright held up a staying finger. "Three...two...one..."

The twin jungle vents automatically flared to life once more.

"Hmm," the doctor said, frowning. "One of the few times in my life I've been wrong. I was sure it would have taken you three seconds more to finish him."

The Menace looked down at the colonel's prone body. "Oh, he's not finished," he said. "He's got a little more work to do, starting with getting us out of here."

The Red Menace picked up Ivan Strankov. There was almost no weight to the sickly Russian. Casting a sad eye at the lifeless body of

Ameriga Blanco, he carried the former Motherland head to the window.

"Just a moment," Wainwright said, snapping his fingers impatiently. "I need those coordinates."

In all the excitement, the Red Menace had forgotten one last detail. He supplied the doctor with a set of coordinates, longitude and latitude. Wainwright hastily dumped them into the Russian system and hustled over to the masked man's side. The dead weight of Colonel Ivan Strankov blinked helplessly as his mortal enemy lifted him like an infant out the window.

As the Red Menace suspected, the alarm had cleared out the barracks. They quickly located a uniform that fit Wainwright and they found Ameriga's truck where she had left it. Wainwright took the driver's seat and the Red Menace propped Strankov up in the passenger seat before climbing into his hiding spot in the rear.

There was no doubt in the Menace's or Wainwright's minds that Strankov desired more than anything on Earth the power to scream out a warning to the succession of guards who waved them down the road, but the Russian colonel could only stare straight ahead. In this case, as had happened before in his career as Motherland director, Strankov's supreme arrogance was his undoing. None of the soldiers they passed found the colonel's haughty demeanor unusual, none dared stop him.

They departed the base with ease and headed back to Havana.

The paralytic that froze his limbs was higher than the doses the Red Menace had administered in the past. Strankov seemed to wander in and out of consciousness. He was aware of events going on around him, but seemed not a part of them. When his mind eventually began to clear he discovered that he was in a room alien to him.

It was a bedroom, expensively decorated with garish furnishings. A lone figure lay snoring beneath a veiled canopy.

The figure in brilliant red was very close, and Strankov could see a smile below his mask as the Red Menace held a shushing finger to his lips. And then he was gone, his red costume turning black as he disappeared into the shadows of the darkened bedroom.

Strankov was standing near a tall window which was open on the night. A warm breeze sent trailing fingers of thin white drapes dancing around the Russian's shoulders.

Strankov twitched when he felt the gauzy drapes tickle the back of his neck and it was only then that he realized he was shedding the effects of the paralytic. He could feel a fresh scratch on his hand. The Red Menace must have given him something to counter the paralyzing injection. When he opened his mouth he realized he could now speak.

"What are you doing?" Strankov shouted furiously. "Where am I?"

At the sound of the raised voice, the figure in bed snorted and sat bolt upright.

When Fidel Castro saw the silhouetted man standing near his open window, the Cuban dictator's eyes grew wide. Without hesitation, he dove with both hands for his nightstand. Castro returned to a seated position, a revolver at the ready. It was only then that Colonel Ivan Strankov felt the weight in his own hand and realized too late that the Red Menace had placed a gun in his own bony fingers. The Russian quickly raised his hands and shook his head violently.

"*No!*"

Six shots exploded from Castro's gun, three shattered windows or thudded into the wall; three more hit their target. At the window, Strankov reeled, twisted on his heel and became entangled in the drapes.

"Hah-hah!" Castro bellowed in triumph.

The Cuban dictator began to hop to his feet but stopped dead when a brilliant figure in red appeared as if by magic beside him.

"Hold that thought."

A scratch to the neck, a shove to the chest and Fidel Castro fell back onto his mound of satin pillows.

The Red Menace flew across the room. He had barred the door on the way in, but the soldiers would be here soon. As if on cue, someone began pounding on the bedroom door.

Strankov had dropped his gun and was attempting to hold his belly together with both bloody hands. The end was here for him, he knew. Finally here. Yet even in failure there was one mystery in this life the answer to which he could not bear not knowing.

"Wait," the Russian colonel gasped. "I must know who you are."

The Red Menace nodded. "Die wondering." And with a tiny shove he toppled the dying Colonel Ivan Strankov backwards out the third story window. The gauzy white curtains entwined the late Motherland director like a burial shroud and the torn drapes trailed him in tattered fingers over the sill and out of sight.

The Red Menace was back across the room before the body thudded to the patio. Castro's desperate eyes followed him, but though he strained mightily he could not force his muscles to move.

"A loyal Cuban friend of mine would be ticked at me if I missed this chance," the Red Menace said. *"Con permiso."*

And the screams of thousands of his own victims were a death chorus in the evil dictator's head as he watched helplessly the approach of the pair of glowing red gloves.

24

WAINWRIGHT was smoking a cigarette and repeatedly checking his watch in the lobby of the Revolucion Grande Hotel when Podge Becket at last came down in the elevator.

Dawn had broken. Their bags were packed. A cab had just arrived.

"It's about time you woke up," the doctor said for the benefit of anyone who might be in earshot.

Wainwright signaled their cabbie, who began loading their luggage in the trunk of an old Packard.

"You took long enough, Patrick," Wainwright said, sotto voce. "We'd best hasten. The good news is that your private jet was permitted to land an hour ago. Don't give me the evil eye, I had them come. I thought we might need a rapid getaway, and I hate flying commercial if I can help it. Besides, the Cubans didn't bat an eye when I asked. You really made an impression on your friend Fidel."

"You can say that again," Podge said, and smiled.

Wainwright knew enough not to ask.

They were climbing in the cab when they heard the soft rumble.

The eyes of the native Cubans in the street and all the guests in the hotel who were enjoying breakfast on their balconies turned heavenward, searching for the source of the strange sound. Many an upturned face grew shocked when in the distance appeared a tiny dart of black; a single missile rising on a plume of flame from some unseen spot in the far-off jungle.

Those who witnessed the launch thought in horror that they must be seeing the opening salvo in World War III. But if that were the case, the missile should have flown north to the United States. So why was this missile flying east over the Atlantic?

Only two men on Earth knew the answer to that question and they were already in their ancient Cuban cab and heading out into the busy street on their way to Havana's Jose Marti International Airport. And home.

Aftermath

IDI AMIN sat at a wrought iron table in the courtyard of his Kampala fortress and allowed Captain Robert Mpala to pour him his third bloody Mary of the day. The Ugandan dictator's version of the drink did not include tomato juice, but did include the blood of a woman called Mary. It also substituted Tang and rum for vodka.

Amin took a sip and nodded appreciatively.

"Delicious," he enthused, smacking his lips.

Life for Uganda's glorious leader had recently gotten even more wonderful than he could have imagined. Idi Amin was the first world leader not in Washington's back pocket with bragging rights to the latest high-tech equipment from Becket Security. Oh, Castro had summoned Patrick Becket after he was finished in Uganda, but Idi Amin was number one. On Amin's recent trip to Moscow even the Russians had taken notice.

Life was truly good. The only minor blip was the sudden disappearance of one of his aides, Captain Edmund Nwatoo. Rumor had it that Nwatoo had defected to the West, taking his entire family with him.

Uganda's Leader for Life was slurping his drink when he heard a whistling sound. It was not coming from the grounds of the Command Post. It sounded as if...

Amin squinted up at the sky. Something small and dark was flying across the thin white clouds. The whistling grew louder and very quickly the object grew larger.

Robert Mpala gaped at the sky for a moment and then jumped in the bushes.

"What is that?" Idi Amin asked, five seconds before the Russian missile with its conventional explosives landed on his terrace and, in a massive explosion that rocked the poor African nation's capital, reduced the Command Post and all who were in it to a pile of twisted rubble.

CLAPP HOPPER rolled the bald tractor wheel through the dust and leaned it carefully against the front grille of the Hoyt-Clagwell.

He slapped dirt from his hands as he walked over to his Ford. The headlights from the truck were on and illuminated the area where Clapp was working.

Clapp was embarrassed when it took him two tries to climb up onto the tailgate of the truck. He was glad Gladys was still asleep in the house or she would have had a real chuckle at that. Gladys had years ago taken to laughing at their advancing old age. "Laughing beats crying," his wife often said.

Clapp was neither laughing nor crying as he struggled to undo his own knots from the rope that held his replacement tire in place. Burt Handley had helped Clapp load the tire in town the previous evening, but there was no one on the farm to help unload it. He certainly would not enlist Gladys. As it was, this was one of the few mornings in their long marriage that he had managed to sneak out of bed without waking his wife.

Clapp had waited weeks for the tire and now that it had finally come in he was danged if he was going to leave that old tractor out to rust one more day. Before dawn he'd get the tire on and the tractor stored away in the barn even if it killed him.

"Gravity, do your stuff," Clapp said.

He gave the tire a push and it rolled off the tailgate, bounced when it hit the ground and rolled a lazy semicircle before coming to a wobbly stop near the tractor.

"Bingo," he said, smiling.

Clapp climbed down carefully to the ground — it was a long time since the last time he'd hopped down from anything — and walked over to the tire, pausing to pull his polka dot handkerchief from his back pocket.

He mopped his brow as he looked at the Kansas sky. The horizon had turned a pale reddish-gray.

Dawn would come soon, as it had come every day of Clapp Hopper's life on the farm, since as far back as he could remember. The roosters would crow, the cows would need milking, the livestock would need feeding, the traffic would pick up on the narrow lane that ran by the north field. No fanfare, no excitement. No Russian missiles dropping from the sky. Clapp Hopper, America and the entire free world would deal with the monotonous sameness of just another day.

And in the next day's paper, delivered on time for a change by young master John MacLeren, Clapp would read about some trouble way off in Cuba and in Africa.

"Glad it's somewhere else for a change. Give me another strip of bacon, will you, Gladys?"

PODGE AND WAINWRIGHT were delayed at the Jose Marti Airport. Word had gotten out that el Jefe, the greatest hero of the communist revolution, Fidel Castro himself had died during the early hours of the morning. Wainwright was concerned at first that as foreigners, and particularly as Americans, they might be detained in the country for questioning. That was, until he heard the details.

"There was at first an assassination attempt," the airport official who was checking their papers confided. "Some insane Russian infiltrated el Jefe's modest home and el Jefe bravely defended himself. Unfortunately, in the struggle el Jefe somehow swallowed his own beard and el Jefe, he choke to the death."

Podge grinned. Wainwright rolled his eyes.

"I'll be hearing about this the rest of my life," the doctor muttered. "Or at least for the rest of *yours*. And before you gloat too much, remember it was my idea to send that Russian missile to Uganda. If it wasn't for me, they would have eventually found all those bombs you planted around his palace and the world would have gotten word that Becket Security is in the dictator elimination business. As it is, they've been obliterated along with the cannibal king, assuming he was home and assuming, of course, there is any justice in this world."

"Oh, there is justice, doc. There is definitely justice."

When they settled in their seats on Podge's private Learjet, Wainwright was anxiously checking his watch.

"Infernal communists. Can't even trust them to get the planes out on time."

"We have time," Podge said, closing his eyes and settling his interlocked hands contentedly over his belly.

The plane was at last given clearance and they were in the air in minutes.

Wainwright shut the shades ten seconds before the brilliant flash came from the jungle to the northeast of Havana. The turbulence that hit the plane rattled the fuselage but the pilot managed to ride it out. When Wainwright opened the shade a few minutes later, Podge turned a lazy eye to the window.

A sinister mushroom cloud rose on a column of dust from the middle of the jungle.

"Should I be worried?" Podge asked.

"Trust your doctor. You're exposed to more radiation flying from New York to Los Angeles," Wainwright assured him. "As for the Cubans, they should be fine. The area was unpopulated but for the base. The wind should carry the cloud out to sea. All in all, a job well done. And I trust that the Red Menace can now safely retire for good."

"Yeah," Podge said. "About that. You know, doc, I've been thinking…"

"God save us," Wainwright interrupted, and refused to listen to another word. He turned his face to the mushroom cloud.

Podge closed his eyes once more.

And even as Patrick Becket drifted off to sleep, the contented smile never left his face.

Epilogue

MIC Director Simon Kirk always picked up the morning paper at the newsstand in Union Station as part of his daily ritual. This day, he stuffed the fresh copy of the *Washington Post* along with his highly polished leather briefcase under his arm and fished around in his pocket for change. Throughout it all, Kirk whistled a happy tune.

It was unusual for the young man to be in such high spirits, and his mood was infectious. The newspaper vendor smiled as he accepted payment and a generous tip.

"Having a good day, sir?" the kiosk vendor asked.

"Excellent day, Sam. Exceptional, terrific day."

He was still whistling as he walked through the station and trotted up into the sunshine. Kirk shook the paper open as he walked.

The front page story was about Cuba again, as it had been for the past three days.

The Cubans were furious with the Russians for the nuclear blast that had taken out a large chunk of jungle. The Cuban government was claiming ignorance about the true purpose of the base, saying that the Russians had told them it was a simple barracks. The Russians were blaming the Cubans for sloppy stewardship of the secret installation and claiming they were not to blame, as they were only in the country as advisors. The strategic partnership between the two nations looked to be at an end. There would be no more nuclear missiles in Cuba. Fidel Castro was dead, as was Idi Amin. Thanks to the non-nuclear missile that had leveled

Amin's Command Post, the Russians were having to explain themselves over in Africa as well. And the *New York Times* and the CBS Evening News with Walter Cronkite were having a devil of a time trying to pin the entire mess in Cuba and Africa and Moscow on the United States.

"If you boys only knew," Kirk said with a happily evil chuckle.

On the bottom of page five Kirk found a story that caught his eye. A diplomat at the Russian mission in New York City had gone missing the previous day. When he saw the name, Kirk recognized the man as a Russian spy, a KGB stooge. But then, who at the New York mission wasn't a spy? It was not mentioned in the paper, but rumor had it this particular KGB agent had been working to turn a high-ranking CIA officer. One Russian interviewed for the story claimed to have seen a figure clad in brilliant red stalking the hallways of the embassy just before the KGB man went missing.

Simon Kirk shook his head and grinned. "Welcome home, fellas," he said.

He folded the paper crisply and slapped it back up under his arm.

It truly was a wonderful day to be alive.

Simon Kirk resumed whistling as he wended his way through the heavy Washington, D.C. sidewalk traffic toward the Treasury Building.

About the author

JAMES MULLANEY is a Shamus Award-nominated author of over forty books, as well as comics, short stories, novellas, and screenplays. His work has been published by New American Library, Gold Eagle/Harlequin, Marvel Comics, Tor, Moonstone Books, and Bold Venture Press. He was ghostwriter and later credited writer of 26 novels in *The Destroyer* series, and wrote the series companion guide *The Assassin's Handbook 2*. He is currently the author of *The Red Menace* action series as well as the comic-fantasy *Crag Banyon Mysteries* detective series.

He was born in Taxachusetts, and wishes he were an only child — save one.

Other books by Jim Mullaney

Crag Banyon Mysteries:
- One Horse Open Slay
- Devil May Care
- Royal Flush
- Sea No Evil
- Bum Luck
- Flying Blind
- Shoot the Moon
- The Butler Did I.T.
- X is For Banyon
- Sleep Tight, Wake Dead
- Habeas a Nice Corpus
- Banyon Investigations, Inc (*Crag Banyon anthology*)

The Red Menace series:
- Red and Buried
- Drowning in Red Ink
- Red the Riot Act
- A Red Letter Day
- Red on the Menu
- Red Devil

Note from Jim:

If you enjoyed this book, please tell your friends and family about *The Red Menace*. Positive reviews on the web will help get the word out as well. Dr. Wainwright, who will one day invent the Internet, thanks you. — *Jim Mullaney*

Made in the USA
Monee, IL
13 January 2022

88854134R00128